The Summer Hunt

The Summer Hunt

Joseph Monninger

NEW YORK ATHENEUM 1983

The excerpt from "Thirteen Ways of Looking at a Blackbird" from
The Collected Poems of Wallace Stevens, by
Wallace Stevens © 1923, renewed 1951, by Wallace Stevens, is reprinted
by permission of Alfred A. Knopf, Inc.

Library of Congress Cataloging in Publication Data

Monninger, Joseph.
The summer hunt.

I.Title.
PS3563.0526S9   1982   813'.54   82-71062
ISBN 0-689-11325-0

Published simultaneously in Canada by McClelland and Stewart, Ltd.
Composed by Maryland Linotype Composition Company,
Baltimore, Maryland
Manufactured by Fairfield Graphics, Fairfield, Pennsylvania
Designed by Mary Cregan
First Edition

For Amy

I do not know which to prefer,
The beauty of inflections
Or the beauty of innuendoes,
The blackbird whistling
Or just after.

> *"Thirteen Ways of Looking at a Blackbird,"*
> —WALLACE STEVENS

Upper Volta,
West Africa

One

Noel Simpson saw the wild pentard emerge slowly from the brush at the side of the road. The bird paused at the sound of the truck, its color holding it to the cover of dry grass and sand. Except for its motion it would have been invisible. But its head bobbed as it tested the air, orange-tinted legs bent backward in a crouch. From behind the wheel of the truck Noel caught a glimpse of one eye turned to face him, locked for a moment onto the rush of the truck. He was dimly aware of the sun slanting behind the bird, the cooler night air waving the light to the horizon.

Without thinking, he swerved the truck toward the bird and pressed down on the accelerator.

The bird moved. It ran straight ahead on the road, too surprised to start the weaving motion that would have come if it had been given more time. The truck closed on it, gradually obscuring the body of the bird by the acute angle of the hood, so Noel could not see the first contact but felt it through his hands, his legs, his feet. He braked sharply afterward, careful to keep the wheels straight. He did not want to ruin the meat any more than necessary.

Finally, he stopped the truck and slipped it into park. He was not prepared for the final heat of the sun as he stepped out. It pressed on him immediately, settling on his shoulders and baking the sweat that held his shirt to his back. He was conscious of the change, moisture to dryness, but the heat did not diminish.

The road around him was pale and dusty, gouged here and there by old traces of runoff. One side of the road had crumbled, forming large clods of dirt that had turned almost white in the dryness. There were no trees for shade.

He walked along the road until he found the bird fifteen yards behind the truck. Its body had been rolled in the dust beneath the chassis. A brown scab of blood and dirt covered a bruise on its head. Otherwise, the body was uninjured.

He lifted the bird and felt the dead slouch of feathers, organs, weight without movement. He carried the bird to the rear of the truck, lifted a spare tire, and pinned the wings beneath it. The bird settled, its head bent to one side along the rubber tread. The steel paneling was still hot under his hands.

He walked back to the cab of the truck, reaching in his pocket for a cigarette. As he brought the cigarette to his mouth, he noticed a dab of blood covering one knuckle. The blood lined the creases of his skin. He bent and rubbed it in the road silt. The blood turned brown, gradually becoming just another spot on his hand.

He climbed behind the wheel and drove. He did not feel distance except in the height of the sun, which sank be-

hind him toward the west. The land was flat on either side
of the road. Light fell over it, simple, pure, distilled by the
evening heat, the sugared dust. There were few trees. The
horizon was constant, neither retreating nor advancing. He
watched the land pass, sensing it in his nostrils, feeling its
touch in the thin gauze of dust that covered his arm. He
could not imagine people here, though he saw one or two,
small boys or old women out collecting wood, their bodies
stilled by his passing. Instead, he thought of snakes and
scorpions, desert creatures living close to the soil, worlds
existing beneath a clump of brush, insect hunts, the stomach slide of a a snake. It was a dry life, a life honed by the
absence of water so that motion demanded economy. In this
stillness he was conscious of the truck noises, his own intrusion, and pictured the sound droning out in a wake which
arrested even the slight motion of a scorpion, sent its pinchers high, started some quiver of stalled predation. To cover
it, he tried to whistle but found he couldn't. He did not
want more sound. He watched the form of a lone tree come
nearer, its size increasing until he was under it. He slowed
the truck then, looking up, and saw the dust-covered leaves,
a wind now sorting through the branches. He thought:
Night begins here, seeing the topmost leaves already
golden, the sun's rays held a minute longer and connected
to the earth. The land seemed old, its stillness a require-
ment of age. He watched in his rear-view mirror as the last
strands of light escaped the tree's top leaves, saw two or
three beams, refracted by the prism of dust, creep into the
sky, an earthen rainbow, and signal evening.

In time he entered the outskirts of Tenado, a small village on the Koudougou road. Mud huts lined the road. He
slowed the truck, his feet working automatically on the
pedals. He heard the wooden thump of women pounding
millet, smelled wood smoke, saw children playing soccer

with a discarded can. He could not, at first, reconcile the activity surrounding him now with the stillness he had passed through. The horizon was broken. There were trees here, one or two gardens staked out near huts. The sights he passed were familiar. He found himself wanting to drive still more slowly, thinking: I am not a stranger here. These thoughts were supported by several people turning, waving, their greetings somehow suspended by the sound of the truck so that their hands hung limply in air, surprised by such motion and noise.

He took the Koudougou road a mile past his compound and stopped at a bar. The bar had no name and was marked only by a sign nailed to a banko wall, reading BIÈRE. As Noel stepped out, an African man came toward him. The man was tall and thin; he wore a dirty white booboo. "Bernard," Noel said, but the man was already close to him, saluting, the ceremonial scars on his face settled in a smile.

"My captain! *Vive la France! Vive la France!* There is *canon* now. *Canon*, over the hills. *Vive la France!*"

Bernard bent away, laughing, ducking in a madman's posture. Noel saw his eyes roam wildly, his face twitch, heard: "I am an older warrior now. Ancient. *Vive la France!*" And then he backed off, standing in front of the bar door. He presented arms to Noel, standing rigidly, giving himself over to inspection, only his eyes unsteady.

"At ease," Noel said.

The man slumped. Noel saluted him. Bernard trembled, started to say something, then quieted.

"How is the war?" Noel asked.

"*Canon! Oui*, my captain."

"Do you have time to guard my truck? Could you do that for me?"

"*Oui*, my captain. The truck, of course, *oui*."

Bernard jerked to attention again. He put his hand over

his eyes, beginning to cry, but Noel said sharply: "Bernard, attention!"

"Yes, yes," Bernard said. "The truck, of course, the truck."

The bar was dark. Stick tables, lashed with gray gut, lined one wall. There was a stone bar in the middle of the room. Noel walked toward it. He nodded to a blind man, a griot, who sat in one corner, strumming a stringed instrument. It was a useless gesture, but the man detected his presence. He poked with a walking stick a young boy who was sitting on the floor next to him. "You there," he asked. "Who's there?"

"Nassarra," the boy whispered.

"Ah," the man said, but nothing else. He strummed his instrument softly.

Noel waited at the bar. He felt the closeness of the room, saw straw breaking through the weathered banko. The floor was packed dirt. There were plates behind the bar, a few covered with chicken bones. He heard men laughing in the courtyard behind. Their voices carried through the room, and Noel turned to watch the blind man cock his head. A young girl came in a moment later. She was barefooted. She raised her head, asking by her movement what Noel wanted.

Noel said, "Four beers."

The girl didn't answer. She walked to a large clay cistern near the blind man and fished out four bottles.

"Do you want to see if they're cold enough?" the girl asked in French.

"Do you have any others?"

"No."

"I'll take those then, won't I?"

"Some customers . . ." the girl began, then shrugged and carried the bottles back to the bar. Noel paid and left. As he came through the front door, Bernard saluted. He was still at attention when Noel handed him a piece of change. Bernard started to cry. Noel reached out to touch Bernard's arm. He felt himself pulled forward, heard the whisper in his right ear: "We must kill the Germans. Yes? The Germans." Noel felt dry lips press his cheek, the whisper repeated, the words a moment in the man's life.

"Now . . ." Noel started to say, but Bernard composed himself. He backed away from the truck, holding a salute, saying again: *"Vive la France. Vive la France!"*

"Yes, all right," Noel said, and climbed into the truck. He started the engine, his mind already drifting away from Bernard, thinking now: Kathy will be waiting. The thought had no effect on him. He wasn't sure how she would react, could never tell until he determined what kind of day she had had. The beer would help, he decided.

He drove back to his compound and saw the lanterns had already been lit. He reminded himself that Kathy didn't like it to be dark in the house. She was afraid of snakes or scorpions, afraid to reach into the potato bin or pick up a shoe without shaking it first. He could not define for himself where prudence gave way to fright.

He parked the truck in the compound and honked the horn. Before she could come out, he ran back to the truck bed and picked up the pentard. Quickly he wedged a cigarette into its yellow beak and propped it, like a puppet, on the hood. Squatting down, he tucked one wing around a beer bottle, then waited. He squinted beneath the truck to see her legs appear.

It seemed to take too long for her to come out. He thought: She's cooking, but then he thought she might imagine him unloading the truck. He crept back to the passenger side and leaned across to honk the horn.

"Noel?" she called.

She followed her voice out. He squatted back down, just his eyes above the hood. In his first look at her, he saw the timidity, the fright which so often marred anything spontaneous between them. She touched one hand to the cement wall, the other to her breast and throat. She smiled a moment later, but still, it was too late.

"How about a beer, lady?" he made the pentard ask, wiggling it enough to give it life. His heart was no longer in it, and he felt himself performing in a situation he could not bring off.

"Noel, where did you get that?"

The beer slipped in the bird's wing, almost falling on the ground. Noel stood. He threw the bird back into the truck and reached into the driver's seat for the bottles.

"I hit it," he said finally.

"Where?"

"Just ouside town."

She nodded. She walked out to the truck and took the bottles from him. He kissed her once.

"Is the meat good?" she asked.

"The best."

"I mean wild pentard," she said, turning back to the house. "Is it good?"

"It's better actually. They forage."

"Well, you'll have to pluck it. I sent Cooca home."

"All right."

She called something about dinner, but he didn't hear her clearly. He carried the pentard to a small charcoal grill he had built near the chicken coop. He heard the domestic birds flutter as he came near, roosting, their clucks low-throated. He raked some sticks and straw into a pile and lit it. When it was burning well enough, he began plucking the bird. The feathers pulled stiffly from the skin. He wanted to chop the head off, but he had no knife. When he was down to the pinfeathers, he held the bird over the flames and singed them off.

"Whew, that stinks," Kathy said behind him. "About ready?"

She held out a bottle of beer. He took it and smiled.

"Can we eat this tonight?" he asked.

"I don't think we'll need it. They killed a steer in the marketplace today. But I can still cook it. It will stay until tomorrow."

"I could get the livers out for breakfast."

"If you want."

He noticed she wasn't drinking. He handed her his bottle as he scorched off the last feathers. The pentard would have to be gutted, but he didn't want to bother with it now. The flame burned lower.

"Oh," Kathy said. "I forgot for a minute. There's mail. That gendarme brought it, from the *préfet*'s office—you know the one—what's his name?"

"Kuliba," Noel said, taking back his beer. He kicked some more straw at the fire and watched it rise. "So what did he bring?"

"You got one from your dad. I got three from friends."

"Anything new?"

"Nothing much. Alice—you know Alice—is pregnant. She's due in August. She says her husband plays a lot of golf and she spends most of her time around the house. She sounded envious of me, I think."

"Anything else?"

"Nothing really," Kathy said. She was staring at the fire.

"Well, let me take a shower then. I'll be right in."

She turned and walked to the house. Noel carried his beer to the shower, a screened-off portion of the yard with a water bucket attached overhead. He took off his shirt and pants, surprised as always at the whiteness of his chest and upper thighs. He pulled the chain, and the water came down. It was still warm from the sun. When he was completely wet, he soaped himself, massaging his muscles as he did so. The calluses on his hands were rough. He rinsed longer than he needed to, standing for what seemed a long time under the warm spray.

He shook out a towel and dried himself, then slipped back into his sandals. He walked around the courtyard into the house, the towel wrapped around his hips. For a moment he felt a sense of satisfaction. The house was warmer now that Kathy was here. She had bought new furniture— wicker chairs, a sturdy dinner table, two kerosene lamps, wall hangings—which made the tin roof and cement walls less severe. It was more of a home, he concluded, more of a place to live. She had supplied some touch, some attention to detail he had missed. There were fabrics now, texture. The house no longer echoed.

Still, as he looked at the furniture, he realized a subtle exchange had been made. He understood he had not gained the comfort without sacrificing something. He had not paid proper attention to detail and had detected in himself a need for it. Kathy had been in Africa only five months, but in that time she had changed him, had merged her comfort with his so that they were now inseparable. He did not blame her, though he felt the house was not as free. An order had been imposed, a sense of time passing, counted by meals, counted by washings. Days were no longer fluid. He thought: I wanted this, yet was surprised by the reality, the translation of thought to cloth and wood.

"Dinner's ready," Kathy said from the kitchen. "You should get dressed."

"I will."

He walked to the bedroom. It was freshly swept. Two

ropes were suspended lengthwise across the room to serve as a closet. He put on a clean shirt and pair of shorts, then walked back to the kitchen.

"Are you going to have a beer?" he asked her.

"They're warm."

"Ice is a problem."

"I don't care for warm beer."

"Ah so," he said, making a Japanese bow.

At the same moment he bowed, he realized he was tormenting her. He was surprised at how natural it had become. He saw her flush, saw a few strands of hair come loose. She looked tired, fatigued by the patience she showed him. He found himself wanting to draw further on the patience, to test her, to drive her to some place where he would know her entirely or else reveal himself. He was not sure which he would prefer, could not tell if it was Africa or himself she reacted to in these moments. He suspected it was both, though he could see Africa weighing on her, the actual heat draining her, and he wondered if this, after all, was not what he had hoped for when he asked her to come. He had wanted to see something drained from them both, obstacles removed, so they could see one another clearly.

Except, he realized, the heat had remained between them, the dryness had wedged them apart. And now, he told himself, it was beyond frankness, discussion. Africa had become an element between them, the third corner of a triangle which could not be shaken by words or compromise. If there was blame for this, he accepted it, though aware, at the same time, he could do nothing to remove it. He felt as a child might feel showing a new playmate something novel, only to have the playmate find the object stupid, of no importance. It did nothing to explain, the object was either admired or refused. The power for her approval was within her. He could think of no new way to present his case.

He thought this in seconds, was not finished even as she asked: "Would you help me take up dinner?" Her voice was tightly controlled.

"Sure."

"There's time to read your father's letter if you want. I can hold the meat."

"I'll read it later."

"It might . . ." she said, then paused, "it might give us something to talk about if you read it now."

"I'd rather read it afterward. Here, I'll take up the potatoes."

He drained the potatoes outside, the boiling water seeping into the dirt. When he was finished, he carried them back into the dining room and set them on the table. Kathy came out with a pan of meat and tomatoes.

"Is that it?" he asked. "Did you get everything?"

"Yes. Would you bring the lanterns closer?"

He placed a lantern on the table. The light was uneven. It threw shadows on the dishes, then pulled them back. He smelled the meat, warm and fragrant. As he sat, he heard a woman pounding millet. The sound was dull, wooden, ancient. He thought it sounded oddly like a heart-beat.

Kathy finished clearing the dishes while Noel smoked. She dunked the plates and glasses in a bucket of water and left them for Cooca, their houseboy. She piled the scraps to feed to the chickens later. She did this unconsciously, knowing food could not be wasted. In Africa nothing went to waste, she realized. Cans were recycled. Small bits of cloth were stitched into blankets; shoes were patched and worn; bicycle tires turned into slingshots. Everything was in a state of evolution, the original use of a product no more important than the last.

When she was finished in the kitchen, she returned to the table. Noel still hadn't opened his letter. He was sitting in the same spot, his legs up on the table. Seeing him, she understood he was conserving the letter, holding it until just the right moment to read and absorb. He did not do things quickly, he was more like an African in that. She thought once of her own opened letters and was annoyed.

"Do you want coffee?" she asked.

"Are you going to have some?"

"I think so, yes."

"Then I will, too. Why don't we take it outside? It's too hot in here."

She went back to the kitchen. She heard him pulling out the wicker chairs and a coffee table. The sound disturbed her. It was the sound Noel had told her about, the very moment: the quiet after dinner, the long coffees underneath the stars. It had sounded romantic then, exotic. On cold winter nights in New Hampshire she had thought: Yes, the heat. Because it was the heat that had drawn her, the image of a different land, the seasons scrambled, foreign. She had not been satisfied, had given in to some misguided sense of adventure. I am a teacher, she had told Noel when they met, hearing even then, in her own voice, some disappointment, heard, underlying it: I could be more. She had fallen in love then, yet it had been with Africa as much as with Noel, had been, more truthfully, a love of the image of herself, with potential. She tried to think now what she had actually imagined. She wondered if she had included terraces, overhead fans. She didn't know.

Any dream she might have had was too far from the reality. Her ideas of Africa seemed ludicrous now, her expectations absurd. Her impression was mitigated by heat, washed by unending days of long sun, dust, insects, ridiculed by dawns and dusks of unforgiving temperatures. Her energy had been sapped, her dream cruelly analyzed until she often thought: Sleep holds dreams. Awake, they are nothing.

She shook herself and found she had been staring at the cement wall above the stove. She heard pits of cement fall, a scratching. She looked up, scanning the wall for a lizard, some insect whose tread was revealed by the slow erosion of material. Finding nothing, she lit the fire under the kettle and filled two cups with instant coffee. She lifted the lid off a can of infant milk and poured some into Noel's cup. She picked out an ant, a brown spot that flowed in the middle of the fluid, then quickly walked outside.

"My father has cancer," Noel said.

Kathy felt air removed from her lungs, thought: This, this now. She could not speak. She waited for him to go on, watched his face to see how he had taken it. She wanted to say: No, don't tell me like that, but she was aware of the comfort the silence provided, the freedom it gave. She glanced down and saw the letter open on the chair beside him. He was staring straight ahead, his eyes in shadow. She waited for him to say something more, but he didn't speak. She went to the chair finally and picked up the letter, sitting in the same motion. She couldn't think, said only: "Where?"

"All through him, I guess. It isn't clear. He's going to die. He said as much himself."

"How old is the letter? He can't know that yet."

"I think the cancer is advanced. He didn't give many details. Go ahead and read it if you like."

"Why didn't he send a telegram?"

"I don't know. Read it."

She read quickly, blurring the lines. She knew she would have to read it a second time to understand it fully. Her eyes kept coming off the page to watch Noel. Somehow she felt deprived at not having been near him when he read the letter. She had been robbed of some emotion, some entrance to him. She folded the letter and put it down carefully.

"Did you see the part at the end?" he asked.

"Which part?"

"He wants me to come home."

"Will you?"

"I don't know."

She heard the kettle come to boil.

"I'll get it," he said.

"No, sit."

"Let me," he said.

He stood and walked into the kitchen. She stared at the letter, then unfolded it and began reading again. She forced herself to read more slowly. The words still seemed unreal: word shadows, half-formed thoughts. She wanted to cry but realized in time it would have been only a mechanical reaction, some concession of sympathy. Instead, she imagined the man, Noel's father, sitting down to compose this letter three thousand miles away. It had taken almost a month to arrive. She wondered what state the man was in now, how he had chanced such news to the mails.

"Here you go," Noel said, and handed her a cup of coffee. She looked at him, trying to see how he had taken the letter, but his face was impassive. He sipped his coffee as he sat down, then lit a cigarette. He was silent. Kathy heard a cricket calling. Far away a bullfrog sounded. The noise was out of place in the dryness.

"We won't get out of there right away if we go home,"

Noel said finally. "There will be things to take care of. I don't know."

"What about your brother, Grant?"

"He lives right there. He'll do everything that needs to be done. I'll wire him tomorrow. He should be able to tell me what the story is."

He stared straight ahead at the lamp. He looked tired. She listened to the sounds of his smoking, watched the red light of his cigarette move forward and back.

Then: "I should gut the pentard," he said.

"You don't have to do that now."

"*C'est Afrique.*"

"It doesn't have to be right now."

She wanted to say: Wait, stay, finish, but he was already standing. He walked into the house and came out with a second lantern. "I'll be right back," he said. She watched the light, a yellow circle moving along the ground. She saw him swing it back and forth, checking for snakes and scorpions, his feet deliberately shuffling a warning of his approach. She lifted her own feet onto the coffee table and settled them near the lantern. Moths hit her toes as they launched themselves at the light, but she let them fall on her, feeling their impotence, the powdered resin of their wings.

Soon she heard the chucking sound of the knife. She saw Noel spin and throw something into the chicken pen. There was a murmur: chickens coming down from their roosts, a squawking, hen-shuffles. One chicken screeched louder than the others, but the sound was covered by the quick beat of wings and the dull thump of flesh and intestines on dry ground. Above her, the tin roof lost the final heat of the day and buckled.

Then Noel was coming back toward her. He carried the pentard in his left hand. She glanced at it quickly and saw only a stark white body. She knew that when she went inside, she would find it safely covered in a pot. Beside it, Noel would place the head and feet for Cooca. She had seen it before: the head covered by small feathers, its neck an open tube; feet yellow and curled, menacing, scaled, looking old the minute they were cut from the body.

"Just let me wash up," Noel said, passing her again. "I'll be there in a second."

A few minutes later she heard him bathing, heard underneath his splashing the chickens still unsettled. She wondered if he would get the blood out from beneath his nails, blood left by the cleansing sweep up the bird's backbone.

He returned to the table and set the lantern on the ground. Kathy was conscious of their sitting in a pool of light. She could no longer see the trees, except as dark outlines. She looked at the stars, thinking: Now he will want me to begin. Now, in his grief, he will assign me mine. "So," he said over her thoughts, sitting. She let the silence deepen, would not puncture it to satisfy him. She watched the insects still coming at the lantern. Something buzzed, its wings tapping the light at incredible speed. The tin roof buckled again.

Then, unbidden, she had a brief remembrance, a quick image of his arriving at her apartment in the States, his jacket too light, his hair blown and snow-covered. He had been tan, his skin and shirt like a vacationer's, like some of the children she taught as they returned from Christmas holiday. He had arrived shyly, reserved, yet with some serious intent, saying: I thought I might drop by. Do you mind? Are you busy? And she had said: No, sensing in him escape, a pass to a different life-style, his rumored departure increasing, somehow, his quality. And she had invited him into her apartment, a dim notion working on her that it would be him leading them out. He had sat quietly, accept-

ing all efforts to make him comfortable, gradually beginning to talk about Africa. He had talked with reluctance,
not at all selling, underlining at every opportunity that
they were in the real world here, allowing Africa to linger
like some fantasy half-remembered, half-anticipated. Her
interest had been piqued, she could admit it now, could
even see her own face as it listened while beneath the skin
thoughts whirled, schoolgirl dreams flourished, so that the
next day she had said to a friend: An interesting man came
by last night. I met him at a party, and I didn't think he'd
take my invitation seriously, but— And in the telling she
detected her own enthusiasm, was ready to say: This was
different. This was something unlike the others. But it was
not only Noel: He was part of an upheaval, a growing dis-
content reflected at her each day in the faces of the children
she taught, the smell of chalk dust, faculty meetings. There
had been the daily ritual of the ordinary, expected turns,
known replies, her life outside the classroom sounding like
repeated lessons to her own ears. She had felt it all, had
discovered in it a betrayal of herself, long overlooked and
partially forgotten, which had been consumed by linking
days of normalcy, numbed by comfort.

Noel had touched this, had reached some remnant of
desperation, returning each time to her apartment, trading
his experiences for the fringes of Christmas: eggnog,
brandy, cookies. She had been conservative, had consciously
lured him by her own solidness, though allowing him to
see more, hinting, always hinting; it was a beginning with
her, not an end. Once she had started to speak of it, had
started to say: You see, I'm twenty-seven, and I never
thought I'd end up like this. But she had cut the thought
off, had swayed to silence. His visits increased. A friend
stopped her in the hallway during lunch to say: I hear you
are leaving us. Is that true? And Kathy had looked aston-

ished, though inwardly pleased, reveling in the mixture of fright and envy on her friend's face, but answering: No, no, I don't think so. Not to my knowledge.

But she had gone. A month and a half later, a whirlwind, married, leaving, an expatriate. She had lost sight of Noel in this; he had become just another item, a key one to be sure, but only an element in the separation, divorce from her old life. Wanting love, she had convinced herself of it, and she had followed him, had come away, only to find this land waiting, the heat. She had been caught and now could not be a traitor to her dream, to the smiles of friends who sent her off, the gleam of knowledge they shared which said: Yes, you are different.

"Kathy?" Noel said beside her.

She turned, feeling lost in her thoughts, remembering his father's letter, thinking with guilt that they could return now. It would not be failure.

"Kathy?" he said again, this time lighting a match. A piece of sulfur broke off and flew in a soft arc to the ground.

"Yes."

"Talk to me."

"About what?"

"About anything. Your work at the dispensary. Just talk if you would."

She heard something loosen in his voice. She thought: His father is dying. She watched him for a moment without speaking. He was leaning back in his chair, his head tilted to look at the stars. She tried to follow the line of his sight, but there were too many stars.

Finally, she spoke. She told him about her friends' letters. She went on, not remembering what she said the moment it left her, but somehow comforted by her own voice, the drone of sound. She was aware of something elemental passing between them. It was not love. It was something simpler than love: compassion, companionship, loneliness. She could not name it to her own satisfaction, yet the feeling grew as she continued, isolating and joining them at once. In time she saw his body relax. He stretched himself in the chair. She asked if he wanted a blanket, but he said nothing. She talked again, telling him a story from her childhood. It was long and involved, and she confused characters, yet Noel said nothing. She knew he wasn't following her story, did not care if there was a story. Her mind strayed occasionally to the sounds around her, to Africa, thoughts of her arrival. She held them off, concentrating, instead, on Noel's posture, the quiet that welled up whenever she took breath.

In the end she permitted herself to be sound. Only when he slept did she stop.

Noel woke without movement. He watched the sun set up a sheen on the mosquito net. He traced the borders of the net with his eyes, searching for spiders or scorpions. He could hear Kathy in the kitchen, smell breakfast meat. Cooca's voice came to him once, but he couldn't make out the boy's words. From the yard, he heard a rooster crow. The bird's call seemed cracked, somehow adolescent. He listened for a second call, but the rooster was silent.

He pushed the mosquito net aside and climbed out. As he rolled the net up, he noticed the sheets were damp. He thought: Night sweat. With the thought came memory of the letter. He imagined his father in sheets like these: cold white, damp from lost moisture. It would take time, he realized, to comprehend that his father was dying. The letter was only a signal, a message. He would have to pick the time, a place, before he could admit it cleanly, accept what he could not yet feel. He was sure it would come, could already feel the beginning locked between thought and emotion.

He walked out into the courtyard, not stopping to say good morning. The sun was up. He saw the treetops turned gold, the soil smoke of wavering heat. A lizard scuttled on the tin roof above him, sending small bits of cement scraping on the wall. The ground was damp and warm. Soap glistened in a small puddle: purple, green, red.

"Noel? I thought I heard you."

Kathy stood with a towel in her hand. She looked fresh. An ease had come into her posture.

"Good morning," he said.

"How are you? Are you feeling better?"

"I feel all right."

He shifted his stance. Damp soil pressed between his toes. He watched three women walk past the compound, wood stacked high on their heads. He heard Cooca call a greeting to them.

"You were tossing last night. I felt you once," Kathy said. "I thought you were feverish."

"No, I feel fine." Then, turning back to her, he said: "I really do. Thank you, though. Thank you for last night."

She nodded. He asked: "Is there water yet?"

"Cooca filled the shower bucket, if that's what you mean. He's doing laundry."

"I'll just take a quick shower then. I'll be right in."

He walked through the courtyard. Near the shower he saw Cooca bent over a bucket of clothes. He was twisting a shirt between his hands, wringing it free of water. Beside him, on a small patch of brown paper, Noel saw the head and feet of the pentard.

"Morning, Cooca," Noel said.

"Morning, Nassarra."

The boy smiled. Noel squatted and picked up the pentard feet. "How are you going to eat these? Soup?"

"I think so. I'm going to take them to my mother after I finish the laundry."

"Ah," Noel said. He clicked his tongue. He held the legs at the top joints and made them dance on the brown paper. Cooca laughed. Noel managed to make them perform a soft shoe on the paper.

"He dances better than you," Cooca said.

"When have you ever seen me dance?"

Cooca shrugged. "Never."

"Did you know that in my country chickens sometimes attack human beings? You didn't know that, did you? They get people with their claws." Noel started to rise. He held the feet out, bending closer to Cooca. The boy backed off a step.

"They come at people like this. They sneak up, very carefully; then they spring. Don't be frightened now. I'm telling you this for your own good."

But the boy continued backing away, laughing. Noel came at him. Cooca held the shirt at his side, swinging it, ready. "They go for the ears first," Noel said. "They grab onto the ears and start to fly. Like this, come here."

And then Noel was running after the boy. Cooca hit him once with the wet shirt. They ran around the couryard, laughing, dodging back and forth.

Finally, breathing hard, Noel said: "You're too fast. Come on, let's check for eggs."

Noel led the way to the chicken coop. He had to turn sideways past the thatched fence to get through. The chickens scattered at the sight of him. He spoke softly to them, watching each as it moved past him. The rooster he had heard earlier was sick. Its comb was covered with blue cysts; its eyes looked rheumy.

"What do you think of that one?" Noel asked.

"We should kill it."

"I guess so. Better do it tomorrow. Be careful it doesn't attack you."

Cooca grinned. Noel felt him take his hand. He touched the boy's calloused palm with his own, surprised he felt no need to pull his hand away. It had made him uncomfortable when he first came to Africa.

"The eggs," Noel said and walked through the small run. He lifted the straw mat propped on bricks that covered the hens and saw three eggs in one nest. A second nest was covered by a brood hen. She clucked at him, watching him warily. He reached down and picked up the three eggs, handling them carefully. They were warm.

"How long has the hen been sitting?" he asked Cooca. "Shouldn't they be hatched?"

"I don't know. It's been a couple of weeks. I'd say any day now they should come out."

"I'd hate to have her sitting on dead eggs."

"We can break one if you want."

"No, we might as well wait."

Cooca nodded, took the eggs, and went back to washing. Noel followed him out. He lashed the matting in place, then stepped behind the shower wall. He stripped off his shorts and pulled the chain, letting the water run over him. Heat shimmied off the walls.

When he finished showering, he dried himself, then slipped his shorts back on. He snapped the towel at Cooca as he passed. The boy splashed water at him. Noel went back into the house. Kathy was waiting. She was drinking a cup of coffee, sitting at the table.

"Chicken man," she said.

He walked to her and kissed her. Breaking away, he shook his head and sprayed water on her. "Tarzan dress now," he said. "Jane happy?"

"Jane happy."

"Good."

He beat his chest, then walked back into the bedroom and put on a shirt. Kathy was in the kitchen when he returned.

"Do you know," she called, "it's over a hundred already?"

"Can't be."

"It is. I watched it climb. It was about eighty-seven when I woke up this morning."

He walked into the kitchen. He grabbed her from behind and kissed her neck. "Love me?" he asked.

"Sometimes."

"Only sometimes?"

"Only sometimes."

"Fair enough," he said, and pinched her. "Let's eat; then I'll drive you to work. Hot as hell, isn't it?"

"How can they stand it?" Kathy asked.

Noel looked at her. She was leaning out the truck window on the passenger side, her shirt billowed from the wind. She rocked back onto the seat and stared straight ahead.

"They move slowly," Noel said. "You get used to it."

"When?"

She said this without looking. Noel slowed the truck. He could not move his legs comfortably on the upholstery.

A bee buzzed against the rear window. He felt his skin warming, felt moisture start beneath his arms and along his spine. The heat pressed on his bare ankles as he shifted his feet on the pedals.

Kathy said: "Even the wind is hot. Do you realize that? It doesn't help to have the wind at all."

"The wind comes from the desert. During the rainy season it comes up from the Atlantic. It's more moist."

Noel drove to the dispensary. It was a mud-brick building with a slanting tin roof. An iron rail had been put around it, though it seemed without purpose. A dog barked as he stopped, and he glanced quickly at Kathy. "Are you okay?" he asked.

"Yes. It's just hot." She opened the door, asking: "So, you're going to wire home?"

"If the *préfet* will let me. I'm going over there now."

A few women came out of the dispensary. Kathy waved and stood. The door pushed a solid block of hot air at him when she closed it. She bent back to the window and said: "I doubt anyone will work all day. Try to get home early if you can."

"I'll try."

She started to say something, then stopped.

"It's hot," he said for her.

She smiled. "You can't get it out of your mind, can you? I've never felt heat like this before. It doesn't seem fair somehow."

She straightened and tapped on the roof. He watched her walk to the women and greet them. He saw her uneasiness; her movements were awkward with the women, tentative. He wanted to call to her, to say something more, but she was going inside. With time he would have said: Don't go in if you don't like it. Would have said: They will see, they will see. Yet she was beyond that now, involved in a job she had found for herself. She went because she wanted to or, perhaps, because there was nothing else for her to do.

He put the truck in gear and drove between the small saplings which had been planted as part of a government project. The saplings were small, withered, their bark stripped. Gradually they gave way to the stand of older trees that marked the marketplace, sharply green against pervading brown. He saw spots of color between the trees, distant shapes of people arriving, heard morning greetings called through dry air. A boy passed on a bicycle, a goat tied to the handlebars, the bleating a brief noise beneath the hum of the truck.

At the *préfet*'s office Noel pulled the truck under a large tree and got out. A line of petitioners circled the front of the white stone building, some carrying chickens as gifts, others leading bulky rams on tethers. Noel walked toward them. He heard them talking, their voices brittle, mingling with dust lifted by feet, tinged by the scent of animals, an aspect of humiliation and request. He could not separate one voice from any other, could not say: Yes, he speaks now, then him, for they seemed grouped in supplication, bowed, their words hushed as if in a church. He was tempted to make some loud noise but, instead, found himself oddly seized by the quiet.

Near the front of the line he found Kuliba, a guard who was talking to a bearded man carrying two white cocks. As Noel approached, he watched Kuliba slap the man on the back, then say: "Ah, the well digger. The American."

Kuliba walked to meet him. Noel saw a few men in line turn to look. They moved back a step or two, making room, clearing a circle for privacy. Kuliba took a bite of kola nut, his teeth and gums already orange. His uniform was wrinkled and splattered with mud around the cuffs. A gun, too big for the holster, bounced on his hip.

"We haven't seen you," Kuliba said. He extended his hand. "Too long, too long. Where have you been? I see your truck pass, but then . . ." He let his voice trail off.

"I've been busy," Noel said. "And you?"

"Always busy. The *préfet* keeps me working. Duty always, as you know."

"Yes, of course."

Kuliba touched Noel's sleeve and drew him away. Noel thought: A bribe, though he could feel no anger, only pity. He watched Kuliba check around him, a petty official checking the perimeters of his own power, knowing that such power extends only so far as an unfriendly ear, then saying: "And you know, I've wanted to see you. We could use a well in Pó—" But Noel was no longer listening. He followed the lilt of the man's voice, hearing it climb and diminish, the folds of a deal dictating rhythm. He watched the breathing patterns, heard air between words, sensing the power the man must hold over his fellow citzens. In the end, gathering it was only a plea for a well, Noel said: "You know it's not up to me. I don't decide where to put them."

"I know, I know. But a word, right? I don't think you can lack a word. Words are everything in these matters, aren't they? People say money, but I say words. Isn't that right? I'd rather have some men's ears than their purses, eh?"

He patted Noel's arm and laughed. Noel laughed with him, feeling the strangeness, nodding his head to show appreciation. Two men in the line joined in.

"Now, how can we help you? Do you want to see the *préfet*?"

"No, it isn't necessary."

"Ah, but protocol. Don't you think you should go in and say hello?"

"I'm in a hurry," Noel said. "I need to telegraph the United States."

Kuliba nodded. "I'll tell the *préfet* right away. It shouldn't be a problem. But if he asks to see you, well—"

Noel watched him leave, then went back to the truck and sat in the shade behind the steering wheel. A dog passed by, its hindquarters rubbed raw. He saw someone from the petitioners' line wave to him, and he returned the wave, sorting through his memory to identify the man. He couldn't. Idly he watched a vulture hanging over the market, its wings motionless, feathers sifting the current. He wondered what they had killed and tried to remember what day it was. Pork, he decided.

Fifteen minutes later Kuliba returned. He said the *préfet* wanted to see him. Noel followed the man to the building. He stepped onto a low veranda and stood in a spot of shade thrown by a patch of bougainvillaea. Kuliba knocked on the metal door of the office, then pushed it open.

Noel waited. He heard the *préfet*'s voice. He did not like the man and dealt with him only when necessary. Once, when a rogue elephant was killed in Pó, he had accompanied the *préfet* to a ceremonial butchering. By the time they arrived, the elephant had been dragged into a clearing and the head already removed. Nearly a hundred men had worked at the carcass. An hour after they had begun, they were still dwarfed by the immense shoulders and hind sections. Flies were everywhere. Noel had forced himself to watch, strangely transfixed, taking in every nuance of the ceremony.

Eventually the right tusk had been given to the *préfet*. The second tusk was sent to Ouagadougou, the capital, and presented to the president. Noel had received a foot. The inside had been cleaned and scraped, and a wire had been attached to form a handle. It was, he had later discovered, an umbrella stand. The hide was incredibly thick.

He had taken the foot back to his compound. After a week the smell had become too strong. The meat soured; the skin turned soft, limp, slowly mushrooming inward. Cooca had taken it then. The boy had climbed a tree and hung the foot from a branch, first painting the bark with a urine mixture to keep ants away. Birds got at it then, pecking the gray skin and causing it to swing. Occasionally during the weeks it remained in the tree, Noel would smell it, and he would recall the huge body of the elephant, the blood and flies, the black men hacking at its limbs with wooden axes.

A month later he had taken the foot down. It was needed for a picture-taking ceremony. Noel had carried it to the rear of the *préfet*'s office and posed with it while sitting on the elephant's skull. The skull had been one of six. The others were old, but the most recent one was dark, skin-flecked still.

But he had shown the picture despite finding the whole incident repugnant. This knowledge bothered him now. He was aware he had allowed the picture to mean one thing to those who saw it, while keeping the image of the butchered elephant in his mind. He had shown it to Kathy. He had shown it to his brother, Grant, watching the wonder come into his eyes, seeing the slight tinge of jealousy register there. It had meant adventure to them, some secret experience out of their realm of understanding, beyond the United States. Yet the truth had remained hidden. He had deceived without speaking, had allowed their thoughts to provide him with a memory he didn't have.

He pulled back from this memory as Kuliba came out and stood at attention. "You can go in now," he said.

Noel walked past him. Inside the office a breeze stirred. An overhead fan moved in lazy circles, its hinges sometimes giving off a rusty sound. Electricity, Noel thought, then turned to face the *préfet*.

"How are you?" the *préfet* asked. He came around the desk and shook Noel's hand. The *préfet*'s color was bad. His skin looked dry, his eyes jaundiced. "Please sit down."

Noel moved to a metal chair placed near the desk. He was conscious of time moving, of the day growing hotter and the need to be polite. The conversation was strained. Noel followed it with difficulty, thinking of his own words as handles, stepping stones for the *préfet* to use. The *préfet* offered him scotch, but Noel refused. He moved several times in his chair so the wind from the fan would touch bare skin.

"So," the *préfet* said after a time, "you need to telegraph the United States? Is it important?"

"Yes, my father is ill."

"I see. Will you be leaving us then?"

"I'm not sure yet. That's the reason I'm wiring. I want to see how serious it is."

"Yes, yes, of course. Well, then, I'll let you go. Kuliba?" he called. Kuliba appeared at the door and saluted.

"Please let Monsieur Noel use the telegraph office. Tell Zungo to send his message."

"Yes, sir."

Noel shook the *préfet*'s hand. He followed Kuliba through a dark hallway into a larger office. Kuliba introduced him to Zungo, a heavyset man with deep scars on his face. When he smiled at Noel, the scars mirrored the lines of his face.

"Would you write down the message you wish to send?" Zungo asked. He handed Noel a scrap of paper. Noel leaned against the wall and wrote in pencil: "What news of Dad? How serious? Send instructions." He signed it and wrote the address beneath it.

"Is that all?" Zungo asked.

"That's all."

"New Hampshire. What is New Hampshire?"

"A state," Noel told him. "They'll understand."

Noel shook hands with him and left. He saw Kuliba walking toward the market. As he was walking back to his truck, the man in the petitioners' line waved again, but this time Noel didn't respond.

Kathy heard the women grunt. She had heard it all morning, but now the grunting had grown in volume, a breath sound lacing it and drawing it tighter. She felt sweat on her own back. Her stomach was upset, and she bit her thumb to distort the feeling. She thought: Birth. It was birth with sweat, birth like an animal. Squatting against the mud-brick wall of the dispensary, the African woman was pushing at the child.

Kathy couldn't move. She let Marie, the African midwife, wipe the woman's forehead and sponge down her back. Kathy could not see the pregnant woman's eyes, but she was certain they would be clouded, pained, almost in tears. The woman had labored for three hours, getting off the delivery table, which she didn't trust, in order to stand at the wall and squat. Each time there would be rapid breathing, a shift in the woman's stomach, then a series of grunts. Kathy had tried to make herself useful but found she couldn't guide herself in any activity. She saw strange details around the room: a pitcher of water, towels, a lizard resting beneath the edge of the roof. She had difficulty concentrating. Her senses seemed locked to the woman, locked to the movement in her womb.

Suddenly Marie laughed. The woman was standing, struggling back to the table. She lay down on her side, her hands draped limply over her stomach, her face turned away from Kathy. Marie dampened her sponge in the water and wiped the woman's shoulders.

"It's work"—Marie smiled—"but the baby is there. Is it like this in the United States?"

Marie pronounced it *U-nee-ted* States.

"No," Kathy said. "We use the table."

"These women, though. They won't use it. They believe in the old ways. They use the table only if there is a problem."

The pregnant woman grunted and rolled off the table. Kathy was surprised at her agility. She was breathing quickly before she reached the wall. Her hands knocked a wedge of dirt free. Her nails scraped.

"Thousands and thousands of babies born here," Marie said, swabbing the woman's back. Her arm moved smoothly yet firmly. Kathy thought of brushing a horse or dog, saw in Marie the same sort of detachment. "I've seen a thousand myself. This one is coming soon."

Marie spoke to the woman in a dialect Kathy didn't recognize. The woman nodded. It had been three hours, and the woman had spoken only twice. She had not cried out. Kathy understood it was a source of shame to cry out at a birth. She watched the black smoothness of the woman's back. Gradually she saw the pores, the muscles clenching and releasing.

The woman went back to the table. This time she lay facing Kathy, who watched her face, saw each flicker of pain, saw the woman cock her head as if listening. Kathy felt she was being exposed to something elemental, something the white of hospitals usually covered. There was risk of death here. She saw it clearly in the woman's eyes: bewilderment, pain, the actual surprise at having another life pulling through one's own.

The woman grunted again and went to the wall.

Kathy stood, feeling she had to get away. She walked outside. She said nothing to Marie but heard a laugh behind her, a quick conversation in an African dialect.

Outside, she became aware of the heat. In the dispensary the heat had been only another force, oddly appropriate for birth, dark, sweet air tainted with sweat and effort. But here the sun was sharp and powerful. The light was as painful as the heat it generated. She leaned against the wall near the door and listened. The woman was grunting again. She heard Marie say: "Ah, ah, now." The words touched something in her own stomach, and she thought she might be sick. She bent to let the nausea pass, putting her hands on her knees and breathing quickly. Her head was light.

She stood after a few minutes. The room behind her was quiet. She was conscious of her mind moving away from the situation, settling back, thinking: Not now, not here. She tried to imagine Noel telegraphing and found some comfort there, drawing his image vividly, his hand writing a message, saying, always in her mind: We will come. She repeated: We will come, seeing suddenly the possibility of escape, the lush green of New Hampshire waiting. Locked in this image was the sense of some struggle's being abandoned, time winning, heat, insects, disease, winning. She no longer felt competition, felt, instead, the intolerable plod of days, hours meshed in sun and night heat, victory relinquished in monotony. Here, near birth, she wished for the old man's death. She no longer cared, could no longer be gentle in her own thoughts, feeling as she did that she had been pushed to the edge of survival, her life beside Noel's vying for identity.

But she wanted Noel. She wanted him in the States. This she saw clearly, the vision sharpened now by her abandonment of Africa. In the blank heat she thought of Noel as an animal perfectly suited to the terrain, the climate, the demands of each day. Thought: I will lose here, detecting even then some need for him, knowing that to return without him would be a loss as well. It was selfish, she knew, but she did not want to return alone, could not, at the risk of disturbing old dreams, lose so completely.

Then: "Kathy?"

She heard this from the room, heard Marie's voice and a lower cry. For a second she could not move. She waited, leaning against the mud wall, touching the sun warmth that seeped into her fingers.

"Kathy?"

She walked back into the room, blinking at the darkness. She arrived just in time to see the baby appear. It dangled between the mother's legs, its arms touching the dirt floor. Marie had one arm on the woman's back, another stretching under to receive the child.

Marie said: "It's here."

Kathy stepped closer, not sure what was expected of her. Marie was saying over and over, in time to the woman's grunts: "Now, now, now."

Kathy moved even closer. She wanted to see. It was not curiosity, but something stronger, a need to be exposed. She said: "I'll take the baby."

Marie nodded, then smiled. Kathy knelt in the dust, her knees touching the moisture of the woman's water. She did not look at the baby but stared, instead, at the woman's bare flank. The baby came into her hands, but even then she didn't look. She had the impression the woman had not given birth; rather, it had been the soil letting something free. The brown legs connected to the soil, the stillness of the hut, all seemed too old for new life.

"A boy," Marie said, obviously pleased.

The woman waddled back to the table. Kathy carried the baby between the woman's legs, the umbilical cord a leash.

In the afternoon Kathy walked to market. She didn't feel well. The heat had not let up. She felt it on her skin, pressing, forcing her to slow. The small hairs on her arms were wet gold, the follicles clogged by beads of perspiration. She walked faster than normal, thinking if she could sweat freely, she wouldn't feel the heat so much. But she was mistaken, the heat flowed with her, her movement pulling air away from her lungs.

She watched her feet. The ground was covered by silt. At times it drifted up to cover her instep, touching it with warmth. In a few spots the ground was cracked. Jagged lines ran for ten or fifteen feet, then stopped, their purpose lost.

She did not think as she walked but accepted impressions as they came. She saw trees, huts, the yellow thatched roofs, new-yellow from the recent harvest of millet. Dogs passed. A sow wallowed in a pool of water near an open bore well, while a woman pounded laundry, the color of her skin identical to that of the woman who had given birth. She heard the muted grumble of the market in the distance, the shrill pipe of a wooden finger flute. She smelled dollo, the strange cidery beer made from millet, and heard men shout, their voices already drunk.

She checked her watch twice, calculating the advance of

time with the position of the sun. She wanted it to be dark.
She was tired of the light, the heat, the strain on her eyes.
She could not imagine things growing in this light, except,
perhaps, bacteria. It seemed to her life would have to be
cellular, infinitely small, to survive.

She entered the stand of trees surrounding the market.
Thin cords had been strung between trees, displaying cloth,
rope, bicycle parts. Women sat behind strips of material,
their vegetables spread out before them. The soil under her
feet changed. It was no longer silt. Instead, it was firmer, a
mulch of countless markets, small piles of seeds and vegetable cores, tiny scraps and threads of material, the residue
of seasons and falling leaves. She had the feeling of entering
something ancient.

She walked through the narrow aisles, careful not to step
on anything. Animals roamed freely. Hogs sniffed at everything while boys chased them, hitting them with sticks,
sending them off squealing. The boys were naked. One,
shorter than the others, had a white piece of cloth dangling
from the end of his penis. The cloth was stained brown
from blood.

Near the center of the market she bought onions and
garlic, each time gesturing with her hands to find out the
price. Once she was forced to call over a young boy to trans-
late for her. She was buying tomatoes. The woman selling
them spoke to the boy, naming a price, which Kathy refused. She started to walk away, but the boy laughed and
waved her back.

"She says you can have them at your price," the boy
said.

Kathy bent and picked up the tomatoes. They felt good
in her hands, warm, their skins polished. She smiled at the
woman. The woman said something to the boy. He
shrugged and moved off.

Kathy walked away, not feeling the heat so severely now. She liked markets, liked buying and bartering, her comfort in the exchange, money for goods. It was contained, final. Even now she was aware of this, aware of her ability here to become, in a sense, a spectator to her own actions so that the uniqueness of her circumstances was not lost. It reminded her of playing dress-up as a young girl, the strange, almost divided sensation of experiencing something while observing herself at the same time.

She left the market and followed the Koudougou road back to her compound. It was still early afternoon, but she knew she wouldn't return to the dispensary. It was too hot. The village women would not make the walk, and if they did, Marie lived close enough to be called. She wasn't needed.

She walked slowly along the road, stopping whenever she found shade. The road was lined by a wall of weeds. She could smell them, dusky, dry, an odor not unlike sage. There were tangled bushes farther off, matted by the sun, compressed into tight balls of hazy green. A lone baobab stood in the center of a field, its branches twisted, the trunk wide and silver. The air wavered, giving the landscape a liquid sheen, sidways chugs of light, movement, vapor. In the distance she could just make out juts of rock, brown-colored, volcanic-looking and porous, pitted by wind and the grind of sand. Stopping, she thought: Age, could hear the sift of dust and sand, the breezes low-sweeping, rooted to the earth, the downturned leaves.

In time she came to the gate of their compound. She opened it slowly, closed it behind her. She wondered, as she walked to the front door, if the pentard had soured in the heat. The chickens clucked at the side of the house, drowsy now in midday. She looked to the sky and saw no clouds, saw the faultless blue run, like the dipping of canvas over tent poles, from tree to tree. Turning, she pushed open the metal door to the house and waited for the lizards to scuttle out of sight. She banged the door with her fist again, not wanting them to fall, as they sometimes did, their fleshy bodies thwacking on the cement floor, when she walked in the house. She was about to go in when she heard Cooca call from the gate. He had papers in his hands and was waving them at her.

"Hello, Cooca," she called, happy to have the quiet disturbed. "What is it?"

"For Noel. It came to the *préfet*'s office. The guard brought it, but you weren't here. I told him I'd give it to you."

Kathy walked to the gate and took the papers. They were telegrams, both from Grant, Noel's brother. Neither had an envelope.

"Did the guard say anything, Cooca? Was there a message?"

"No. He just brought them and said they might be important. That's all."

"Okay, thank you."

Cooca ran off. She noted he was dressed in his best clothes, heading for the market. She read the first telegram, walking back toward the house. It said: "Dad dying. Are you coming?" The second one, dated a week earlier, said the same thing.

Noel thought: Heat. He felt the heat around him, pushing his chest flat and taking air from his lungs. He was sweating. He felt hungry, light-headed, his body depleted.

He bent over the jack and worked it higher. The truck

leaned to one side, wedging itself against the rocks he had placed near the tires. He stared at the base of the jack, watching to make sure it didn't slip. When the truck was high enough, he pulled the tire and threw it into the flatbed. The tire rolled, banging against the side, and the truck shimmied. Noel waited.

When he was sure the truck was steady, he went back to work. He grunted as he held the spare in place.

He screwed the lug nuts on with his fingers, then lowered the truck until the tire touched the road. He took his time with the lug wrench, leaning on it, feeling the solid sensation of metal on metal. The tire turned once, causing the jack to shimmy again, but still he leaned on it.

He finished the job quickly, then lit a cigarette. He could not distinguish the feeling of smoke in his lungs from the heated air. He stood beside the truck, squinting, his hands resting on the door.

It was then he let the image of his father come. It was a deliberate action, an opening he forced on himself, thinking: Now it will start. Still, he did not let memory come whole but broke it down, sifting it as soon as it pressed on him. There were disparate memories, connected only by the life line of his father. He saw his father cutting the lawn, gardening, hammering nails. There were other times, times when his father was dressed for work, his suit looking like shiny business armor, but these did not come as clearly. It was easier to remember his father at home, his presence somehow hardening them all. He recalled boots, the thick stump of them as they walked over the bare wood floors, always the sound of him, even late at night, passing through the house. And now his father was dying. The thought undermined those memories, ridiculing them, scattering recollection until he thought: No, it cannot be. He could not conceive of his father's death, could not accept his father's frailness now, the thick blood he had always imagined just under his father's skin slowed and turning thin. For a moment Noel's mind stopped on this, wondering not at death, but at his father's weakness, finding he could not reconcile the war of intellect and emotion within him, saying to himself: Death, yes, but not weakness.

He took out a handkerchief then and wiped his face. He threw his cigarette away and stamped it with his shoe. He wondered for a moment what his father was thinking, what he had intended by the letter. The question hung in his mind, and he was afraid to go near it, knowing that beneath the question there had been some motive. The letter was not innocent. It had had a purpose, Noel knew, was not sent only to confirm knowledge Noel could have received from some other source. There had been about it something in the nature of a request, a calling in of old debts, saying: Come home. Come home now. He was certain it was not meant to garner pity; the thought did not come close to fitting his father. But it was a debt, flesh calling to its own, a last payment of duty, affection, loss.

Noel wiped his face again, pulled his shirt away from his body. He climbed into the truck and sat motionless behind the wheel. He started the engine, pushing his mind closed, losing recollection in the whine of the pistons. The heat inside the cab was immense. He put the truck in gear and drove slowly, glancing frequently in the rear-view mirror to see how it was riding. He saw dirt curling up behind him, obscuring the road. It gave him an odd feeling to see the road he had just covered consumed that way. It was as though the past were removed.

He stopped twice on the way to Kongoussi. The first time was at a small bush village where he bought two mangoes. The mangoes were large and orange, and he ate them whole without bothering to skin them first. The second time he stopped while a young Fulani boy herded his cattle across the road. The cows separated and pooled around the truck. Noel listened to the boy calling each by name. He smelled dung, skin, the odor of unclean fur. He noticed one steer whose right shoulder was covered by a large sore. Every time the steer moved a swarm of flies broke from the cut, then resettled, their clustered bodies a black spot on the steer's hide.

He drove on, easing past the cattle, heading out into the flat country, the truck sound preceding him, obscuring sight by noise. The bee, still with him, buzzed against the back window, its body sometimes tucked and slapped by wind, the buzzing cuffed to silence, then rekindled. He passed wide fields dotted with millet saplings, pecked by new growth that pushed tentatively from the soil. In sideways glances he saw birds flutter, their colors bright in contrast with the earth, mating, collecting, pursuing activities on razored wings, feathers held stiffly to capture air. He smoked two cigarettes, each time watching the smoke rise and drift across the rear-view mirror, touching the windows in gray, lethargic whirls, only to be pushed aside, then flung out. He followed the tire grooves dug in the road, the steering wheel almost useless in his hands, the direction established for him by countless repetitions of coming and going. The sun was still high, its rays chucking into the new soil like plow blades, vertically, without leverage, the dirt holding secret fertility.

He stopped the truck on a small rise, squinting to see the village before him. He saw the circled huts, thatched roofs, mud walls rising before him like a wave of soil. He paused there, not wanting to go forward. Dimly he could make out the sound of habitation, the collective murmur of survival, the odd leisure of soil-scratch farming: dogs barking, chil-

dren crying, men laughing. The air was still. To one side of
the village he saw a copse of trees, the bark matching the
shade in color, the leaves mottled green.

He pressed the gas slightly, then let the truck drift, only
the tires making noise, the gritty ping of stones on the chassis. He coasted down, feeling himself shedding time so that
he imagined himself going back in age, less descending than
returning. The huts seemed to approach the truck from all
sides, silent, a honeycomb of mud dauber nests. He parked
the truck to the right, at the edge of the village, the soil
already changed beneath the truck tires. He climbed out.
He noticed a small group of boys watching him from the
trees, their bodies stilled in expectation, fear, their whispers
cautious. He pretended not to see them, though they followed him, sometimes giving him sight of their thin, coiled
bodies, naked except for small leather belts around their
waists. They stalked him; his activity, he knew, was game
enough for them, hunting the difference between them. He
heard them call, tracing him with their voices when he left
the copse behind.

He walked to the left, around the village. Three dogs ran
at him. He waved at them, and they came to a halt, unsure
whether to move closer, their claws scrabbling on the dry
ground. From behind him he heard one of the boys yell at
the dogs, but turning, he didn't see the boy. Yet the voice,
disembodied, acted on the dogs, which turned gaunt sides
to him, circling as he walked between them. Skulking with
ears lowered and tails bent, they ran sentry around him.

Near the first line of huts a woman called to him. He saw
her standing next to a gray log, a machete in her hand, her
breasts bare and sagging. He smiled at her and nodded. The
woman bent back over the log and hacked at it. The muscles stretched in her arms, biceps, supple and tense, regis-

tering contact with the wood. She began to hum, dotting the sound with quick intakes of breath and the explosion of chips and wood dust.

He saw the well when he rounded the last hut. Two trees stood in the center of a level field, marking the water. The men, distant and small against the even backdrop, were clustered in the shade. He saw the crossbeam hanging over the open lip of the well, a pulley attached to it by a bicycle chain. The men did not see him. As he came closer, he heard the sound of digging. It was a rhythmic sound, a cadence coming from deep in the earth. He timed his steps to it, wondering as he did so whether all movement wasn't somehow tied to a pulse.

"Nassarra," one man yelled.

Noel was near them now. He saw tools scattered around the work area, saw the men rise, already shifting in uneasiness. He watched a group of men pulling dirt from the well and listened to the pulley squeak as he approached, transfixed, turning in his mind the prehistoric aspect of the scene.

The men were lepers. They came to him, greeting him, their hands extended. He shook their hands, sometimes a proffered wrist instead, touching without feeling the white stumps, the fingerless palms. With each, cataloguing, gauging ability, he noted the signs of disease, saw ears gone, noses missing, toes broken and splayed into wide white paddles, feeling, at the same time, an ancient mourning come into his soul. And while his mind was sharp, he had the sensation of its deliberately dulling certain details, as if it had been pulled in too many directions in too short a time. He passed among them, greeting them by name, touching when he could and feeling the touch bloom in his mind, thinking: In this I am whole. And he again experienced the warmth of return, the continuance of something eternal, as timeless as suffering, so that he lingered longer than necessary, passed the time of day without need to work.

It was only after dollo had been brought and he had drunk that he walked to the edge of the well and asked: "Is there much water?"

He looked down and saw a man fifteen meters beneath him. The digger was chipping at the laterite. Sparks flew when the metal pick hit rock.

"Any snakes down there?" Noel called.

The man stopped digging and laughed.

"No, Nassarra."

"How much water?"

The man held his hands apart, letting the pick drop in the mud. Noel had to squint to see. Three inches. He knew they had probably pulled some while working. Still, it wasn't enough, and he thought of going deeper, calling: "Is it caving in?" He pointed. "Down at the bottom. Are the sides caving in?"

The digger said: "A little."

"I want to take a look," Noel said to the men behind him. "Let's take him out."

He stepped back and watched Ba, one of the three men in the village with working fingers, untie the bucket they had been using and drop the rope down to the digger. Noel watched the digger attach the pick handle to the rope, forming a swing seat. When he was ready, he called and jerked the rope three times.

"He's ready," Noel said.

The men lined up along the length of the rope. When Noel told them to pull, they walked backward, the rope trapped under their armpits, unable to reach hand over hand. The men walked steadily, not glancing behind them until the digger appeared. The digger grabbed the cross-beam and swung himself clear.

Noel took his place, saying: "Easy now."

He sat on the handle seat and nodded to the men. He let his weight fall forward, feeling for a moment he wouldn't stop. Then the rope caught him, and he used his feet against the sides of the well, bouncing with his toes as he descended. Above him he saw the sky shrink. It became a patch of blue, rounded, distorted only by a few black heads looking down at him.

He was in the mud before he could prepare himself. The suck of it surprised him. It pulled him down, clinging to his bare legs, matting itself against skin and hair. Around him the walls were sheer laterite, giving way to dirt only near the bottom. He saw a calcium streak running through the wall higher up, white flakes twisting in lines of compression. The well smelled of mud and sweat. He found the air wet when he breathed it.

He untied the pick and let the men above pull the rope free. He tapped with the metal head in a circle, testing the rock. He saw it would cave in soon and thought of the supplies he would bring: cement, iron re-rod, metal molds to shape a column of cement. He told the men to send him a shovel. When it came, he shoveled out the mud, filling bucket after bucket, his skin wet with sweat, his hands heavy on the wooden handle. He strained to see the bottom, peering through the mud slide of dirt, water, the rock shift of the well bottom. A rhythm came to his movement, discovered and remembered the moment it came, so that his hands and back worked in coordinated motion, his lifting tied to the thought of lifting. After a time he saw a small stream of water near the bottom of one wall. He scraped the last mud away, bending to look, trying to see if it ran quickly enough.

"Do you want a man?" Ba called down to him.

"Yes, send one. We've got some water."

Noel stood in the heat and leaned against the well wall, watching above him. He felt his body chilled by inactivity, the humid air. He wiped his forehead with his sleeve. Mud caked his arms and legs, and he felt it drying, adding texture to his skin, pulling at the short hairs and clinging.

He did not understand what happened next. He saw only that a man was dangling above him, descending too quickly. Beyond the man he saw Ba stretched across the well, leaning against the crossbeam, trying to hold the weight of the man with his hands. Noel yelled. His voice echoed, and he listened to it reverberate, ducking at the same time, trapped by the jangling legs coming at him. But then, more clearly, he heard the whisper cut of the pulley, heard Ba scream, one voice among the confusion, saw Ba's finger snapped by the run of the rope over the raised metal edge of the pulley. He saw the finger fall past the man, a white finger streaming blood as it came. He tried to dodge, but the finger followed him, bouncing off his shoulder and landing in the mud.

He looked up and saw the man who had been dangling now scrambling out of the well.

"Nassarra?" someone called.

Noel didn't listen, could not force himself to respond. He felt sick. He covered his eyes with his hands, feeling a crazed tremor move through his body. He heard the men on top shouting at one another, then a low moan which he took to be Ba. He thought: Now this. He couldn't breathe, felt choked by the sudden knowledge that came, sensing in this event the trappings of dreams, nightmarish visions of a thing fated. "Nassarra," another man called. He listened to the voice, hearing it off cold stone walls. He took his hands away from his eyes slowly. The finger was near him. He turned his head and bent to pick it up, sightless fingers searching the dirt for flesh. He was grateful for the mud which blocked sensation. He did not want to touch skin. With an effort he put the finger in his shirt pocket, then called for the rope.

More confused cries came, then the rope. Noel knotted the handle to the rope, dazed by the demands of muscle, the ordinary. He yelled: "*Taka,* pull," standing ankle-deep in mud, the finger held by cloth against his chest. The mud did not let him go at first. He felt his feet linger, then come free. He spiraled up, his feet playing off the walls, and he gripped the rope tighter, forcing himself to concentrate on the rough texture, the mechanical movement of legs, hands, feet. The sun reached him when he was halfway up. He put his head back and stared into the light. It was warm. As his head cleared the well lip, he saw the men walking resolutely backward. They walked with the slow, plodding steps of mules.

Noel swung himself clear. The men, sensing the weight gone, let the rope go. It fell back into the well, the pick thumping in the mud. Noel stood for a moment, taking the heat, watching them lift their arms to inspect the rope burns beneath. He saw one or two, red welts rubbed raw, the friction cut of hemp and the clamp of skin.

"Ba?" Noel asked.

One man pointed. Noel walked over to Ba. He was slumped against the trunk of the tree, holding his hand against his chest. There was little blood. Noel realized the disease had taken the blood, knew the finger would have been lost eventually.

A man squatting next to Ba moved off. Noel took his place, reaching into his pocket for the finger. He held it forward, offering it. He could think of nothing to say. He was aware of the absurdity of the gesture and saw the blank expression on Ba's face.

Ba took the finger finally and threw it to a sow that was snuffling near them. The sow started, then came back. It inhaled the finger. Another man threw a rock at it, and the sow ran off, its teats wagging.

In late afternoon Noel drove. He was drunk now. He smoked cigarettes in succession, dropping one after another out the open truck window, watching the orange dot fade and diminish in the rear-view mirror. He watched the land go by, sometimes lifting a bottle of beer to his lips, the liquid not distilled from barley but from some cousin of millet. He tasted Africa in this: the grain distinguished beneath the weak carbonization, somewhat flat, yet sturdy, somehow practical.

He continued to drink. Finished with one bottle, he threw it out, heard it fall softly on the dirt, then leaned across the seat for another, holding it between his legs as he opened it, fighting the lid off, and spilling a frothy puddle on his knees and crotch. "Damn it," he said. Again: "Damn it." But he was drinking, too, sucking the suds that climbed the neck of the bottle, guiding the steering wheel with the heel of his hand. For a stretch of some hundred yards he pressed the accelerator, felt the truck respond, and thrilled at the speed, acknowledging the ease of his own death were the truck to have a flat or bounce to one side of the road.

After a time he pulled to a stop near a small unnamed village and located a bar. He parked the truck and went inside to exchange the one empty he had for a refill, paying quickly, making no note of the change. When he came out, he found two boys standing near the truck, one with his hand on the hood. They separated as he came near them, backing up, the older one saying: "Nassarra?"

"What is it?" Noel asked, not ready for conversation.

He tossed his cigarette away, and the smaller boy ran to get it while the first said: "My mother has to go your way."

"Where is she?"

The boy pointed. Noel followed the line of his finger and saw a woman struggling toward the truck, large bundles in each hand. She was old, her skin dry and cracking, her teeth coated orange with kola.

"What is this?" Noel asked, not quite expecting an answer, watching the woman come forward. He felt the alcohol climbing in him, felt the dizziness of hunger, exertion, emotion.

"Nassarra," the woman said, then lifted her arm, dropping one bundle in the process, waving at the road in the direction he had been traveling.

"Yes, yes," he said, anxious to be going.

She pointed again. He nodded, but she hung back, her eyes glued to the truck as though it might continue without either of them. The small boy stepped forward with the butt of the cigarette in his mouth, tripped, and almost fell into her.

"Come," Noel said. He took the bundles from the woman and set them on the flatbed. She still stood quietly, waiting for instruction. He waved her to the other side of the truck, and she circled, going around the back, keeping her distance. She began to climb into the back, up onto the bed, but Noel shook his head and pointed to the interior of the cab.

"Tell her to get in here," he said to the older boy.

The boy said something quickly. The woman nodded, continued the circle, and stopped at the door. Finally, she yanked at the handle, but the door didn't open. The small boy laughed. "Jesus," Noel said, feeling an irrational anger, repugnance at such ignorance, his tolerance broken. He hurried around the front of the truck and interrupted the woman, who was still pulling at the chrome handle, tugging harder, her feet dug into the road.

"Here," he said. He pressed the button beneath the handle and the door sprung open. The woman stepped back, sucking in her breath. Noel started to laugh. The woman smiled, and the two boys jumped up and down, laughing without understanding. The woman climbed in, folding her limbs awkwardly, tucking her dress around her, looking out of place and afraid. Noel shut the door softly.

He walked back to the driver's side and climbed in. The woman was near the passenger door, staring out the window. He took a drink and started the engine. The pistons misfired, then caught. Noel lit a cigarette, seeing in the match flare the profile of the woman, dark face set rigidly, ears halved by the bandanna over her head. He set the truck in gear and pressed the gas. The woman's hand flew out to grip the dashboard, though she didn't turn to face him. She sat sentinel, riding silently, her jaw sometimes working to chew kola. "Where are you going?" Noel asked once. She pointed ahead, not bothering to speak.

He asked no more questions. He drove more cautiously, still drinking, though, his eyes red in the rear-view mirror, which he turned to him now, not wanting to catch her reflection each time he glanced behind him. The countryside was still, gathered for a last push before the deadening light. He smoked cigarette after cigarette, blowing the smoke out and away from her, granting her such courtesies while knowing they went unnoticed. He smelled her, her scent not very different from the land's, her hair occasionally giving off the odor of grease. She turned twice in her seat, each time to check her bundles, then returned to her position near the door, leaning out, unwilling to be contained by the truck.

Near a small gully running between two eroded hills, she straightened. She looked around her, detecting landmarks indiscernible by him, then spoke quickly, waving her hand up and down, the palm horizontal to the floor of the truck. "Here?" Noel asked. She looked at him, nodded. He slowed the truck. She pointed forward, perhaps fifty yards ahead, and he let the truck glide, not understanding the difference between the two places, yet fascinated by her confidence, her homing instinct. He stopped finally, and she sat trapped in the truck, her hands wandering over the door handles, unable to make them work. He leaned across her and flicked the handle up. She pushed against the door and unfolded outward, standing wearily, her eyes still roaming the landscape.

Noel got out. He pulled the bundles down and brought them around. They were heavy, and he waited to see how she would go on. She lifted them, bending with her knees and hoisting, using her straight back as a flexed rod which, once set, would not buckle. She said thank you briefly, turning as soon as the words were spoken. She walked off, down into the gully, her feet slipping on hard dirt. She turned sideways and eased down, the bundles held out away from her body, lowering and rising for balance. He saw a bird take flight above her, heard stones pushed by her feet rattle into thorny bushes. She disappeared behind a bush, then reappeared, finally, on the spine of the gully. He watched her shape grow small, obscured by vegetation.

When she was gone from sight, he walked back around the truck. As he climbed in, he found two kola nuts left on the seat in payment.

By three Kathy had slept and awakened and now lay on her bed, her skin clutched by the sheets, her mind webbed with heat so that she thought: I need water. But she could not bring herself to move, choosing, instead, to listen to the house, the tin roof pinging with sun and insects, the walls grating and eroding under the tread of lizards. She heard all this from the haze of dream cover, able to drift by closing her eyes, locked and released by sleep. She thought once: This could be fever, then dismissed the notion. She did not feel sick. Her ears continued to follow sounds around the house, probing outside as well. Twice she heard trucks pass, expecting each time to hear Noel afterward, his boots clicking on rubber heels. She tried to imagine how she would tell him about the telegrams, phrasing words on her tongue, thinking: He will go now.

Finally, seeing the sun lowered on the walls, she got up and made her way outside. The light was gentle, broken. She stood framed in the doorway, waiting for impulse to direct her, unsure how to fill the last hours of day, yearning again for sleep and night. She watched a small group of ants working over something left by Cooca when he washed the dishes earlier. The ants were swarmed, tugging perhaps, laboring with quiet discipline. She wanted to use her sandal to brush them away, but waited, mesmerized, in time able to distinguish individuals.

A few minutes later she walked through the courtyard to the shower stall. She stripped her clothes and stood under the water, letting her hair get wet, wanting it to hold the moisture to release later. She stood in the open air, naked, vulnerable, smelling the dirt turn wet. The edge of the roof divided the sky above her. Far off, she heard pentards flocking, their calls raucous and shrill.

She let the chain slip back, cutting off the water. She stood in the quiet afternoon, the water dripping from her, dryness and warmth returning. A truck passed, and she listened to it, expecting it to stop, though it went on, its sound fading in a dopplered hum.

She dressed then, pulling on clothes, the trapped warmth of fabric. She walked past the coop, her steps causing a reaction among the chickens, heard the squawking of senseless panic. Back in the house she stopped to sit for a moment in a wicker chair, the wooden rungs hard against her buttocks and back, waiting for release. She reached to a desk table and took up her brush, combed her hair in long sweeps, letting the water fall on her skirt and blouse. Through the door she saw night coming on, watching the light thin and stretch, shadows arching like the shiver of a waking dog. She clipped her hair back, still holding the brush in her lap, thinking: He should be back.

She stood and went to the desk, bending to see her reflection framed in the tiny mirror there. She finished with her hair and stepped into the kitchen, her eyes running to the pot containing the pentard. She found a box of wooden matches on the window ledge and turned on the bottled gas. She opened the oven door. Crickets scrambled up and out, hopping on triangular legs as she reached among them, turning the oven dial with her free hand, smelling gas, then seeing the blue flame that ran over the dots, heating and giving light. She closed the door quickly and stepped to the pot, lifting the top, sniffing for rot and sour flesh but finding none. The head and legs were gone. She poured a dab of peanut oil over the bottom of the pot, rolled the bird once to grease it. It moved from side to side in the pot when she lifted it, the dull weight off balance. She opened the

oven door once more and placed it inside. Part of the gas
runner had not taken the flame, and she blew on it once,
watching the last dots catch and fire.

Turning, she took four potatoes from the bin on the floor
and set them beside the pot in the oven. She walked out of
the house then, dragging a chair after her, and put it in the
shade thrown by the wall. She came back in for a book,
searching for a moment through the house until she found
it near the bed. On her way back she checked the lanterns,
making sure Cooca had filled them with kerosene. Satisfied,
she went outside and sat.

She tried to read, but her eyes skipped entire lines, pas-
sages, jumping ahead to discover what was next. She could
not force them to slow and eventually put the book aside,
marking her place with a turned-down ear. She sat quietly,
almost cool now in the stillness. She felt the past push on
her, begging recognition, the present rooted to old associa-
tions. She centered on one thought: We will go home now.
And with this she smelled wood smoke, could not be sure if
it was the scent of old dreams gone or of cook fires burning
in the village. She remembered now a star-scudded sky,
Noel ahead of her on cross-country skis, the greyhound
length of his strides breaking frozen tracks. They had skied
on the golf course of Wentworth-by-the-Sea, the New
Hampshire coast stilled to icy shards, congealed tidal zones
of rock and kelp, past the long silent holes, greens, bunkers,
summer frozen and dipped in the lace of new snow. Noel
ahead saying then: Are you tired? We can stop. And she
answering: No, I'm fine, both traveling through black
night, the moon sickle-shaped, her breath freezing in a
gauze of white on her cheeks and nose. They had stopped
once by a group of people circled around a small fire, a coven
of suburban people unlocking ancient yearnings within themselves, their voices hushed even in this comparative com-

fort, the flame light catching strange attitudes, arms cast out, legs bent, sounds mixed and sorted by sea breezes. Noel had turned to her, their first real contact coming through heavy coats and sweaters, their first impressions padded by quilted down, a kiss above cloth on red cheeks, ears fragile and burning. Someone had passed mulled wine, the udder warmth of the filled goatskin in their hands, the spray as it hit her teeth and washed down building warmth. She then thinking: I will go with him if he asks, feeling in herself some crystallization. They skied back, tracking along the spined coast, feeling beneath their skis the longer grass of the rough. He had fallen once, stood sweeping snow from his pants, brushing powder back onto the trail, laughing at his own clumsiness. She had been aware of significance of the moment, thinking: This is what we would be, wondering if he understood. He had stepped aside, letting her go ahead, his skis taking up her rhythm, leader and led exchanged. They had skied toward the car, the warmth of the heater, the spell eventually broken by combustion, the fishtailing of the car as they pulled out and away.

They had slept together that night, the chill of their bodies gathered into one another and dispersed. Afterward, in the bed warmth, they had watched new snow fall, she waiting for an invitation of continuance, though it didn't come that night or for many after. Walking barefoot, they had crossed to the kitchen, to brew hot chocolate, half-clothed and shivering, the night given over to a wildness, north winter cold, the house and apartment creaking like pine. There had been warm stirrings, the slightly burned smell of frying protein, the milk combining with chocolate, pulling flakes of brown into white, nourishment given, received.

Later she had listened to him go, boots muffled by snow, his car starting far off, finally mixing with the chained sweep of tires grinding, a plow going by with flashing lights. Thinking: It is time to be joined, suddenly discovering in herself a loneliness only suspected before. Her flesh, untouched now, smelled of him. And she had settled into the covers that winter night, tracing herself through his presence, the thoughts he had forced on her, finding her independence transmuted by age, so that she had thought: It is time now, wanting to be collected, dependent for a time.

In lantern light she cut vegetables into the pot, slicing carrots and onions, smelling the meat close and warm, the skin already brown. She put the pot back in the oven, then went about the house, lighting more lanterns, catching the flames on cloth wicks, shutting and adjusting the glass chimneys. She set the table quickly, sorting flatware and arranging it around the metal plates Noel had used before she came. Darkness pushed through the room, collecting furniture, blank walls, carving shadows where the dim lantern light could not reach. And though she had seen these spaces not fifteen minutes before, she now felt afraid, wondered what creature might linger in the cornered darkness. She did not dwell on this, though once, at the sound of creaking, she lifted the lantern and swung it around the room, half humoring some childish impulse, half-serious.

She was near the table when she heard his truck. She was sure it was his the moment she heard it and wondered briefly how she could have mistaken earlier ones. She listened to the chug of the engine, the identifying wagon-spring rub of the shocks, and walked out to meet him. The headlights caught her unaware, and she shaded her eyes before lifting the same hand and waving it. The lights flicked off. Waiting, she heard crickets; a bat shadow cut overhead. She called: "Noel?"

"Be right there," he said.

She walked slowly across the yard, reluctant to leave the light. The truck door opened and closed, keys jangled. He said: "I should tell you now I'm a little bit drunk."

"I don't care."

"You sure?"

"Yes, I'm positive."

He walked toward her, a bottle in each hand, and she thought once: Death is contagious, wondered if his father's dying had already begun. She saw Noel wobble, the motion swift and corrected almost as soon as it started, then smelled him, his clothes carrying scents of dirt, beer, kola, sweat.

"What a day," he said, putting his arm around her.

"What happened?"

"I'll tell you later. How was yours?"

"There was a baby at the dispensary."

"Sick?"

"No, we delivered one."

"That must have been something. Did you help?"

"A little."

She passed through the door before him. She glanced once at a small wooden bookcase, made from planks and dirt bricks, and saw the telegrams folded, waiting. She wanted to say: Here, and step to them, watch him read, ask afterward: We will go now, won't we? But he was already sitting at the table, his legs and boots gray from hard-packed mud, breathing deeply, still more a part of the night outside.

"Is that the pentard?" he asked, sniffing.

"Yes."

"It smells great. Was it okay—it must have been if you're cooking it."

"It was fine."

He pointed to his clothes, then asked: "Would you mind if I cleaned up later? I'm too tired right now."

"No, I don't mind."

"You're being very—what? What's the word I'm looking for? Sympathetic."

"Noel . . ." she started. He was smiling, leaning back in his chair. She wondered if he was being serious. He looked up, said: "What?"

She couldn't read him. She stood mutely, hearing a lantern hiss. A dog barked. She thought: Now, I should tell him now, but went into the kitchen, instead, gauging his time and mood, sensing in herself a need for care. She could not rush. And in this preparation she felt some slyness, knew it was not only from sympathy she withheld the telegrams. It was more of a gambit, an opening move which, she knew, would set off other moves, a chain of reaction.

She checked the pentard, turning the oven up slightly. She felt guilty for stalling. She stopped in the middle of the kitchen and listened to him move. His chair creaked. His boots slid once on the cement. She said: "Noel?" using the wall to protect her.

"Huh?"

Then she walked out. He was picking mud off his legs and flicking it outside. A beer, nearly full before, was now half-empty before him. "What?" he asked again.

"Here," she said. "These came."

She handed him the telegrams, relinquishing control. She sat in her chair and watched him read, his forehead wrinkled, his eyes socketed by shadow. "How . . ." he started to ask, but then shuffled the papers again and reread them. She saw him slouch, cover, his expression vacillating. He placed them flat on the table and ran his hands over them.

Speaking for him, she said: "I think they must have been waiting in Ouagadougou, and when they received the message from here, they knew where to locate you. It must have been a mix-up."

"They're from Grant," he said.

"Yes, I know."

" 'Dad dying. Are you coming?' " he read aloud. " 'Grant,' " he said.

She waited then, listening for more, silence building. He did not lift his eyes. She arranged words in her mind, let them go. He took his cigarettes from his pocket and lit one. He lifted his beer and stood. He walked outside and she heard him sit in a chair, the wicker rungs giving. She went into the kitchen and checked the dinner.

Two

Leaving.

Kathy thought the word, though its meaning did not come clearly to her mind. She looked around her. Boxes were stacked, the walls bare. Their bed was leaning against the corner, angled to form a dark triangle with the two walls.

She walked around the room. She remembered other moves: apartments cleared out, their contents carried to trucks, to U-Hauls, to friends' cars. There had always been a destination, a place to move to, a continuance. But now she felt the move was more final, the boxes more firmly sealed. The old sensation of having her life reduced, narrowed, only to have it bud again in a new location, was gone. These boxes held. Time was severed.

61

She had been packing for almost a week while Noel went through the official procedure of leaving, the papered finish of their departure. The rooms had come down, apart, in slow, monotonous hours, stripped to hollowness, the house converted to a campground. Noel had packed his things in a large steamer trunk and locked it. He had come with one trunk, he had told her, and he intended to leave with only one. The rest—the wall hangings, a few bronze statues, some baskets—she had wrapped and placed in strong wooden crates. She intended to send them by surface mail. The crates would follow them, a reminder, their sides stamped with stickers of Dakar, Abidjan, or Lomé.

She was standing quietly when Cooca came into the room. Kathy saw him framed against the doorway, his arms and legs sweaty, his chest bare. He shuffled his feet, his discomfort at being alone with her transparent.

"Hello, Cooca," she said.

"Nassarra."

Kathy crossed the room, pointing to a few scattered boxes. She said: "I want to give these things to the dispensary. The pots and pans and things. Do you think they could send a donkey cart?"

"Yes."

"I know Noel wants you to have the chickens. There will be a lot of other things. He should be back soon. Any minute, I think."

"Well, then," Cooca said, and turned.

She started to say something, then stopped. "Nothing," she said. "Never mind."

But she had wanted to ask him if he would miss Noel. She had seen him mechanically accept the odds and ends he had been given, his face blank. She wanted to say: What does my husband mean to you? What will it be like when he is gone?

Cooca left. She heard him close the gate outside, then his voice as he spoke to the children gathered beyond the compound wall. The children had come as soon as the news had spread that Noel was leaving. Other people had come as well. Villagers, in town for market, had passed to say good-bye to Noel, to thank him for his work, for the water he had found. She had watched them, the passage of each quiet and calm, their robes flowing, bare feet or sandals made from truck tires padding on the earth. They had left gifts: chickens to cook, pieces of meat, tobacco, gris-gris to protect them. The sight of the people had affected her. She had seen Noel differently, thinking then as now: He has been an influence here. It reminded her of a time when she had gone with her father into his office and had finally seen the men he worked with, his desk, his chair and blotter. It had left her with a sinking feeling, a knowledge that her father was not particularly important, that he was only one man among twenty or thirty. It had disturbed her then, sensing in his sameness with the men around him her own sameness. But Noel's work was different. She had seen the people, had talked with them and heard their thanks. And she had seen Noel's reluctance to leave, his identity being unraveled. Come back, the Africans told him. Return.

She walked around the room idly now, touching boxes as she passed, feeling warm cardboard, wooden boards. She tied box flaps down, marking each with a grease pencil. She wrote in French when she could, checking her memory for the appropriate words. When she was finished, she arranged the boxes in piles—one for the dispensary, another for Cooca, a third to carry into Ouagadougou for shipping.

Afterward, she walked outside and stood in a thick stream of light. Nothing moved. There was no shade, and she stepped back in the doorway, letting the doorframe block the light, cover half her face in shadow. A drum sounded far behind her, muffled by the cement walls. She leaned against the wall, letting the cement dig into her shoulder, feeling the grit press through her blouse. A wasp buzzed past her, weaving in drowsy light up to the roof of the house, its wings ticking on the tin, finally landing against its mud home. It pulled its body into a small hole in the center of the mud patch, disappeared, reappeared, in flight again, sinking on tissued wings in sound, graceless. She stepped deeper into the shade, then turned and went into the kitchen. She fixed herself a cup of tea, waiting beside the stove without energy to move. She thought once of New Hampshire but could not pull a vision of the place to her.

She poured hot water onto the bag and carried the cup into the larger room. She sat at the makeshift table, her cup ringing the cheap wood. She moved the cup and saw a fly come, drink, test, sip with legs extended like a man panning gold, its body lifting and starting at the touch of shadow. She was almost finished with the tea when she heard Noel come. He was honking his horn, driving fast, the purr of the engine stretched and blooming in the silence surrounding her. She walked outside and saw Noel climbing out of the cab, grinning, his shirt wet with sweat. He waved to her and shouted: "*Glace, glace.*"

She started toward him, but he was already jumping onto the flatbed. She saw him lift the tire iron and bring it down on something. The group of children were jumping up and down behind the truck.

"What are you doing?" she asked when she was closer.

"Ice," Noel said. "Most of these little bastards have never seen the stuff. I promised them I'd find some in Koudougou."

He had a huge block of ice wrapped in burlap. The bed of the truck was wet from melt. Noel cracked the ice again, and Kathy saw it splinter and break.

"Come on," Noel yelled. "Come up. Look at these kids."

Kathy climbed onto the flatbed. The children were jumping around, slamming into one another. Noel handed the ice out, grabbing chunks and giving the smallest children their portions first. The little ones let the ice drop, finding it too cold. The older boys hooted and snapped their fingers together.

"They don't know cold like that," Noel was saying, almost shouting. He was excited. He kept slamming the ice with the tire iron. "Here, have some," he said in French. "Here."

The children laughed at Noel's tone of voice. They were inventing new things to do with the ice. One of the larger boys was rubbing it on people's backs, causing shrieks and retaliations. Another put some ice on the ground for a dog, but the dog took one lick and ran off. The children threw ice at it, laughing.

"Where's Cooca?" Noel asked when the excitement had settled some. He was still handing out chunks and sometimes slamming the block with the tire iron.

"He's down at the dispensary getting a donkey cart."

Noel sat on the tailgate of the truck. "You know," he said, suddenly more serious, "I don't think he's ever had ice. But I took him into Koudougou once. Did I ever tell you about it?"

"No, tell me."

He spoke then without looking at her, caught in some reverie, saying: "I took him into this French guy's house that used to live there. I realized at one point he had never seen electric lights. He was shy—he was only about ten then—so I took him around the house and watched him flick the lights on and off. He stood at the switch and flicked them on and off, on and off, and he never did get his fill of it."

The children were shrieking again. Noel stopped for a

moment, then said: "You know, it was just like taking someone from the eleventh century and jumping with him into the twentieth. Cooca listened to a stereo, played with a fan, even flushed a toilet, all for the first time. I don't know what he thought of it."

"That's a wonderful story," Kathy said. She watched him hand out more ice. He looked sad. His head was cocked to one side as if remembering. He seemed to turn gentle in front of her, and she thought: I fell in love with this. His hands moved more slowly. The children quieted. They sucked at the ice, shifting their pieces from hand to hand.

"It's all coming to this continent, and they don't even know it," he said after a time. "Well, anyway." He stood and chopped at the block. It was almost gone. He handed out more, throwing one piece up in the air and watching the children jump. He saved one large portion, saying: "That's for Cooca."

He climbed down off the truck. He helped her down, then walked with her into the house. She heard the children still laughing. Noel stopped in the center of the room.

"Is that everything?" he asked.

"Just about."

"I'm sorry I couldn't help much. Thank you for doing it."

"That's all right."

"I'm going to fix some coffee," he said. "Would you like some?"

"I just had a cup of tea."

He walked into the kitchen. She sat at the table, and traced his movements by sound, heard the sugar come off the shelf, coffee spooned out of a tin. She called: "What did the director say?" but he didn't answer right away, leaving her words hanging while he finished fixing the coffee, then answering as he came out: "Nothing really. There's no problem at all."

Noel sat. He stirred his coffee, said: "They have a new chicken project at the center. They ordered a bunch of French chickens, but they didn't have the pens built in time, so now the chickens are in a small coop and they're pulling the tail feathers off each other. I don't think they were even debeaked, and there's too little space. They've all turned cannibal."

"So they're dying?"

"Most. They keep pulling the feathers off each other and running around the coop. The Africans think it's hysterical."

"Who gave them the chickens?"

"The World Bank, I think. Who knows?"

"What can they do?"

"Nothing. I told them to put some salt in the coop. Sometimes that helps."

"Isn't it just a case of too little space?"

"Probably," he said. There's no roof on the pen either, so they're dying from the sun and disease brought in from other birds. The chickens probably think it's Dachau."

He grinned at this. She laughed. He drank his coffee, lighting a cigarette and letting the match fall on the floor. A lizard passed by the open front door, stopped, raised its head, then skittered off. Kathy checked her watch and saw it was close to four-thirty. Noel blew smoke straight up, watched it circle. She watched him, feeling the sullen heat, the day limited to sweat-smooth movements, languid gestures. She wanted to ask about his father but could not begin. She could not comment about the future, feeling as she did that the present was not yet done, that Africa still held sway.

In time they heard the donkey come. It brayed as it entered the courtyard, and they walked out together. Cooca walked beside the ainmal, a small stick in his hand. He had the donkey by two reins, which dangled from the animal's neck. Cooca led the donkey past the doorway, stopping when the cart was directly in front of the door. The donkey closed its eyes immediately, dozed except for skin shivers set off by flies.

Kathy stood to one side as they packed. She rubbed the donkey. The hair bristled under her hands; the warm smell of it reached her in full sun. She patted it once and saw small throws of dust fly up, swirl, rejoin the earth. The donkey shifted feet, lifting one in slumber. A row of pentards came onto the brick wall of the compound, called, were gone in a clatter of noise, their bald heads jogging through the bush like quail.

Noel and Cooca worked at loading the cart. Kathy watched the piles inside the house reduced, thinking: A third gone. It occurred to her they could have used the truck, and she thought to mention it, but it made no sense to bring it up. She held the donkey's reins, looking on, idle, suspended in thick heat. Flies buzzed close by, one touching the short hairs inside the donkey's ears, setting off a twitch, a fold of drowsiness. She waved her hand to clear them.

"Is that it?" Noel asked after a time. "Is that everything for the dispensary?"

She stepped forward, bending from the waist, and looked inside. "Yes, I think so," she said.

Cooca took the reins from her. She watched him hit the donkey's flank, heard the dull thud of wood on flesh. The donkey came to, pulled from sleep, its leg moving and lowering in a clop of imbalance. Cooca said: "Heah," and hit the animal again. The donkey heaved, its chest cut in leather bands by the traces, hooves clicking on the hard dirt. Kathy moved back, letting one hand trail over the donkey's fur as it passed, dust rising again between her fingers. "Heah," Cooca said. He pulled the animal's head sideways, jerking quickly while the donkey turned in slow precision, its head bent cheek to shoulder, melon-shaped slices of dirt working free under its feet.

"Will there be someone to help you unload?" Noel called after the boy.

"Yes, Nassarra."

And with that the children waiting at the gate took up after the cart. They ran behind it, laughing, towed by the slow plod of the animal, by Cooca's official air. Kathy watched until they were gone from sight.

"I forgot to give him ice," Noel said. He lit a cigarette. His shirt was wet from sweat. He wiped his face with a handkerchief.

"Let's get inside," Kathy said. "We should be in the shade."

"It's hot, isn't it?"

They walked inside. There were fewer boxes scattered over the floor. She wanted to say: It's almost done, conscious of some mental tally, finding in the packing process a rhythm of collection and release.

"So tomorrow's the day," Noel said. He sat at the table. Kathy fought the impulse to glance at her watch. She felt the room was sealed somehow, cut off from all intrusions. She sat opposite him, watching from the corner of her eye. He asked once: "Where did I leave my book? Did you see it?" But he made no move to get up, stayed slouched in his chair, quietly smoking. She thought of sleep then, though it was too late. She did not want to be awake that night and so sat in the warm silence, half dreaming, her eyelids thick.

She repeated: We are leaving, to herself, her mind taking it up like a chant, the heat peeled back by the sound of the words. A wasp reappeared above her head, and she studied it, heard its wings marking summer, heat, days of even sunlight and darkness.

The air was cool when Noel woke. It was not quite dawn, but he smelled the morning, sensed it rising toward him. Chickens murmured, probed by the release of light or by the wind coming across the land. He thought of the Sahara, imagining a vast sea of sand, salt, caravans, dunes moving in rolls. The wind seemed to him a whisper of the continent, laced with smoke and brush smell, containing and held by the history of lives unshared, unknown. He looked up, cocking his head on the pillow to catch the breeze, recalling at the same time how they had pulled the bed out into the compound the night before, Kathy saying: This is your last night here. He remembered it now, thinking it was something of a ceremony, that he was supposed to remember the night and hold it. He was conscious an ending had to be marked, that in order to begin, something had to be closed. And they had made love late into the night, with the stars beyond, the clench of darkness and skin, he thinking: This communion. He had held her, feeling Africa closed within her, their leaving rendered a formality, a step onto an airplane. Later he had come awake next to her, the covers off, and pressed against her, listening to night-baying dogs, a chill somewhere in his soul asking to be touched. In sleepless night he had held one strand of her hair, his fingers woven through it, fear and old dreams surrounding him. He had said: Kathy, quietly, hoping to reach her somewhere among her own dreams, his voice stretching through time, past and present, his fear bathed by her breath.

Now the stars were pale. He could make out the Southern Cross falling to the approach of the sun, a new moon rising too late. He pushed the covers off and lay naked. Far away he heard a flock of pentards call; beneath it, a dog barked twice, then quieted. The morning seemed to him power, night the absence of it. He waited until light appeared in the sky, then climbed out of bed and dressed. He walked to the shower and splashed water on his face and hair. The water was cold, and when he straightened, it ran down his back, touching his shoulder blades and spine. He crossed the compound, careful to be silent as he passed the bed. He opened the gate and stepped out.

Immediately he saw the light was distilled, drained somehow by its appearance through the trees. He waited until he could discern a barb of sun, then walked to it. He stood lizard-still and let the sun climb his body. It warmed him as it passed, his blood responding. A faint shadow appeared behind him, and he turned to watch it, seeing his form take shape in new shade, his identity excised from the land, pulled together by exclusion. He heard the village come awake, stalling and starting as if from dreams. He heard women calling, their voices rope-gathering children while the children responded in cries and wails of morning harshness. He heard someone chopping wood, the metallic twang of a machete blade counting things conquered by the sun. Standing this way, he reminded himself to remember these things, though understanding at the same time that he could not predict what memories would stay.

The morning was established in pulses, in movement. He stood a moment longer in the sun, sweat beginning, the cloth of his pants touching his skin with the warmth of a fresh cut. He stretched. His bones rocked; his spine shifted.

He yawned as he walked back to the compound. When he opened the gate, he saw Kathy sitting up, her outline clouded by the gauze of the mosquito net. She smiled and asked: "Where were you?"

"Just outside. I was watching."

"You're a romantic, aren't you?"

He shrugged and grinned. He watched her climb out of bed. She was shivering. She shook out her clothes before putting them on.

"Do you want to eat or go?" she asked. "I can cook some eggs. There should be some left."

"Let's just go. Is that all right with you?"

"Sure, I'm ready."

While she washed, he finished loading the truck. He tied ropes over the top, pulling and tightening them until the ropes vibrated under his hands. He checked the oil and brake fluid and added water to the radiator. Kathy came out as he was finishing, a small bag in either hand.

"Is there room?" she asked.

"We can keep them in the cab with us. Is that it?"

"I think so."

"Then let's go. We can eat lunch in Ouagadougou if we hurry."

"*Brochette* sandwiches?"

"If you like."

He helped her carry the bags to the truck. There wasn't much room in the cab, and he was forced to set the bags behind the seat, blocking the rear window. When they were in place, he went inside the house to see if they had left anything behind. He was surprised to hear his feet echo and thought of the hollowness returning. Sound moved around the room, preceding and following him at once. The cement walls seemed older now, grayed by osmosis from his own experience. He saw how badly the tin roof fit the house, saw lizards moving in and out at will, their eyes round-socketed and crazed with new tenancy. He clapped once to make them move and watched them scatter for cover like seed thrown against a blank wall. In the kitchen he found two mouse traps left set and sprang them both, kicking the second one against a chair leg until it triggered and flapped against air. He waited then, leaving his mind open to impression, hoping half-heartedly, for some omen, a clear dismissal. He heard: "Noel?" but let her linger, aware of the thin edge between drama and honest emotion, reluctant to believe departure so simple. He left the kitchen and walked the perimeter of the house, his fingers sometimes grazing the wall, thinking: It cannot be this easy. Rounding the last corner, turning back toward the door, he watched the doorway grow larger at his approach, saw again the vision of day held framed, heat rising. He walked out into new sun and locked the door.

"Noel?" Kathy asked.

She was waiting in the truck, her arm outside the window, a suitcase toppled near her shoulder. She wiped her face with a red bandanna, said: "Find anything?"

"No."

"Do you want to stop by Cooca's?"

"No, I said good-bye already. He knows I'm leaving."

He climbed in. He started the engine. He was conscious of himself in a way he had never been before. He saw his feet move on the pedals, watched his hands turn the steering wheel. He had a brief image of his father wrapped in sheets, the man somehow a destination. He closed his mind to it.

"Hot," Kathy said.

He honked once as he drove out of the village, and saw

Bernard saluting as he passed the bar. He saw the two lanes of huts on either side of the road grow smaller in the rearview mirror, finally linked together by some trick of light and distance.

Through time and distance Noel drove, watching the land cancel itself, fold away under the wheels of the truck. He had no memory of the road between Tenado and Koudougou and now knew only that they were entering the outskirts of Ouagadougou, the capital. There had been animals—herds of cattle, thin and sickly looking even at a distance, their humps sagging to one side; sheep and goats, the goats sturdier, sometimes holding down a sapling with their hooves, biting and pulling the green leaves—and woven through it all were earlier memories. He thought more than once: I am traveling to the past, but he was not sure he phrased it correctly, thought perhaps the past was moving to meet him. Kathy remained on her side of the truck so that her words reached him in fits and starts, touching one part of his consciousness but never the whole. In the drone of wheels on dirt he went back, lingered in a past without image, until he recalled a drive through the New Hampshire countryside, crossing dirt roads similar to these. He remembered a walk through a wooded hollow, the leaves orange, sugar-laden with sun, tired and dropping to earth. He had walked with his father, carrying the fishing poles, the water a chill before them. The sun had tucked in and out of shadow in an October forest; their steps had been a stick walk, their boots crackling leaves and mulch, like the scrapings of a winter chisel. Then white rocks, gray water, the bone-chilling sensation of cold water through waders. His father saying: Fish toward the white water. You want to get it into the pockets just behind the rocks. They hang there, waiting for the current to bring it to them. And Noel had fished, propped on a rock, receiving the water on his Achilles tendons. He had watched, too, his father's line go out, heard sometimes the whip crack of the tippet as it snapped back and forth too fast, seen the line dance on the water, the insect swing as it bobbed. Locked to the rock, he had fished mechanically, following his father's lead, watching even as a breeze came and snapped his father's fly sideways, setting and securing itself in his father's neck. He had seen it: a white barb, a Quill Gordon, an insect body protruding from the neck, streaked red with blood. His father had taken out a pair of pliers and cut the hook free, leaving the steel embedded, a silver pin near the throb of neck arteries.

There were other memories, but this one stayed, rocking with him in the truck, creating a second world around him. He came out of it only when they were forced to stop in the first bind of traffic, then retreated to it again when they were moving, remembering his own wonder at the man with a pin in his neck wordlessly casting, sometimes scratching the hook as if it were a mild annoyance. And he had asked: Does it hurt? Of course it hurts. Wouldn't hurt you? But we should go to a doctor or something. Why? This word, the last spoken, came to him through memory: Why? He realized now he had never understood the question, he wondered if his father had, wondered if he had seen its implication, the hardness it had conveyed to his son. Don't feel, it had said. Ignore. It had not been a lesson. It had been merely an extension of a life-style, a firmness almost of neglect. Suffer, if need be.

At a light Kathy bought two oranges from a vendor. The vendor was a young boy. He made change, though it was incorrect, and Kathy let him keep it. Noel watched her peel the orange, the pulpy sections causing a clean smell in the heat. He ate one, spitting the seeds out the window, his free hand steering.

"Do you want more?" Kathy asked. He shook his head. The orange had turned sour in his stomach. The activity around him had obscured his memory, and he felt in control again, ready to go deeper into the past or present. He thought: This is the beginning of grief. I can start it now. Yet he held back on it, choosing instead the motion around him, saying: "It's crowded. I've never seen it this busy."

"It's almost noon, that's why."

The streets were narrow, choked with mopeds, their tinny horns coming at him from all directions. The heat in the truck swelled, it surrounded them, letting in only sound. Once Kathy said something, but he didn't hear. He didn't pursue it. She was silent beside him then, her eyes on the people.

He drove to the AID office and parked. His motion was mechanical, slowed in order to record it. The sun was full. The white building in front of him seemed sterile, almost antiseptic. He knew it was air-conditioned, could hear the hum of small engines sucking air.

"I don't believe we're here," Kathy said. "Do you?"

"I believe it. I have to see Peplin. I wired him last week."

"Should I come?"

"Sure. It will be cooler inside. I'll get someone to unload the furniture."

They walked inside. An African woman Noel didn't recognize went to see if Peplin was busy. She returned a moment later and told them to go in. Kathy hesitated.

Noel said: "No, come with me."

Peplin was short, about forty years old, a black man. He

smiled first at Noel, then at Kathy, sadness working around his lips.

"Noel, Kathy, how are you? Please, sit down. I received your wire, of course. I'm very sorry."

They sat while Peplin walked back around his desk. It was cold in the room. A plant waved on a green file cabinet to one side of Peplin's desk. The windows were covered by venetian blinds, half-drawn, sun slanting through them and striking the far wall. The floor was bare, tile, flecked by some indiscriminate browned sequins which grated on Peplin's dragging feet. A constant hum ran beneath everything. The air conditioner sucked air and recycled it through blowers aimed at the ceiling.

"I really am sorry," Peplin said even before he was seated, moving papers off his blotter, clearing, it seemed to Noel, the way for condolence. "We'll miss you."

"Thank you," Noel said.

"Now, do I take it you're not coming back? We could make this a leave, you know? We like your work."

"I don't know yet. I have to see what condition my father is in. I wanted to bring the furniture in anyway in case we don't return."

"Oh, is it out there?"

Peplin rocked back in his chair, the springs braying, and looked out the window. "I'll have someone unload it then. We'll store it until we know more, all right?"

"Fine."

Peplin talked about flights, tickets, a ride out to the airport. Noel understood that they would fly via Paris, but that was all. He was no longer listening. He let Kathy speak for them, her voice oddly out of place in the chill room, as if heat had been a quality of her speech. He watched the venetian blinds riffle with air-conditioned wind, saw a draw cord bounce on its plastic end, the rhythm in tune with the subtle throb of electricity. "Well," he heard Peplin say in response to Kathy, heard Peplin's throat clog and release, words swallowed perhaps, then saw him rock forward again, standing this time.

"Well, then . . ." he said.

Peplin led them out. The African secretary smiled, half bowed over her desk. Peplin called to a few men to unload the truck. The men jumped up, their lethargy gone, and began pulling at the ropes. Noel watched to make sure they didn't take anything that would have to be carried back on the plane.

"I'll leave you now," Peplin said. He shook hands with them both and stepped back inside, the door silencing the hum, heat returning.

"Let's get some lunch," Kathy said. "I'm starved."

Noel nodded. He left her and went to arrange their baggage, putting it to one side of the furniture in the small storage warehouse. When he returned, he stopped to study her, wondering if they weren't now closer to her world, the return to the States something she had long anticipated. Already she had become more animated. He saw this now as he walked, saw that a heaviness had been lifted from her. Her face looked lighter, fresher, and he thought: She is happy to be in motion, pleased to be going back. He looked for something to hate in this, but found nothing, thinking: She has never left.

Kathy couldn't finish her sandwich. The meat had been tough, chewy, the bread stale. Her hunger had disappeared after the first bite, but she had eaten some anyway, feeling guilty. Noel had said once: There are starving children in Africa, then laughed. She knew the food would be eaten in the kitchen. It would be passed out the door to waiting hands, or sold, the waiter pocketing the change.

Noel had eaten quickly. He had eaten as though it were something to be done with. She had watched him soak up the gravy with bread, his jaws clicking softly, aware that in Africa one must pay attention to replenishing the body. There had been times when she had regarded her own body as she might a machine, judging proper food, proper oil, proper elimination.

Noel lit a cigarette when he was finished. He rocked back in his chair. An overhead fan was twirling slowly. Flies buzzed in lazy circles. Heat came up through the dirty tile floor. Through the front doors, held open by back-turned chairs propped under the handles, she could hear the beginning of siesta, the slow dullness coming even to motors.

"Tired?" Noel asked.

"Yes, a little."

"We should get a room soon."

He made no move to get up. She watched him smoke. People were leaving the restaurant. They passed from the comparative darkness into bright sunlight, squinting, hands raised to fend off wakefulness. She felt sweat begin on her body, sluggishness invade. She wanted a nap. She wanted silence, coolness. Her stomach seemed to tighten over the lump of sandwich. Even the flies, which she could occasionally watch with interest, held no appeal for her now, and she waved at them listlessly, driving them off.

"Do you feel all right?" Noel asked. "You look pale."

"I'm okay. I feel a little light-headed, that's all."

"We'll take a taxi then."

"I'd like to."

She wanted to say something then, though she wasn't sure what it was. Perhaps: It's over. Perhaps: I'm glad it's done. But she couldn't bring herself to form the words. She watched Noel, wondering if he could bolt somehow, retreat from the movement already begun. She felt that to stop or go backward would be too difficult for either of them, that return was impossible. Yet this thought lingered unspoken, though she was aware it would have to be broached eventually. She watched him take his last puff on the cigarette, the coal glowing close to his knuckles. She felt faint watching this, wondered in numbness how they had covered so much ground so quickly. She thought: I do not know him, yet she did not believe it, amended it to say: I will not know him, because she found she could not picture him away from Africa. She was startled at this, touched her hand to her lips, and concentrated, trying to draw on an earlier vision. It came, pieced together from discordant images, linked only by the sense of loneliness she had found in him even in his own home. She narrowed on this loneliness, conscious of the similarity between Africa and his home in New Hampshire, the quiet mirrored by quiet three thousand miles away, thought, finally: He cannot be touched. And here she discovered a vague truth, suspected but never realized before, saw his austerity as heritage, Africa was a kind of breeding dish. She pursued this line of reasoning, following it through days half-remembered and scorched by sun, until she heard him say: "We should go."

He put his cigarette out, called the waiter over, and paid him. The waiter took the money and cleared the dishes. As they walked out, Noel said: "Let's get drunk tonight. Would you like that?"

"Sure. Where?"

"The Cayman. How about it? There will be people there. It's Friday, isn't it?"

"Yes."

They were outside. The street was quiet. Kathy saw a young boy sleeping face up in the sun. Everywhere she looked she saw someone sleeping, limp arms and legs dangled in feline repose. The sun was brilliant. She felt it on her skin, melting resistance to sleep. I want to lie down, she thought. I want to be cool.

She followed Noel through the Grand Marche. It was crowded even now, the small aisles packed with merchandise. She saw chicken wire covering tables and stands set up with knives, machetes, files. They passed through a section given over to rope, another selling pig bladders skinned and tanned, one with its sides wet to prove its cooling properties. She saw mosquito nets, hammocks, seeds, sunglasses, here and there radios and calculators. In the meat section she saw a row of vultures clinging to a steel rafter in anticipation. One flew down, landing on feet that jumped in a running dance. She heard its wings, lacelike, almost feminine, the feathers luminous black. She reached out and took Noel's hand. It was considered wrong to do it in public, she knew, but she wanted to touch him. He glanced at her once and let her hand remain. In the few open spaces she closed her eyes and let him guide her. She opened them only when someone approached, a boy or old man waving produce, saying: "Nassarra, Nassarra." She heard Noel say: "No, no, not today." He said it twenty times, thirty, but people still continued to come. She bumped against a few, feeling their skin for an instant, their heat and closeness. She could not rid herself of the feeling of strangeness and found the air hard to breathe, the atmosphere acting on her.

"Noel, I don't feel well," she said, and he squeezed her hand, pulling her faster.

"We'll be out in a second. Just a second."

His words carried her out. The vendors pulled back. Noel gave change to two beggars, one with withered legs tied behind his back. She felt a wave of sickness come, pass, replaced finally by wonder at the pragmatism involved, the man shunting his legs out of the way to have more freedom. He walked away on his hands, his elbows bowed, a strange duck walk of adaptation.

"Taxi," Noel called close to her ear.

Her breath was coming back. Noel dropped her hand, but she stayed close to him, looking at him sideways, seeing him unconscious of her, thinking: This is how he looks when I'm not with him. This is how he was before me. She saw his neck was flushed, reddish brown. His complexion reminded her of men who worked in the sun, brown men stripped to the waist on construction jobs, the smell of tar and wood close to them, their skin no longer tanning but already golden. There was a solidness to him, his legs boot-heavy.

"Taxi," he called again, this time causing one to stop. The car was small. Kathy had to crawl over the seat. The driver had a radio on. The music was Indian, raucous and tinny. Noel gave directions, and the driver started, the music flagged now by the wind, the streets outside passing in torpid calm. The driver hummed a lyric from the song, tapped the steering wheel.

She was not aware of their stopping until she saw the hotel. It was flat, one-story, the rooms clustered around a graveled courtyard. Noel leaned forward and paid the driver, then climbed out, pulling her after him. The taxi went off.

"I'll go sign in," Noel said.

She did not follow but moved to a spot of shade, instead, relishing the idea of being inside, being able to lie down. She stood with her hip jutted out, her weight stretching tendons along her side until they grew tired and she shifted, her body rocking like a work-worn trace horse. After a while Noel returned, swinging the keys on his finger.

"Madame," he said, bowing slightly.

"Is everything all right?"

"He thinks you're my mistress. He winked at me."

"I don't feel well," she said, unable to stop herself in time.

Noel took her arm. They passed palms, the fronds still, new shoots arching up sleeved in green covering. Lizards moved on the walls, their yellow heads ducking and raising, their tails hanging down to plumb. Noel stopped at the door and showed her the key. It was a skeleton key, large and old. He fitted it in the door, turned it, then pushed. The door vibrated open, twanging, sending chips of cement onto the bare gray floor.

"Madame," Noel said again.

The room was furnished only with essentials. There was a table, a chair, a shower, and a bed. The shower smelled of mildew, the wetness out of place in the dry heat. The bed was old. It sagged in the middle. A mosquito net was held up by four rough sticks lashed to the bed legs.

"It's not the Ritz," Noel said.

"It doesn't matter."

Kathy lay down. She did not undress. From the doorway Noel said: "I'm going to get our bags. I'll be right back. You rest."

"Thank you. I don't feel well."

A third time. She wanted to pull the phrase back, but it was already out. She watched it go to Noel, saw his head nod. He flicked on the overhead fan, saying: "That should help some. I'll be back."

He pulled the door closed. She rolled on the bed, gradually falling toward the center. A mosquito stirred from the mattress and buzzed in her ear. She sat up and pulled down the net, but the mosquito was already inside. She raised one arm, lifting it like an animal trainer, and allowed the mosquito to light, let it stick with its mandibles before she crushed it. The mosquito rolled under her blood-stained fingers, and she wondered momentarily if a stranger's blood was now mixed with her own. She pushed back on the mattress and heard the ticking rustle, felt the straw beneath her back wedge and fall in place. The fan caused the net to wave, and she watched the room through shifting holes, her vision refracted and bent like a fly's. Her breathing slowed. Coolness came with dried sweat until she rolled onto her side, tucked, and slept.

Noel accepted the voices like a bath. They warmed him, pulled at him. He listened to words breaking all around him, French and English mixing together in a pool. He pulled random words to him, dissected them, let them go. There was enough noise here to lose oneself in, enough to cover any embarrassment, rudeness, drunkenness. He listened in a half-hearted manner, hearing music as part of the voices and the whisper slide of moving feet. Heard, years ago, his father saying: In a bar you should always buy a drink for the people on either side of you. You never know when you might need a friend. Heard his father's voice, speaking through the letter delivered a week ago, saying: I hope you will come home to me and help me now that I need you. And Noel told himself, hearing his own voice blend for a moment with the sounds of others: This is an old debt; this is a debt made for me at my birth.

But he could not concentrate. His senses were full,

drunk. He had had three quart bottles of beer, accepting drinks from the table. Three friends, all male, clustered around him now, telling tales of his past to Kathy, who disturbed him slightly by being polite and listening. He watched her, knowing somehow each of her gestures before they were finished, saw the napkin on her lap shredded, her back straight, rigidly receiving news of past indiscretions. He saw plainly she did not fit, though she tried, though she was the most attentive listener at the table. He wondered once again how he had brought her to this, how he had expected it to be otherwise.

And now Frank, a stocky man who did irrigation projects near the desert, said: "So really, it was strange. I swear, there were Jews doing irrigation for Moslems. But the Moslems kicked them out after the whole Middle East business. The Jews were the best irrigators I ever saw."

Kathy nodded. Frank, looking proud of himself, slightly flirtatious, if only to have a reaction from a woman, drinking beers in long pulls, continued: "Jews for Moslems."

"Jews for Jesus," Simon said. He was smaller than Frank and revolved around him so that they seemed to be always in combination.

"Oh, man, you're in for it, Noel," Frank said over the rest. "It's crazy back there, in the States. There's the Moral Majority, book banning, the KKK, Nazis marching in the Midwest, everything. It's a zoo."

"Jews for Jesus is what kills me," Simon said. "Do you believe that?"

Noel smiled. He watched flies move on the table, their black bodies tracing the rings, the puddles of beer. He reached forward and drank. He was drunk, he decided, though it was only the beginning, the first flush of warmth. He crossed and recrossed his legs. Around him, people were dancing. Some were barefoot; others in sandals. There was a sanding sound, feet like scrape boxes dotting the rhythm. He saw three whores sitting at the bar, their clothes better than most, bright, made of cloth sent up from the coast. One wore a foulard over her hair which made her forehead look incredibly large and glowing. He was aware of heat moving through the room, fanned by swaying bodies. The record skipped, suspended motion for an instant, then caught again.

"—so this guy Alan," Frank was saying, "he just disappeared after his two years in the Peace Corps were up. Nobody knew where he was. It was a matter of International Concern, they said. They sent people all over the desert looking for him. Somebody finally found him up by Lake Chad. He believed he was a Tuareg warrior. He was brushing flies away from his face with a severed horse tail."

"I've got one. I've got a horse tail," Simon said.

Noel looked at Steven, the third man at the table. He was drinking quickly. Noel didn't know him well but from his silence felt some kinship with him. Once or twice Noel tried to catch him looking at Kathy. It was not from jealousy. It was something more elemental, a need to see Kathy being seen by another, as though only in such observation could he remember her objectively. He felt he had lost the ability to see her clearly, yet the thought, no sooner formed, was lost in the shuffle of people around him, the jangle of limbs thrown out in harsh electric light, the smell of weekend lotions applied to unclean bodies. He lit a cigarette.

Frank called the waitress over. She was a tall woman with a pagne around her waist. She was listless, her arms too long for her body. She took the empties off the table and replaced them with fresh ones. Frank reached for his wallet, but Noel called him off, saying: "I'll pay. I'm the one leaving."

"That's true, that's true." Simon laughed. "Anyone leaving this pisshole should have to pay. It should be a tradition."

"Why do you stay if it's a pisshole?" Kathy asked.

Simon shrugged.

Then Frank, too serious, said: "It has its points, you know. There's something real here."

"What do you mean?" Kathy asked again. Noel saw her sit straighter, her posture saying: Now, I want to hear this.

"Well," Frank said.

"Well?"

"It's just that there's a lack of bullshit here. Everything is pared down, you see? The problems here are real."

Noel didn't listen. He had heard it before. He had even used it on Kathy, breaking it down, covering his pride with facts and statistics, making it sound fine and pitiful at once. It had been a stance, a device to set his life before her. Come, see, he had said. But now, looking back, he could not quite understand what he had meant by it. He had wanted Kathy to come, had wanted, perhaps, only to have someone to introduce to Africa. He had wanted to transfer his knowledge of Africa, to prove through her that his life was worth something. He was upset by this thought because it undermined notions of love, replaced love with more neutral words. He thought: Perhaps I was lonely, knowing as he thought it how unfair it seemed. It had been a false premise to build on, even if true. He accepted this as a statement of fact. It could not be made an excuse, despite his understanding that loneliness was no less a motive than love. He smoked now, saying once to himself: I was lonely, finding in it some final truth.

Around him the conversation stalled. Noel glanced at Kathy to see if she had learned something. Instead, he saw in her face the wide expression of comprehension, the familiar slouch that indicated her willingness to learn, to receive. He admired her for it, perhaps loved her for it, he couldn't tell. He thought briefly that she was better than he. He knew she had acted on purer motives, had come to him originally from a love he could not quite equal, or feel he deserved. Seeing her this way provoked a tenderness in him, a sense of loyalty. He wanted to say: I will try, wondering at the same time if effort held any sway over emotion.

"—Noel? What do you think?"

"What's that?" Noel asked. Frank was leaning across the table. He was taking a cigarette from Noel's pack.

"I think we should ride the crocs. How about you? What do you think?"

"No, no, thanks."

"Come on," Frank said, then turned to Kathy. "I've seen him do it."

"What's this?" Kathy asked. "What are you all talking about?"

"You'll see," Frank said, standing. Simon was up, too. Noel saw they were both drunk, weaving, their faces red and flushed.

Steven made no move to get up, said: "I'm going to stay here."

"Come on," Simon said, and punched Steven on the arm. Then, seeing Steven shake his head, he said: "Come on, Noel. Wait till you see this, Kathy."

"What is it, Noel?" Kathy asked once more. "I want to see."

Noel stood. "I guess we don't have a choice. Do you really want to?" he asked.

"Yes, what is it?"

Frank and Simon were walking ahead, turning sideways

to squeeze past the people dancing. Noel watched them, following slowly, Kathy at his side. He concentrated on their backs. He saw their blue work shirts seep through the crowd, the Africans sometimes turning to watch them. Frank bumped into one woman and bowed slightly, saying something quickly in an African dialect. The woman looked surprised. She laughed, shaking her head, saying to her partner: "Americans."

A moment later they were outside, behind the building, the music already stilled. There were tables and chairs set up in a circle around the patio. Green plants lined the perimeter, their shapes dark now, waving. In the center of the patio was a large cage, sunk into the tiles, and, inside it, three crocodiles. Noel listened to the water slosh, saw that a small puddle had leaked and spread over the patio, when it was caught by light and turned into a mirrored pool. Near the cage Frank said: "They are ugly. Ugly, huh?" He laughed and bent toward Kathy.

Far away, Noel heard the music, dancing, someone singing. He walked toward the cage. Kathy was giggling, though it was a nervous laugh, something between fear and excitement. Simon was quiet. Only Frank was speaking, saying: "Crocodiles. They got three of them from the sacred pool of Sabou. Who wants to ride them? Anyone?"

"I didn't know they were back here," Kathy said.

But Frank was already rattling the screening. The crocodiles moved slowly, their hides faceted by diamonds of water that settled in grooves along their spines. One, a huge male, puffed its throat. Small waves washed over them. Noel stared at the eyes on top of their heads, watched his stare being returned in soulless scrutiny.

"What's the difference between an alligator and a crocodile?" Kathy asked.

"Alligators are found only in the Americas. And crocodiles—now, which is it? One of them has its incisors inside the top jaw, and the other has them outside? Which is it?" Simon asked.

"Who's going to ride one?" Frank asked. "Noel?"

"Nope, not me."

"Kathy? How about you?"

"No, thanks."

Then Frank started climbing. Noel said: "Be careful." But Frank already had one leg in the enclosure. The closest crocodile backed in the water. Its tail moved to one side, cocked, held stiffly in a lizard curl. Frank was straddling the rail, laughing, saying: "I'll run over these like logs. Just like the cartoons."

One crocodile opened its mouth and hissed. Frank said: "Now, now," but he was still swinging his leg over, finally standing inside. He stayed against the wire mesh. Noel watched him wobble, thinking: He's drunk. Thinking: He's afraid. The three crocodiles were facing Frank. Frank started around the edge of the cage, keeping his back against the wire, ready to jump out. Noel moved closer, finding his own thoughts clogged by drunkenness, watching as the crocodiles swung with Frank, shifting mechanically, like turrets.

Kathy said: "Don't, Frank."

"Ha, this is adventure. This is what we come out here for, isn't it?"

"You're fucking crazy," Simon said. "Do you know how fast those things are?"

All the while Frank was circling. Noel felt sweat beginning, saw in this man's foolishness something of his own. He saw one crocodile duck under the water, the eyes disappearing, the body hidden by the glare of light. He heard a whisper of music work through the quiet, linger for a moment in the slosh like a radio heard through the drone and steam of a shower. "Frank," he said, thinking he could stop him, but Frank was still moving, trying to work behind the animals.

"These are sacred crocodiles," Frank said. "They won't hurt humans."

Noel nodded, hearing the nervousness in Frank's voice. He recalled now the one time he had gone into the enclosure, the sick, sweet feeling of danger. He had circled just as Frank was doing, then sat finally, his fingers touching the rough hide, waiting for the slash of tail, the wild thrashing he somehow invited. He had felt then some sickness, some revulsion at the knowledge he was forcing an event, acting recklessly. The tail had not come, but it made no difference. It had been a token, an indication, had been a testing of his own spirit so that he had thought: I seek this. Standing outside the enclosure now, he was nervous for Frank, pained by Frank's transparency no less than his own.

"Jesus," Frank suddenly shouted. "Did you see that?"

One of the crocodiles had skittered past him, brushing his leg, its tail flicking. It had kept going in a circle, running incredibly fast on four legs, water rocking in its wake. Noel barely saw it, could not speak before the other two reacted, backing in the water, their tails twitching, legs pushing at the slick bottom.

"Get out," Kathy said. "You're being stupid."

"I know I am," Frank said. "So that means I'm not."

"Oh, just get out."

Noel saw Frank grin, then reach one foot out and touch the male. The male arched, then slapped its tail on the water. There was a loud thwack, water spraying, Frank squatting close to it, reaching his hand out to rub the crocodile's back. Noel said: "Don't," but the male was swinging its tail again, raising it like a scorpion, venomous, muscles tensed in anticipation. It brought its tail down, almost catching Frank. He slipped forward, his foot going into the water. The smallest crocodile came at him, its mouth open, and Frank jumped, vaulted the railing, suddenly laughing hysterically.

"Did you see that?" he asked. "Aren't they evil?"

Simon handed Frank a beer, while Kathy said: "You shouldn't have gone in there. It's so stupid. Did you ever really go in there, Noel?"

Noel nodded, feeling sick now. He walked back toward the bar, the conversation still going on around him. When Simon opened the door, he heard the whisper scrape of feet move out to meet him. The room was airless. He smelled bodies, exertion, a urine odor seeping from the bathrooms. A light above the dance floor was jiggling, swaying in beat to the steps, the music.

Once back at the table, they ordered more beer. Noel lit a cigarette. Frank was still laughing nervously, not sure, Noel realized, if he had been brave or merely foolish. Kathy was shaking her head, grinning. At the bar he saw Steven talking to one of the whores. The whore had a hand on Steven's arm and was whispering. Steven shook his head, and Noel wondered what had been said.

Beside him, Kathy was saying: "They feed them chickens? When? Whole, just like that?"

"It's a sacrifice," Simon said.

"But why?"

And Noel drifted, lulled by their words, their completeness without him. He saw his father coming across the front lawn, leaves blowing, wood smoke in the air. He saw, too, Grant standing next to him, soft, his flesh fuller than it should have been, saying: The car hit it, Dad. It hit it and drove off. Noel stood, marking the spot along the road where the squirrel had been hit. He saw where the back of the squirrel had been crushed while the front legs continued to move. Leaves blew across the road, making skidding sounds, giving air an identifying voice. There had been something solemn in the day: gray clouds, dark, heavy tones of light, and his father's progress across the lawn, Grant anxious and pulling at his side:—hit it, but I guess the driver didn't see. Just drove off, Dad, going right by. Then they were near him, his father looking disheveled, roused from an afternoon nap, coming to witness this small catastrophe. Where is it? he had asked, and Noel had pointed, vigilant, though the squirrel was still circling, its hindquarters tethered and useless. His father had looked both ways along the street. Noel recalled that, remembered the caution, the prudence, then saw his father stepping off the curb. You could have done this, his father had said. You should have known not to let it suffer. And then there was only the vision of the boot in Noel's memory, the careful set of it above the squirrel's head, the slight lift of his father's arm for balance, while he and Grant stood in long shadows, somehow afraid to miss the next motion. But the squirrel moved, twirling, and his father adjusted, still rocking on one foot and heel, his arms out. You just had to— The sentence was never completed. The boot came down, ending it. It was startling in its rapidity, in the bone sound that accompanied it. His father wiped his boot on the curb, while behind him the squirrel was still, flattened, the mark of a tire tread notched into its fur. Grant had started to cry. His tears were blubbery, even though he was the elder, even though he had gone to get their father in the first place. Finally, his father had walked back across the lawn, his size diminished and outlined against the white clapboard house.

"See?" Frank said. He was reaching across Noel's lap for another cigarette. Noel noticed Kathy looking at him. Steven had not returned, and when Noel glanced toward the bar, he didn't see him. Simon yawned. Noel wondered for a moment if he had been addressed, if some response was in order. But the conversation went around him, somehow, Noel realized, in deference to the news about his father. Again he felt the slight exhilaration, the freedom his grieving entitled him to. He was conscious of the others' treatment of him, the caution that sometimes filled their voices.

At midnight Simon said it was time to go. They all stood, paid. Noel was drunk. He followed them outside, saw the street through dust kicked up by a passing car. The moon was up. At one side of the door tall stalks of bamboo rubbed together, making a wooden click, a soft, quiet sound. Frank and Simon left, laughing and stumbling a little, promising to see them at the airport. Kathy waved.

Noel walked beside her through narrow streets. Twice they tried to get a taxi but couldn't. The cars passed, their headlights tinted yellow to reduce the numbers of insects hurtling at them. It was cooler. Kathy took his hand, let it go. He realized she was not sure how to perceive him, was not sure of this middle ground. He was dimly aware of his own desire to get back to the hotel, to lie beside her and be free to follow his memories. He was aware of beginning to live the new life, which was older than she imagined, which came to him even now, walking dark streets, his wife beside him.

"The butter is rancid," Noel said.

"I know. I already told the waiter. He says they don't have any more."

"Wonderful."

"The bread is good, though," Kathy said.

The patio they were sitting on was hot. Kathy could just see the street between two buildings. It was brown, unpaved. She saw cars flash past, their colors almost painful. There were other people having breakfast: couples, two African businessmen wearing long flowing gowns. The waiter, a short man who was sweating heavily, wove through the tables, accepting criticism and pouring coffee. Kathy found herself wanting to look at a thermometer. She needed to check her own feelings of oppressive heat against the factual record of mercury and gradation. Seeing it, she thought, I will know how to feel.

"What did you think of Frank last night?" she asked.

"About the crocs?"

"Yes. Or just in general."

"He's all right. He does good work, I know that. I went up to see one of his projects. He had a dam that held water longer than any of the others near there."

"But what about the crocs?"

"Everyone was drunk. Weren't you?"

"I guess. Not that drunk, though. I wouldn't have climbed in there like that."

"It was just one of those things."

"Men things?"

"If you like."

Noel dunked a piece of bread in his coffee. She saw him glance away. He looked tired. A fly buzzed over the table.

Kathy thought: It cannot be this still this early. She looked out at the road again and saw the restaurant sign on the metal gate. She tried to read it, though the letters were reversed. She just made out the arcing name: Croix du Sud. The waiter came to their table then, walking across the gravel, holding a tray extended in one hand. He put a small check on one end of the table, then covered it with a dish.

"Anything else?" he asked.

"The butter was rancid," Noel said.

The waiter shrugged. From his side Noel said: "How can you serve rancid butter?"

"It's what we have."

Noel paid. The waiter walked off. Noel said: "Christ," then laughed.

Kathy drained the last of her coffee. "Well," she said, "what would you like to do today?"

"I don't care."

"We have to use it up somehow. Are you tired?"

"Not really."

They both were silent. Kathy ate the crust off her last piece of bread. She felt nervous. She brushed some crumbs off her skirt, sipped her coffee. Finally, she said: "Well?"

"We can do something. Whatever you want is all right with me. It's just one day."

"You know the city, though. Is there anything to do?"

"Not really. Not that I can think of."

"Frank said they have pedal boats out at the reservoir. Would you want to do that?"

"Are there really? Sure. Whatever you like."

"Are you sure you want to?"

"Time has to be spent, right? We have to do something."

He took a large chip of crust and put it in his eye, squinting to make a monocle. Then, in a Viennese accent, said: "Time must be spent."

The crust dropped out. Noel smiled, his own joke humorless to him. Quieter, he said: "Let's go."

They walked across the gravel courtyard, out into the street. Kathy felt the heat lurking. It met her as soon as she stepped out of the shadow of a building, touched her, glanced away. Merchants and vendors were walking here. She heard a moped being revved, stalled, revved. A horn honked somewhere, the sound unraveling, muted by the shameless glare. Close by a man yelled: "Nassarra, five francs. Five francs." She did not turn, knowing it to be a beggar's plea. She was conscious of Noel moving off, returning, saying: "You have to give to the first beggar of the day. Bad luck not to."

"All right."

"We'll have to walk a couple of blocks to catch a taxi. Do you feel okay?"

"It's just so hot."

"I know. It feels like rain. But this is Africa, isn't it?"

They walked two blocks. Kathy watched the people, saw vendors passing, their goods tied around them. As they passed an open door, she heard loud music. The noise confused her momentarily. A little boy danced, his knees scraped and scabbed. He said: "Nassarra," though it was not a question or request, but simply a statement. Kathy smiled. The boy smiled back, then spun, dancing alone. Farther up she saw a coffee bar. There were five men seated around a picnic table, each with a piece of bread and a cup in front of him. At the head of the table a young girl tended the fire under a huge kettle. Kathy smelled wood burning, smelled heat. The air wavered around the young girl, distorting her outline, making her seem liquid, a beam of light held by smoke.

At a larger intersection Noel finally stopped a taxi. The driver was gruff. He drove without speaking. Noel smiled at her, started to speak, but his words were lost in a blare of horns as the taxi skidded to a stop. The driver stuck his head out the window and shouted at the car that had cut him off.

Kathy sat back. She was sweating. She felt ill. The interior of the car was suffocating. She could not control her thoughts, felt them pulled and pushed by the heat, slowed until they lingered too long, consumed too much. She stared out the window, watching the scenery pass, realizing Africa was no longer strange. She knew it. She was accustomed to its shape, its landscapes, the people.

In time she smelled water. The taxi pulled over, and beyond the windshield she could see two lakes, an earthen dam dividing them. Noel opened the door, and she slid across the seat, her legs touching the hot leather, small bits of Styrofoam padding. The driver took the money silently, then backed up, the tires stirring dust.

"This will be good, you'll see. Come on," Kathy forced herself to say, though she no longer believed it.

They walked along the dam. The water on either side of her was flat, the sun a green sheen across the surface. She smelled damp soil, the sad odor of wash, unclean lappings. Here and there she saw fishermen wading hip deep in the water, pulling inflated inner tubes behind them, occasionally casting circular nets. She watched them pull the nets closed, one or two fish caught in the mesh, silver bodies set, gasping, onto the cache of the inner tube. By the side of the road women were selling dried fish, which were gray and bent in circles, their tails clamped in their mouths.

"It's cooler, isn't it?" Noel said.

"A little."

"But the insects. Christ. This is where the mosquitoes breed."

He bent to pick up stones, then threw them, one by one,

into the water. She watched the ripples. At the end of the dam they found the pedal boats. A young man was renting them. The boats were painted bright colors, though the paint had chipped in places, revealing metal, rust.

"There's something obscene in this, isn't there?" Noel asked, then laughed. He went to talk to the boy. Kathy saw the boy nod a moment later, then point to one of the boats. The boat was red.

"Here we go. Did you see?" Noel said, coming back, motioning with his head toward the sky. "There are clouds forming to the south. That's where the rain comes from."

"Do you think we'll get any?"

"I don't know. But that's the right place for the clouds."

Noel helped her down the bank of the dam while the boy pulled the boat up sideways. Kathy held Noel's hand as she climbed on. The boat shifted. It was open at the bottom and she saw the green water beneath it. She sat, lifting her feet onto the pedals. Noel's weight rocked her slightly, and she glimpsed the clouds hanging near the horizon.

The boy pushed them off. Noel was giggling. He steered with a small rudder between them. "Which way do you want to go?" he asked. "They can't be serious with these things."

"Out toward the middle."

"Pedal boats. Just what the developing nation needs."

Kathy pedaled. The boat rocked. The pedals kicked back small splashes of water. They passed a fisherman and slowed to watch him. He smiled at them. The inner tube behind him was moving, and Kathy thought of the fish down at the bottom of the crawl writhing, tangled in the strands. The fisherman cast his net twice without catching anything. Noel pedaled.

"We might be scaring the fish," he said.

They were near the center of the reservoir then. The

clouds had darkened. Once or twice Kathy felt a puff of wind and turned to face it. The breeze smelled of land, dust, trees. Along the banks she saw people walking, saw cars pass, their windows throwing barbs of light.

Next to her Noel said: "It's raining over there."

"Where?"

"Look, can you see it? You have to squint a little. See?"

She saw it. The clouds were darker to the south, and she could just make out the rain falling, tinting the sky gray, the trees dangling on puppet strings of water. Breezes came, stronger now, turning leaves up. There was no lightning, yet she felt it, static energy stored in the scrape of soil on air.

"It hits and skips," Noel said. "It might rain ten miles to the south but miss us completely."

They had stopped pedaling. Kathy watched the storm. She saw fishermen glance over their shoulders. Some had already left the water, and she could see them climbing out, pulling their fish onto the bank, women coming to meet them. Watching them, she was not prepared when Noel said: "I'm sorry you didn't like it here."

She could only answer: "What?," not understanding, thinking at first he meant the present, the pedal boat. But then the meaning of his words came clear. She wondered at his opening the conversation, broaching the subject that had been silent between them. Comprehending, yet wanting to hear him say it again, she asked: "What, Noel? What did you say?"

"I said, I'm sorry you didn't like it here. You didn't, did you?"

"No. Not like you like it."

He sighed, stretched, seemed nervous. She was reminded of their first days together, the silence that sometimes slipped between words.

Then: "You did fine work here," he said. "I haven't told you that, have I?"

"No."

She listened, not sure how to go on. She wanted to ask: What will happen now? What was it you wanted from me? She realized now that she had never known. She saw him grow quiet, his eyes on the storm, and she knew he was embarrassed by the conversation, almost shy. Then, not sure what to say but wanting their voices to continue, she said: "It wasn't like I thought it would be."

"How? What did you think it would be like?"

"I'm not sure anymore. Maybe I thought I'd have more power—something, I don't know. But now I don't think anyone can change things here. It's made me more selfish. I don't want to give up my life here. That's what it would take."

"You lack a good dose of Catholicism."

"Maybe."

He pedaled. He took her hand without looking at her. The storm was behind them now. The boat was drifting. He smiled, and she thought: Don't go away. Don't retreat. Then he shook his head and smiled once more.

He said: "Except once you know this exists, how can you go back?"

"I refuse the responsibility."

She said this, feeling in the words a confirmation of thought. She had never expressed it that way before. Now it startled her only for a moment. She repeated the words to herself.

"Yes," he was saying, "I guess we can do that."

"Don't be superior."

"I'm not trying to be."

She was aware of the conversation's being closed, looked for some way to prolong it. Noel was still pedaling, the boat moving easily over the water. She saw people ahead of them scrambling for shelter. It was not raining, but the boy who had rented them the boat was whistling to them, waving for them to come in. Now, she thought, sensing the need to go on. Now, again, but this time the word brought back images of the woman leaning against the wall, her nails scraping, birth. She felt angry suddenly, repulsed by Africa, by Noel quietly pedaling beside her. She asked: "Are you coming back, Noel? What do you want?"

"Would you come?" he asked, surprising her.

"How important is that?"

He did not answer immediately. She waited, partially grateful he did not lie, did not give the expected reply. Staring at him, she felt her mind divided. She tried to remember them before Africa, but the image wouldn't come. It seemed to her they were inseparable from Africa, that they had always been aware of its presence. She could not say herself how she would feel when it was behind them.

Noel said: "I love you."

"Do you? Are you sure of that?"

"Yes."

He tried to take her hand again, but she moved it, leaving his dangling. She watched him, wondering if he believed it, wondering: Can he believe such a word? Then the bank seemed to be advancing toward them. The boy was wading into the water, pulling at the chain attached to the front of the boat. The streets were empty, the women gone from the banks. Kathy stood and looked behind her. The water was sugared white from the wind.

"It's going to rain," the boy shouted.

"Yes, all right," Noel yelled back.

Kathy climbed the bank. Noel paid the boy, counting out change slowly while the boy shifted from foot to foot, sometimes glancing at the clouds. Kathy took deep breaths, thankful for the coolness.

When Noel reached her, he asked: "What's wrong?"

"Nothing."

"There's something. Why did you pull your hand away?"

"Because . . ." she started, then stopped.

"Tell me what you're talking about. I don't understand."

"What is it about you? Why are you like this?" she cried. Nearby she heard the boy stop temporarily; the boat he was pulling up skidded to a standstill. She felt the wind on her, felt suddenly the day seem to pause. Wind ceased, her own blood stilled, breaking to motion again with the first peal of thunder. She looked up once at Noel and saw him extend his hand, retract it, extend it again. She smelled his body coming closer.

"What?" he was saying. "What's this all about? We're just a little confused with all this. We're leaving."

His arm came around her, him saying: "I'm scared, too. It's just this confusion."

She leaned against him. For a moment she did not recognize his arms, the shape of his body. The feeling frightened her.

"Ahieeeee," the boy suddenly yelled.

She looked up and saw the rain coming. It moved across the water, pecking the surface, the wind a wedge dorsaling. It reached them as they hurried across the dam.

From memory, Noel woke. The rain still sounded on the roof of the hotel, louder now, the storm more established. Kathy was beside him. He heard her breathing, the slow, even intake of her lungs. The room was cold. He could see a puddle of water underneath the only window, drops sometimes flecking it. He lifted his arm away from the mosquito net, seeing the bites he had gotten through the mesh. Two mosquitoes swirled away, then were caught by a crosscurrent and disappeared over his head.

He closed his eyes, drifting back. Remembrances came, distilled by time so that only the outlines remained, and he felt he could fill them as he wished. Once, briefly, he recalled his mother's funeral. He remembered the undertaker's parlor, the sight of the long black coffin. He heard people crying, someone saying:—with children. How will he care for them without a wife? There were other words, some less clear, but he could not push his mind to remember them, could not bring them forth. He sorted through scattered images until he came to the grandfather's clock in the lobby, heard again the slow drag of the pendulum. He had stood next to it, wedged into the narrow triangle it formed with the wall, smelling wood, flowers, counting the swings of the gold-plated ball through the glass. He was always there, in time for the chimes, listening, beyond the sight of the casket, pressing against the wall, repeating quietly after the chime: One, two, three, four. There had been skirts then. Perfumed visits from different ladies, each bending to find him in the triangle, gemmed hands reaching out, the litany of condolence: Oh, you poor lamb. You sweetheart. The words had run together, becoming senseless finally, somehow thrown to the weave of the rug beneath his feet, twirled in patterns punctuated by the steady swing behind him, time passing. His father had come later, his hands different from the others, pulling him free, severing him from the heartbeat of the clock. Let's go, his father had said, though Noel's jacket was provided by a woman, his buttons closed by long nails wrapping him in cloth;

then a quick hug, another, the final touch a push from her hands on his shoulders, propelling him forward with reluctance. All set, his father had said, his words including Grant, who had moved up beside Noel. Grant had taken his hand, suddenly maternal, yet still too soft, too fleshy. He had been crying, and Noel could smell the tears, the wool of his blue blazer; he smelled them again later when Grant bent toward him in the final cold of the back seat and said: The casket means she's dead. She won't be coming home again.

Kathy stirred beside him now, sighing and waking almost at once. She opened her eyes. Noel said quietly, trying to cheer her: "We'll be leaving soon. Tomorrow."

"I know," she said.

"Should I give you a countdown? Hour by hour?"

"No. Not unless you want to."

"I want to leave," he said then, not sure what he meant, but thinking of truce, a settlement between them. He looked at her, dreams still matted in his mind.

"It's time to go, isn't it?" he asked.

She nodded. He turned his head and watched the ceiling. The fan twirled slowly. He put his feet under the covers. Kathy stretched, and he heard a bone creak, a gristle snap. The rain let up slightly. Noel could hear a gutter draining somewhere in the distance. There were no car sounds.

"How long did we sleep?" Kathy asked.

"I don't know. An hour or two."

"What time is it?"

"Almost four. It just looks late because of the storm."

"I hate waiting," she said.

Noel closed his eyes, almost retreated again into memory. He found himself wanting a drink. He wanted dullness, the sense of time passing without being noticed. He pulled the mosquito net away and climbed out. He walked to the window. Evening was coming. The darkness of the clouds was deepening, a night hush passing through the trees and hedges. When he turned back, he saw Kathy sitting up, putting on her sandals.

"We could take sleeping pills," she said. "Wouldn't it be nice to sleep until we had to leave?"

"You can if you want."

"No, I wasn't being serious. Let's go out. Is it still raining?"

"Some. It's going to break soon."

"Good. Then we'll go out, have dinner, then come back and take pills."

She laughed. He watched her, feeling a barrier had been removed between them. She made a face which he couldn't see clearly through the net. She said: "I knew a lady once who kept her kid in a net like this. It was built like a tent, and she always put it over him when she was gardening or working around the yard. My mother thought it was awful. He looked like a dog penned up, and my mother stopped bringing me over there. The lady used to say, 'But he gets the sun this way.'"

She laughed again. She went on about how the boy got a speckled tan every summer. Noel listened, finding it difficult to conceive of Kathy as a young girl. He could not imagine her summers, could not see her young, careless, alive in a life before him.

"So," she said, "he'd press his head against the net, and his face would look like a man wearing a stocking. He looked gruesome, you know, his eyes pulled back and his hair flattened. I was afraid to go near him."

Noel smiled, wondering why he had not heard this story before. It occurred to him they did not know each other well. There had been too little time, too much to contend with. He had asked her to come to Africa—she had come.

It reminded him now of men on the frontier writing east for wives, not seeing their own crudeness, but wanting company, the comfort of a woman. He shared with those men the same surprise at suddenly finding his wife human, no longer a name in letters. He watched her still, buckling her sandals, her hair mussed from sleep. He could just make out the slight swelling sleep had brought to her face, a reddish tint of her skin where she had rubbed against the pillow. He felt the beginning of knowledge, thought: This is her. He was startled by this sense of recognition and almost said so. But he kept his silence, not wanting to disturb the new perceptions, wanting to let this new understanding work into him.

She climbed out of bed, pulling the mosquito net free. She rolled her side up and said: "Would you do your side, Noel?"

He crossed the room and stood on the other side of the bed. Together they pushed the mosquito net up and tied it. Noel ran his hands down it, funneling away any mosquitoes that might be trapped in it. Kathy smiled at him.

"Were you listening to me?" she asked.

"Of course."

"What did I say?"

"You were talking about the boy they kept in a net."

"You did listen, didn't you? Sometimes I think you're not listening at all."

Suddenly she laughed, put her hands over her head. She danced a moment on the far side of the bed, saying as she formed each position: "Pirouette, à pointe." She danced bits of ballet, arching and bending, finally finishing by saying: "We're going to Paris. That's something, isn't it?"

"What would you like to do there?"

"How long do we have?"

"A day. A little longer, I think."

She said: "It's almost like a parlor game, isn't it? What would you do with one day in Paris? But it's not long enough. What should we do—wait, I'm trying to think."

He moved around the bed to her, wanting to hold her. But when he reached out his arms to her, he noticed the slight hesitation in her body, the stillness entering her posture, and he was able to cover only by speech.

"We can do anything you want for one day."

"I don't know," she said. "There's so much. What do you think? You've been to Paris."

"Museums?"

"I suppose we could. Will they be crowded?"

"It's tourist season."

"Spring and tourists, huh?"

He let her go, his arms falling weakly, taking comfort in the distance. She bent to straighten the covers, distracting him by movement. He heard the gutter running behind him.

"There has to be a way to get the feel of Paris without slogging through the lines at the museums," she said.

"In one day?"

"I know, I know," she said, standing and lifting one leg again, slowly spinning on her right heel. "But there must be something. Let's just not sleep, all right? Let's stay up all night."

"Is this the woman who wanted to take sleeping pills a minute ago?"

But she wasn't listening. She said: "But we can speak French. That should help. I'm not going to let you sleep. We're going to watch the sun come up over the Seine. Does it come up anywhere near it?"

"It must."

Her leg came down. She moved to where her skirt was

hung on the back of a chair. "I can't believe I'm going to Paris. Tomorrow we're going to Paris."

She dressed, pulling on her skirt and a top. She walked into the bathroom, while he stood quietly, listened to her brush her hair. She was humming something. He tried to identify the tune, but it remained nameless, a background to the crackle of her hair and the gutter running full.

He dressed, then lit a cigarette. He sat in the chair by the window, feeling the coolness, smoking slowly. He put one foot up on the window ledge, brought it down. He waited for Kathy to come out. Outside, street sounds began, quietly at first, then building gradually until he could not remember the stillness. He lifted his foot again and poked it through the window slats, watched as the rain caught his boot and turned the leather brown.

"Has it stopped?" Kathy asked, coming out.

"I think so. I can't tell if the trees are just dripping or if it's still raining a little."

"Are you hungry?"

"I could eat."

"Well, I'm finished in the bathroom."

He flicked his cigarette out the window. "All right," he said, standing. He went to the bathroom and washed his face. He brushed his teeth, using bottled water to rinse his mouth out with. When he came out, Kathy was by the window. He saw her turn, bend to check her purse. When he was ready, he said: "Okay."

"Cab?" she asked.

"If it's not raining, maybe we should walk. Time, you know."

"I forgot how early it is. At least it's not hot. Not like before."

He opened the door. As she passed, moving almost imperceptibly to avoid brushing against him, he felt his mood changing, marveled at his own temperament. But he let this thought go and tried to maintain the equilibrium he sensed between them. He shut the door.

"See?" he asked. "The rain's stopped."

"Sticky, though."

There were puddles in the courtyard. The gravel was wet. A breeze touched the leaves, shook them, and they dripped. The gutter had slowed, but he could still hear it far away. A dragonfly hummed past on waxed wings, trailing mottled blue light on its body. Noel moved to Kathy's side and let a hand rest on her back. She checked once more in her purse, then looked up, smiling.

"How do you feel?" she asked.

"Fine. You?"

"I'm hungry."

"So am I. We didn't have lunch."

"What should we eat? I don't know if I can stomach another *brochette* sandwich."

"Wait, I'll take you."

The road outside the hotel was deserted. They walked two blocks up, stopping for a moment at the large intersection and looking both ways for a taxi. Kathy asked twice where they were going, but Noel refused to tell her. He led her along the street, watching the banko houses pass and merge, leaving only the impression of brownness, weathered dirt. At one turn he caught sight of the moon, flesh-colored in the damp air, and he walked toward it. Cooking smells came, indistinct at first, the charcoal sweated with rain water. Beside him, Kathy stopped, asked: "What is that?"

"What?"

"That sound. Listen."

He paused. She said: "Do you hear it? It's eerie, isn't it?"

Noel heard frogs, their drone momentarily obscured by the very silence they violated. Their croaks came from every direction, throat swells and violent exhalation, the sound rocking back and forth as if they had taken their cues from one another, as if they had asked the ear to follow. In time it became one sound, faceted only by distance. He listened, hearing it not as she heard it, but rather as an echo of seasons gone, Africa closing to him.

"I never heard that before," Kathy said finally. "Not that loud."

"It's the rain. You should hear it in the middle of the season. I heard one once that sounded exactly like a human calling 'Help, help.' "

"What did you do?"

"I went out and looked for someone. I realized they wouldn't be calling in English anyway. But it was strange."

"They're beautiful."

Night was coming. As they walked, Noel felt it, smelled again the smoke from cooking fires, the heavy, dense odor wrapped around the moisture in the air. Closer to the center of town he saw people passing, signs of commerce. There were small cigarette stands on each corner, some already with their lamps lit. Mopeds cruised by, edging cautiously through the mud on either side of the road. A car went past, its interior yellow from the last slant of the sun, and for a moment Noel saw the people inside, a large man in a white caftan chewing on a wooden stick, and beside him, a young girl close to the door, staring out.

Noel led Kathy past the market, the stalls empty now, the vultures departed. He looked in and saw a guard standing sentinel, a rifle cradled in his arms. To one side of the guard a dog rubbed against a cement pillar, whetting its fur on the roughness, stropping its lean body forward and back.

"Where are we going?" Kathy asked.

"It's right here. Here we are."

They stopped in front of L'Eau Vive, beneath a hand-painted sign displaying the image of Christ walking on the Galilee. They were met at the door by an African nun, a small woman in white robes who walked them barefoot to their table. "Here?" she asked, putting down a menu. When she left after taking their orders for drinks, Kathy said: "I love this place. Look at the parrot. Did you see it when we came in?"

"Yep."

"Now, what's the story behind this again? I don't remember. Are they all nuns?"

"They run it to make money for their mission. It's been here a long time. It has good food, and it's clean. It's the cleanest place in the country."

More couples were coming in. Noel saw a Frenchman he had worked with once on a small project and waved. The man waved back but made no move to come to their table. The nun came back and served them drinks. When she left their table, she went around the small courtyard, lighting Japanese lanterns. The lanterns gave off a weak light, the colors blending. The nun continued around the courtyard, this time lighting candles on the tables. Noel watched, sometimes blurring the lights with his eyes, trying to make the beams from the Japanese lanterns meet with the shine from the tables.

He said: "See if you can do this."

"What?"

"See if you can get enough moisture in your eye to blur the lanterns until the beam meets with the candles on the tables."

"You're nuts."

"No, I mean it. Try it."

He watched her squint. She smiled, cocked her head,

said: "Almost." Then: "There, that's it. I used to do that with streetlamps when we were driving home at night. I could sit in the breeze coming through the window and make the light from one streetlight meet the next."

Kathy opened her eyes and held up her glass. "A toast?" she asked.

"To what? To leaving?"

"To leaving."

They touched glasses. Noel drank, feeling the scotch burn his tongue. He set down his glass and lit a cigarette. He saw Kathy start to say something, then stop. He leaned forward. "What?" he asked.

"Nothing. I was just thinking about Paris and going back. Do you think Grant will meet us in Boston?"

"He won't know what plane we're on."

"We could wire him from Paris."

"Somehow I'd rather just arrive."

"I guess," she said, "but we have the bags and everything. We'll have to lug them around."

"We'll make it. We can get one of those airport limousines. Remember, we get in at something like four or five in the morning. I don't think Grant would like to hang around waiting."

"You're right. You know, I'm anxious to get to know Grant and Mary. I never really had the chance before. What are they like? Can you describe them?"

Noel smoked, thinking: Yes, yes, this now. He wanted to say: I am my father; Grant is my mother. For an instant he pictured Grant: heavy, large, somehow kinder than them all. He remembered long lashes, an almost feminine quality about him. Except this image was real only in connection with the larger image of his father, softness compared to hardness. Finally, Noel said: "Well, you met them. You know what they're like."

"But not really. Grant just seemed—what? Jolly and kind. What's Mary like?"

"I don't know her that well. I was in Africa when they married."

"But you must know something about her. Come on."

"I do know some things, but not much. They're conventional. Grant's in business right near Hampton, in Portsmouth. It's where my father worked."

"So you're the black sheep, right?"

"No, more like an exile. Grant always said I'm the product of the friction between him and Dad."

"So they didn't get along?"

"They did. It's just that Dad always tried to toughen Grant up. Do you know what I mean? He rode Grant. Grant was the kind of kid who wanted to be an Eagle Scout while the rest of his friends played football."

"Like you?"

"Like me. But can you imagine little Grant in shorts, those fat knees and that kerchief around his neck? He was a prize."

Kathy giggled, drank. Noel watched the nun come to the table, relieved he did not have to go on. He felt the past with him now, felt he could step toward it and arrive. He pushed it away and concentrated on the menu. The nun asked: "Are you ready? Do you need more time?"

"No, I'm ready. I d like the steak and vegetables," Kathy said.

"They make onion soup here," Noel said.

"I want to wait for Paris."

"I'll have the steak, too, with potatoes," Noel said.

"It will take some time," the nun said, then walked off. Noel realized his cigarette had gone out in the ashtray. He lit another and took a drink. Noel looked at Kathy, wondering if he could say: We are returning to old ways. I am not sure how I will be in that past. But he was drifting, too, seeing Grant, long ago, standing outside the door to the elementary school auditorium, Grant dressed in a Cub Scout's uniform. He recalled Grant's fleshy face above the yellow kerchief, the other boys around him. There had been boy smells, dirt, grime, things protruding from pockets. They had slammed into each other, giggling, nervous, waiting until they heard: I ASK FOR THE CALL OF THE WOLF. It was the den master, speaking over a microphone from inside the auditorium, calling to the boys. Noel, near the water fountain, tucked back in shadow, had watched Grant bend with the other boys. He had heard the first howl come. The boys moved, swayed together, glancing at one another as they let their voices mix. Noel had watched Grant, had seen his brother's eyes widen, the veins along his neck grow blue. He had heard Grant's call above the rest, purer somehow, less self-conscious. Again from the auditorium came the sound of the den master, saying: WE OF PACK SEVENTY-TWO— But Noel had missed the rest. He watched, instead, the boys who were waiting now, trying to pick up a cue. Finally, they howled again, this time eloquently, louder. Grant had turned then, had seen Noel standing by the water fountain. Their eyes had met, and Grant, perhaps sensing some disapproval Noel couldn't remember, had bent again, howling even more forcefully than before, until the other boys turned to him. Noel recalled now there had been a wildness to the call. It exerted pressure, forced him to move back, away from the water fountain. The other boys had stopped, their mouths still open, until only Grant's call rang in the silent hallways, and the den master's voice, laughing, said: WE HAVE ONE VERY ENERGETIC WOLF OUT THERE.

And Noel remembered thinking even then there had been something about Grant's expression, his defiance, that

had been aimed at him. It had established something between them: Grant's softness and their mutual recognition
of it. Walking home that night, neither of them had mentioned the howl. Grant's silence reinforced Noel's feeling
that he had just seen his brother participate in something
shameful, ludicrous, had witnessed his own brother's willingness to sacrifice something unspoken between them in
order to join. Because, then as now, Noel knew that had
been the meaning of the cry, the plaintive wail masked by
ceremony. Let me in, it had said. Let me join. And, of
course, with this newly gained knowledge there had been
the glimmer of a second knowledge, this more unsettling, so
that Grant's wish to join was a clear expression of his
understanding that he did not belong at home, that he was
a subtle outcast. The cry had included all this. It had placed
Grant forever outside his father's world, if merely by the
harsh comprehension it forced between them as brothers.
The guilt Noel felt then was generated by his own belong-
ing, his own inclusion. It had generated from his own silence that night while his father had inspected Grant, looking at the pack badge he had just received, saying: So scout,
you're a Scout. Saying other words, words that stung by
their own softness because it was apparent the softness was
not intended. And this theme was repeated: Grant bringing
home his small accomplishments, increasing them as their
insignificance increased, receiving wounds of parental in-
difference, near scorn, until the cry Noel had heard that
night deepened and furrowed in his mind, eventually becoming the full expression of Grant. Grant the Scout.
Grant the Soft. And as the howl became the core of his own
brother, the howl repelled Noel, had driven him, by example, farther away, closer to his father. He had become
less vulnerable. He had become a silent complement to
Grant, both of them teetering on the fulcrum of their fa-

ther, unfairly matched in personality, in love either given or refused long before they had the power to earn or lose it.

Thinking these things, Noel was uncomfortable. He moved in his chair, pulling back to feel the pressure of the metal rungs on his spine. He felt time dropping away, his mind propelled forward at too fast a rate. He became aware again of his surroundings, of Kathy sitting across from him. The parrot called. There was a burst of laughter from an unseen table and voices speaking rapidly in French. There were breezes, small cross winds that pulled at the branches above them. He was surprised when Kathy spoke, surprised her words could be simply conversational.

She said: "I think I could sleep again. The heat keeps you drained."

"It does."

"Could you?"

"Sleep? Sure, I think so."

Noel could not respond to her tone. He waited for their meal, checking twice behind him for the nun. He wanted another cigarette but remembered he had already smoked two. He thought: Time, feeling time had become more important, that he had entered into a series of moments, of clearly marked days and hours. Some continuity had been disturbed, and he knew it would remain this way, fractured, unlinked.

"How are we going to get up tomorrow?" Kathy asked. "We don't have an alarm clock."

"Are you worried? I'll wake up."

"Are you sure?"

"We're both used to getting up early. It gets too hot to sleep late anyway."

The nun returned, carrying plates on a wooden tray. The meal was plain but good. They were interrupted at six o'clock when the nuns gathered at one end of the courtyard, arranged in rows according to height, with one French nun standing before them. A record came on. It was scratchy with static and the amplification was poor. Then the song came, melodic, solemn. The French nun motioned for the diners to sing along, but few voices responded. Noel found the music too sweet, too thick. He tried to recognize the song but couldn't. He listened, thinking now of Christmas, thinking of going home.

When the song was finished, the French nun made the sign of the cross. A knife clattered. Noel watched the nuns disband and heard the various conversations spring up again, quickly it seemed, trying to fill the silence. The parrot squawked once more, but it did not disturb the swell of sound, the quiet that lingered just beneath it.

"Is that it?" Noel asked.

"I think so. Did you pack your shaving things?"

"I've got them. We should go."

Kathy looked once more around the room. Everything was packed. Strangely, she felt no nervousness, no anxiousness to be gone. Now that the time was on her, she felt some luxury of appraisal and observation. Leaving had become a formality, a motion to follow her mind's movement. She experienced no reluctance, only a desire to see the last hours clearly, thinking: I must know how this ended. Thought: These hours may be called back.

Then, seeing Noel's impatience, she said: "Let's go then. I'm ready."

A taxi was waiting. Noel had gone out ten minutes before and had guided the driver back. Now, when he opened the door, she heard the engine running, saw the driver leaning against the car fender, smoking. Noel went ahead of her, carrying their bags. She closed the door and went after him.

"Here, Nassarra," the driver said when they reached him. He was tall and thin, young, wearing a shirt unbuttoned to his navel. He spoke French rapidly while he put their bags in the trunk. "Okay?" he asked once, smiling, hoping, Kathy knew, to surprise them.

"American, right?" he asked. "My brother went to America."

"Why?" Noel asked.

"He was in school. In the university. He said America is a very large country."

Kathy opened her door and sat in the back. The heat was there. Noel climbed in, then the driver. He asked over his shoulder: "To the airport?" Kathy knew he was speaking to Noel, that he had seen somehow Noel's comfort with him. She had seen it before, had seen Noel's ability with strangers, his knack of putting people at ease. She didn't listen to the conversation. Instead, she watched the road pass, measuring distance, thankful for the air streaming in through the window. She felt her mind roaming forward and back, and the trip took on a certain timelessness. She tried to think of Paris but could not. Neither could she think clearly of Africa; because they were leaving it, it was already shrinking. She knew once they entered the airport terminal, Africa would be shut off, the last grip of its soil obscured by cement, by airplane tires and the metallic body of the plane.

The driver stopped once to let Noel buy cigarettes, then continued on. It was half a mile to the airport. Once Kathy thought she saw the terminal from a distance, but it proved to be another building, equally modern, its shape incongruous against the surrounding mud huts. But except for this mistake, she saw everything else with a clarity that surprised her. She did not look at Noel. She felt now she had looked too long at him, that their marriage had become blurred. She was conscious her attention had been drawn to him, that it had been she reacting to him, if only because Africa was his. Her own past had been consumed, had languished in the heat and closeness of Africa until it disintegrated, falling apart in the advance of each day. She wondered, too, how she had permitted this, thought: Me to him, though she was not sure what this meant. She wanted to say: This is the risk women take, yet she was not certain it was true, could not set down rules larger than her own experience.

She felt the car slow, saw the driver motioning with his hand to someone near the airport doorway. Kathy looked up. In the distance she could see the plane waiting and trucks moving over the runway, dragging hoses and baggage.

The driver said: "Look at all these people. Everybody leaving now. Nobody come in anymore."

"Is that true?" Noel asked.

"Yes, even at the railroad station. Everyone leaving."

Then there was the commotion of climbing out, unloading bags. Kathy stood on the sidewalk feeling the comfort of cement, thinking: Africa ends here. Children pressed up against her. Some were deformed, carved by disease, malnutrition, selling their own misshapen bodies. Vendors circled her. She stood in the center of the beggars, watching Noel tip the driver, slap him on the back. "Noel," she said out loud, but her voice was too low. She wanted rescue, wanted Noel to remove these children from around her because she could not trust herself any longer to be gentle, kind. She clamped her purse under her arm, making sure it could not be opened.

"Ready?" Noel asked. "We have time for a drink or two."

"Are you sure?"

"Positive."

He carried their bags, and she was left to untangle herself from the vendors, the beggars. She felt for a moment like some prey being circled. She attempted not to turn her back, though she bumped into different children, felt arms and legs, skin touching hers. "—*cinq francs.* Nassarra, Nassarra. Buy, Nassarra."

She hurried through them and caught up to Noel at the entrance. He was waiting, smiling, saying as soon as she was near enough to hear: "They like to get you when you're going out. We should give to one, though. Good luck and all that."

"Please," she said.

"Well, there will be others inside."

An electric eye opened the door for them. Kathy was shocked to see it slide open, then shut behind them. She almost asked Noel how the airport had managed it but let it go. She looked back and saw the beggars turning to meet someone else, circling the door of a second taxi.

"We'll check in, then get a drink. How's that?" Noel said.

They moved to join a long line of people. Kathy saw that they were mostly Africans. She stood beside Noel, feeling the beginning of sickness stir, wondering if they could board the plane early, sit in the air-conditioned cabin.

"Do you want to get a drink? Wait for me in the bar?" Noel asked. "I can check us through."

"Don't I have to show my passport?"

"Maybe you're right. You'd better stay."

The line moved slowly. Kathy sat on one of the suitcases. Her legs were weak. She closed her eyes and, for a moment, wished time away. It was a game she had played as a child, making deals with herself, pretending if she saw the color blue when she opened her eyes, the deal had been agreed to. Except now she did not open her eyes, no longer trusting enough to play the game out, reserving for herself some margin of error and disappointment. She lingered then, her eyes closed to everything but the impression of light working under her eyelids. External consciousness was cut off, her mind tucking back on itself. She thought: I came here not long ago. And she remembered the first day, her arrival with Noel, their taxi ride to the hotel. They had driven through first light, Noel saying: We're fifteen degrees from the equator, his words not finding her as she watched life spring up, replicating pictures in magazines she had glanced at long ago. Up in the room they had settled, she showering in a dark bathroom down the hall, then returning to him, a bride, a virgin to this continent. There had been three moths poised over the bed, their wings spread to camouflage themselves on the wall, and she watched them as Noel came closer, saw them remain still, instinctively, even as she and Noel went to bed together, shook, copulated. In the rhythm of their bodies she had sensed a mirrored procreation, so that the animal richness of their smell had heralded the onslaught of a primitiveness she did not fully understand. Rolling off her afterward, Noel had said: Hello, thinking it coy perhaps, yet it had been a greeting, possibly their first, while in her mind had grown the image of them molting, shedding old skin in coupled ritual. She had whispered his name, hearing it in her marriage bed, tracing the contours of the sheets with her fingers, until she said: Husband and wife, wife and husband, heard him settle to his own sleep, fall away.

She recollected this now, her mind pushing to form a circle of coming and going. She sat quietly, the metal buckles of the suitcase digging into her leg, wondering what would leave her, what would remain. She opened her eyes in time to see Noel go up on his toes and peer over the heads of the people in front of him. He had their tickets and passports out.

"Here we go," he said finally.

Another ticket window had been opened. Half the line moved over. She stood and pushed the suitcase forward with her knees. "Ready?" Noel asked.

"Go ahead."

"What?"

"It's our turn."

"Oh," Noel said, turning back. She lifted the bags onto a dolly as Noel talked with the airline official. She watched to see them tagged. She wiped her brow with the back of her hand and heard the airline official ask Noel: "Boston? In the United States?"

"Yes."

"Ah," the man said, then nothing else. He stamped their tickets, circled numbers. There was only one gate, Kathy knew, but the agent pointed it out anyway.

"Thank you," Noel said.

The bags were gone. Kathy could not accustom herself at first to their being gone. As they walked, she found herself wanting to check something, to make sure nothing was missing. She kept her purse cocked under her elbow.

"Jesus," Noel said when they came onto the bar. It was full. Noel found a chair for her against the wall. She sat and watched him force his way to the bar. When he returned, he carried two beers.

"I'm sorry about the beer. They were faster to get, that's all. Do you want something else?"

"No, I don't care."

The beer was warm. Kathy drank it, sip by sip, blocking the flow of liquid sometimes with her tongue. "What time is it in Paris?" she asked after a few minutes.

He looked up, stopped speaking, then checked his watch. "The same, I think," he said. "The same time, I mean. We're on the Greenwich meridian, aren't we?"

"I don't know. That's why I'm asking."

"I'm not sure. I was just trying to say—"

"I'm sorry," she said. "I didn't mean to snap."

"No, that's okay. I can find out if you like. They'll know at the check-in desk."

"It doesn't matter. They'll tell us on the plane."

He nodded, holding up his beer. "Want another?"

"No, I'm fine."

"I'll be right back then."

She watched him push through to the bar. He stopped once on his way, bending to ask something of a French couple. When he straightened, he yelled: "Eight o'clock." He smiled. She propped her beer on her lap, stared at her watch and calculated the time change. She was strangely satisfied to move the hands, thinking, somehow, that Africa could be eliminated so easily. When Noel returned, she heard him say: "It's eight there. It's already dark."

"Is it?"

"We'll be there by sunup." He made a small show of raising his beer. She could not tell if he was serious or mocking her. "To sunrise in Paris," he said.

She started to raise her beer, then heard the flight called. She looked at her watch, frowned.

"You should have waited to change it," Noel said. "But it's time anyway."

The people in the bar were moving through the door. They were pushing. Noel put his hand on her shoulder, his gesture telling her to wait. She controlled herself, though she wanted to rise and run into the crowd, to push to the front. The air seemed drawn by the crowd, removed in spurts of effort and exertion. She smelled the people, the tainted smell of alcohol mixing with the odor of perfume and powder, the musky scent of dirt and sweat. As the bar emptied, she saw it was only a cement cube. Two fans circulated the air above them, keeping the heat down, forcing it between the bodies. She felt faint. She rubbed the bottle on her forehead. A drop of moisture came free and ran down her temple like an insect crawl. She thought briefly of screaming, wondering whether they would let her on the plane first if she did, carry her to the air conditioner like meat kept from souring by the fog of a freezer. She was mildly shocked to find herself considering it seriously, yet the idea lingered even as the crowd temporarily stalled in the jam of the doorway.

"Noel," she said, only to get her voice working, using his name as a chant to block sensation.

"What?"

"Shouldn't we go?"

"No, not yet. They just don't realize they have reserved seats. They think whoever gets on first gets the best seat."

"But it would be cooler in there, wouldn't it?"

"If we could get on. Are you all right? You look flushed."

"I'm fine."

"No, you don't. I mean, you don't look fine. Did you take your Aralen?" he said, naming the drug they took once a week to suppress malaria.

"Yes. I took it yesterday. I'm fine, honestly."

He was squatting next to her. He put a hand on her forehead, but his hand was cold from the beer. He shook it, then replaced it. "No, you're not hot," he said. "It's just stuffy in here. You'll be okay."

"I'm fine, really. Don't worry."

She counted the people as they passed through the door. When she was up to twenty, she realized she had no reference point. She didn't know how many had already left. The counting made her feel worse.

Finally, Noel said: "I guess we can go now. It won't be so crazy."

"All right."

She did not trust her legs as she stood. Noel held her under the elbow, asking too frequently: "Are you okay? Easy now. Are you sure?" But he was guiding her, taking her to the rear of the line. In front of her, she saw some sort of group standing to one side. They were all men, all dressed in traditional costume: long robes, caftans, white shoes with long, pointed toes. Three of the men chewed sticks which shredded green matter on their teeth. She asked: "Who are they?," immediately regretting her own curiosity.

"They're making a pilgrimage to Mecca probably."

"By way of Paris?"

"They make a connection there. They hardly ever go straight across the desert. See?" he said, pointing out one man by nodding his head. "He's El Hadji. He's gone before."

"And that brings him luck, doesn't it?"

"And holiness."

She watched the men as the line moved forward. They were excited. The airport official, a woman this time, passed them through, wishing them luck. Noel presented their tickets in turn; then Kathy followed him outside onto the runway. The group of men were lined up for a final photograph.

Noel asked again: "Are you all right?"

"Yes. How do you feel?"

"I don't know yet. I can't tell."

The plane seemed too large, too modern. Kathy had trouble believing it was for them. She paused at the steps. A stewardess at the top of the stairway said: "Hurry now." Kathy climbed. The stewardess greeted them, but by this time Kathy could think only of the coolness, sleep perhaps. Noel turned once at the door to look back. Kathy thought: Now done. She walked into the plane, looking for her seat.

New Hampshire

One

Frankenstein walked. His green shirt stuck to his back. A line of sweat trickled down each temple. He turned once and watched his footprints fade. He thought: Dew steps, water tracks. The dew was disappearing faster than usual, sinking down to the roots where it was needed. He opened his shirt and rubbed his chest. His chest was gray and curly. A wind kicked up for an instant and ran over him. He flapped his shirt open wider, taking a breath.

It was still a half hour to light, still the best time to kill. He reached his hand to his knife, pressing its outline on his thigh. The knife was as wide as a bookmark.

He ducked under the first branches of a rhododendron patch. He took out his slingshot, making sure the brace was firm on his forearm. With his right hand he took a pebble *from his breast pocket. He rolled the pebble in his palm, touching the smoothness, taking satisfaction in the white color. He lay flat out, his stomach receiving the chill from the night ground. He wondered what kind of track he would leave if he belly-crawled across the park lawn, thought of silver remaining on both sides of a snake mark, a sea monster returning to water. The cicadas called, marking the temperature. He put his head down on the mulch, dead leaves that blanketed the roots of the rhododendron. He did not want to sleep. He stretched his arm out in front of him and steadied the slingshot.*

He waited. He watched a beetle crawl through the leaves, pinchers reaching out, hoisting and lowering its body, its mechanical progression through the humus. With his left hand he buried the beetle with leaves, then watched it again as it climbed free, its body tilting a strand of grass gently. He saw it stop, mark his shadow. He lifted his hand and moved it so the shadow it created touched the insect's back, then removed it. The beetle retreated under another leaf, its wide-set legs burrowing.

He shifted then, easing the pressure of his belt buckle off his stomach. His legs were stiff. He could feel sleep still gathered in his eyes. He rolled onto his side and pulled a whiskey flask from his hip pocket, drank. The liquor burned, caught in the pores of his tongue, and rested, unswallowed, on the roof of his mouth. He let it drain down his throat, rising first on his forearms and tilting his head back like a bird. He coughed, shook, felt the liquor. He wanted to hawk but could not break the silence now. He took another sip and put the flask away.

A ray of sun broke through the leaf cover, took up its spot on the mulch beside him. He moved a hand into its path and let the heat work on him. He tested the air with his breath, looking to see it curl in frost, but it was too warm. A wind puffed, died. Through the green of the rhododendron bank he saw a man walking on the street beyond, heard the clop of shoe leather on cement. He sighted the man with his slingshot, let him pass.

It was then he heard the gull coming. It called once, then flapped to the ground. He saw the orange beak, the black eyes, the crisp white of its body. He didn't move, made no effort to take the gull in his sights. He stared straight ahead, waiting for the gull to come into the V. He aimed between the garbage can and the gull. He pulled back on the elastic, feeling the muscles on his forearm knot.

He fired just as the gull stepped into range. The follow-through was right—a slight downward snap of the wrist. He saw the white rock flash in half-light, white to gray, white to the white of the gull. He saw the gull spin to face him, its beak smiling. It took three steps before its wings would accept the weight of its body. Then it ducked low over the water, its wings rowing the river. He thought: No kill, picturing then a white gull that would sink to the bottom of the river and hang there, gill-less, the sea flushing it inland and pulling it back.

He stood, separating the branches with his hands and body. Branches cracked around him, and he smelled green sap. He pushed through to open lawn and walked toward the garbage can. Bending to a crouch, he sifted the grass for feathers, found five, six, the seventh flecked with blood. He took a plastic bag out of his pocket and set the feathers inside, thinking already of Farley, the hardware man, who would take the feathers for money and turn them into trout flies. He wrapped the plastic around them, folded it all into a neat package, tucked it back in his pocket. He hung the slingshot around his neck and buttoned his shirt over it.

Noel lay flat on his back, staring at the ceiling. He felt Kathy beside him, her body damp, her breathing regular. The window behind him was open, the shade drawn almost to the sill. A lawn mower droned somewhere in the distance. He tilted his head back and took a quick breath. The air was hot. He smelled the grass he had piled next to the garage the day before. It reminded him of winter hay piled chest deep, its core turning gently to flame.

He had dreamed of the finger. He had seen in the night the black finger falling, the African heads staring down at him from the top of the well shaft. The finger had fallen slowly, end over end, severed by the grind of the pulley and the weight of rope. The stream of blood drew lazy lines in the humid air: red lines against the rust of laterite, the well a blood cave. In the dream he had picked the finger out of the mud and tucked it into his pocket, then called to the men to pull him out. Going up toward the sun, bouncing off the walls like a mountain climber, he had seen streaks of blood on the rope, the heads gone now to pull, the finger throbbing against his chest.

On top, he had given the finger back. He handed it to Ba, the leper, a man in the dream with a white cloth over his mouth to hide where his jaws had been eroded. Even as he stared, Noel saw the cloth sucked in and out, pulled and released by the man's quick breathing. Then Ba took the finger and threw it to the sow. The sow started, grunted, then came back, the bristled snout inhaling the finger.

The finger gone, Noel had opened his eyes, thinking: This past returned to me. He hovered between dream and waking, felt himself divided. He wondered at the return of this dream after a month, the release of it now signifying something unresolved. He went over it again in his mind, let it go. Beside him, Kathy turned onto her side, tucking a pillow between her legs. The shade billowed out with the breeze, then flapped back. The light that entered might have been a camera flash. He wondered how many times he had seen everything in the room, a boy's room really, while lying in the same position. The plaid wallpaper had been selected years ago. The row of model airplanes was still arranged wing tip to wing tip above the small study desk. A pennant from the University of Maryland. A map of Wyoming, square white except for the hazy yellow around the Tetons. In the doorframe the pull-up bar he had asked for on his twelfth birthday still glistened, its chrome silver white from the wear of his hands. He thought: fifteen pull-ups a morning, saw an image of himself standing before the mirror on the dresser, biceps flexed, a young boy moving to manhood. And to him now, this image seemed no less removed than the finger dream, provided him with a mental photograph, an emblem of other days no longer recoverable by him.

He sat up and dropped his legs over the edge of the bed. Calmly he admitted to himself he wanted a drink. A drink would take the bite off his headache, remove the last grip of the dream. The night before, he had gotten drunk watching television. He had started on beer, then switched to shots. Kathy had come in and gathered the cans without a word. He had listened as she threw them into a paper bag, rattling each in accusation, finally slamming the entire bag down by the refrigerator. She had been loud on purpose, just as he had opened each can with a snap, letting the sound find her in the kitchen.

He stood. His blood climbed, pumping to his head. His stomach rolled once and was still. He walked to the door and let himself out. He paused and listened to the house. A patch of sun warmed the floor in front of him, the leaves dancing in quick shadows. The lawn mower had stopped. A motorcycle passed on the road, followed by the low whine of a Volkswagen. The house smothered each new wave of noise and sifted it, breaking it down until it was absorbed in the rich texture of cloth and wood.

He walked to the kitchen in his underwear. The tile was cool on his feet. He poured himself a tall glass of tomato juice and debated whether to add vodka. Quietly, he reached into the cereal cabinet and took down a bottle of Smirnoff's. He poured in half a jigger and sipped. His stomach rolled, this time in acceptance. Leaning against the counter, he poured in a little more, then put the bottle away. He reminded himself to brush his teeth and gargle before Kathy woke up.

He started back through the house. Old sounds came to him as he walked. He deliberately stepped on a loose floorboard next to the dining-room table to hear it creak, wondering as he did so about such knowledge retained. A crystal vase trembled on the sideboard, the glass chattering on a sterling platter. He saw light, now tightened into ropes, reaching the sofa. He remembered sitting in an easy chair beside it, letting the sun climb him. His knee had been eight o'clock, his belt eight-thirty. At nine his parents would wake, and the light would cease to matter.

He took another sip. His headache was disappearing. Except for the taste in his mouth, he would have felt fine, normal. He realized normalcy was becoming harder to secure and thought for a moment of his body as a combination of liquids, his mood touched and shaped by consumption, by catalysts taken or refused.

He climbed the stairs to the second floor. At his parents' bedroom he forced himself not to pause, not to knock. He opened the door and walked in. At first he couldn't make out his father's form in the bed. He saw the legs set apart, the shoulders still large beside the boned features of the face. He imagined the cancer again as a crab, thumb-crawling sideways, working its way through the salty veins of his father. He saw it nibbling, trapped by the thin wall of skin, clinging for a moment before it was washed to another part of the body. He was sure the cancer had an intelligence; it could not be explained otherwise. Somehow female, the crab was dispersing eggs, bathing them in warm currents of blood, attaching them to arteries by a saliva solution. Mounds of eggs were formed in his father's joints. Only the eggs kept the body from collapsing in on itself, falling into a saclike shape which could be rolled and kneaded.

He stepped closer and touched his father's forehead. His own fingers were wet from the drink, and he wiped them against his ribs, the chill raising his flesh. He saw there was no change. The lungs moved weakly, the chest barely rising. He sat in a straight-backed chair and took a large swallow. He swished tomato juice in his mouth, thinking: This debt, his ears still tuned to his father's breathing. He leaned forward, unable to recognize the man, seeing him as an outline, his bones marking the remains, a soulless diagram of tissue, muscle, cartilage. He had not come in time, had had no last opportunity to speak, and now felt as if his father had retracted into himself, had sunk from acknowledgment, sealing himself in coma. At this, Noel felt pity, felt emotions unnamed. He watched the skin tented by blankets, saw the solar plexus knot, expand, sensed himself in wordless dialogue, reconciled to the belief that his own soul was begun by this man, caught by flesh in his mother's womb years before. He wished to speak, envisioned his words sinking into nerveless flesh until they were heard, recovered by his father, sent back to him. In the same moment he thought: He is dying, dead, looked around him to the familiar furniture, saw briefly a picture of his mother set on his father's bureau. The picture touched old grief, made him lean closer still to his father, while he caught, from the corner of his eye, his mother looking on, waiting.

He finished his drink and stood, idly tucking the sheet tighter, inching his fingers under the mattress. His father's breath halted momentarily, perhaps instinctively, at Noel's proximity, then continued in a rasping sound which forced the ear to listen. It could stop any moment. The last movement could be missed. It seemed to Noel like a strange performance when the audience isn't sure the act is finally over. He hung in the dim light, looking for some clue, something that would demand a reaction. But the lungs continued winding down and sinking until his father seemed to gain another thought and pull back to life.

Noel backed out of the room. He stopped in the bathroom to wash his face. He pulled on a pair of cutoffs that he had left on the doorknob. Kathy's powder and shampoo were scattered on the back of the tub. He wondered whether the house had a new smell since they had come. There was the medicine smell, of course, but there was also something else. He couldn't name it exactly. The odors from the kitchen at night were not the smells he remembered. Perhaps, he thought, it was as simple as the choice of a spice.

He went downstairs to the kitchen and began preparing coffee, his hands working automatically. He lost count of the scoops and judged them to be four. He added another. He rinsed the glass out, sniffing it to see whether Kathy would be able to detect vodka. Satisfied, he shook the glass dry and put it in the cabinet.

He opened the back door. The morning fell into the kitchen, heavy, panting. The screen held light, making it difficult to see the lawn. He turned on the radio and heard the DJ predicting more heat. It was to be dry and hot, temperatures in the nineties. The station switched to a helicopter report, and the pilot said cars were overheating up and down the major roads. Hoods were lifted, and steam poured out of drained radiators.

The coffeepot chugged. He set the timer for ten minutes, then went into his father's study. The room was dark. A worn Oriental rug covered the floor. French doors opened to a view of the pool, which was bordered by pine hedges, fifteen yards beyond the house.

Noel pulled a pack of cigarettes from a carton on the desk. In the corner of the room he saw a globe, held in cross brackets on its own stand. He walked to it, remembering the game he had played with his father years ago. His father would let him spin it, then stick a finger wherever he wanted. They both would bend to see where he had traveled to. Then, together, they would see who knew more about the place. The game had always begun the same way: language spoken, continent, religion, temperature, industry, political stance, folklore. His father had been unbeatable. He was a shipper, a man who dealt in boats and storage. He knew the world without ever having traveled it.

Now Noel spun the globe once, watched while the colors flashed by. He put his finger down on California, spun it again.

"Noel?" Jenna, the nurse, called from the kitchen. Noel let the globe spin and took his cigarettes, wondering why he hadn't heard her car. It was an old Ford with a muffler problem. He could always hear her coming.

"Jenna?" he asked, coming into the kitchen. She was outside the door, her forehead pressed to the screen. She looked, for a moment, like a little boy peering inside for a playmate.

"Why didn't you just come in?" he asked.

"I don't like to just come in. It's not my house," she said

as she opened the door and blinked. She was dressed in slacks and a loose blouse. She set a large shoulder bag on the kitchen table and sat down. "Coffee?" she asked, already searching in her bag.

"It'll be ready in a second."

"Good. Last night I was up until three with Willy. He can talk forever. You haven't met Willy, have you? I think you two would get along. He's always asking questions, just like you."

"Am I?"

"See?" she said, and smiled. Noel looked at the things she was putting on the table: cards, a novel, a nail file, tweezers, a transistor radio, and a spiral notebook. Noel thought of them as time games. She could sit for hours in a sickroom and keep herself amused. She dug deeper in her purse and pulled out a dozen scraps of paper, saying: "I brought the receipts for everything. I know you don't care, but it keeps everything flat on the table, you know what I mean? I worked for a woman once . . . shit." She stopped and pulled her blouse free. "It's too hot for stories."

Noel took the receipts and tossed them in a junk drawer. He had read the first batch, but they depressed him. Jenna had purchased diapers, rubber matting, tissues, gauze. He didn't look at them anymore.

"How's your father? Did you look in on him?"

"He seems fine. I was worried he'd be too cold without a blanket."

"No. We have to keep him warm, of course, but it's hot enough. No reason to make him too hot."

She started putting the things back in her bag. Noel watched her hands. They were feminine but incredibly strong. He had seen her roll his father around easily. Dr. Zitch had recommended her. Since then she and the Doctor had carried on a running conversation through him. He would carry bits of information back and forth and watch each accept the other's message with a nod. The prognosis never changed. It was always death. Time was the only factor, the only thing to risk an opinion on.

Jenna pinched her bag closed and tucked it over her shoulder. "I'll just run up and look in on him," she said. "Too damn hot for coffee, but I'll come down in a few minutes. Kathy still asleep?"

"Yep."

"I'll be down."

Noel listened to her climb the stairs. He stood next to the stove, watching the slow reach of bubbles in the pot.

Kathy carried a breakfast tray out the back door. The screen door bounced once, then hissed closed. Birds broke from the feeder, scattering sunflower seeds with their feet. They took to branches far enough away to be safe, calling the danger. A blue jay swooped above her, warning.

She followed the short path down to the pool. The patio stones were already hot. She stepped off into the cooler grass, careful to keep the tray level. The heat was building. She could feel it against her skin as she walked. It was a pressure, a web she could stir simply by moving her hand.

The water was blue in front of her. She heard it lapping and thought of the pool alarm. Noel had taken it out when they first moved in. Several groups of kids had come late at night and jumped in. Noel had let them swim. But he had put the alarm back in when he found a mound of feces on the diving board. The next day he dug out his brother's BB gun and propped it by the French doors in his father's study. He was ready now, but they had stopped coming. The pool was quiet all night.

She set the tray down on a steel table and adjusted the legs of a lawn chair. She was tempted to dive in and cool off, but then the food would be cold. She lifted the lid off her poached egg and saw it had already soaked into the whole wheat bread. A small yellow moat of egg rimmed the plate, obscuring the floral design.

She took a bite of egg and bread, the two textures playing off each other. She leaned back in her chair, chewing slowly. The birds came back to the feeder one by one. A gray squirrel came straight down a tree trunk, and she threw a piece of bread a few feet away, trying to lure it closer. She had forgotten there were animals in the suburbs. Noel had drawn an image of a wasteland, saying: Birdies and eagles on the golf course, that was all. But there were animals everywhere: squirrels, mice, gulls, dogs, cats, skunks, and raccoons. There was even a beehive behind the house, giving off a summer drone which seeped inside. Almost every morning they would find something floating in the pool, the body bloated, eyes filmy with chlorine. She thought of these animals as midnight swimmers, skinny-dippers who couldn't find a hold on the round cement edges. Kathy hated to think of them swimming in circles, their heads barely above water, their strokes getting weaker.

"Morning," Noel said.

She was surprised to see him halfway down the path. He carried a white towel over his shoulder. He bent and kissed the side of her neck, then was gone, diving, his body arching for a moment before slapping the water. He swam the length of the pool underwater, his legs curling in cadence with his arms. He came up at the other end, his hair skinned back. He blew into the water, then pretended to splash like an elephant, dipping his hand and throwing water on his back. Then, suddenly, he was a dolphin. He pushed backward from the wall and made a high staccato sound. He held his hand to his nose, a snout, and flipped water straight up. When he came up beside her, he rolled onto his side, showing one eye. It was featureless, an animal eye.

He snorted again and in one motion pulled himself up on the edge. He rolled onto his belly, begging food. She handed him a piece of bread, and he swallowed it. He made the sound again, then slid back into the water, sinking to the bottom. His body coiled near the drain, finally exploding upward until he was above the water, splashing. He gave a high dolphin laugh.

She asked: "Flipper, did you eat this morning?" but he didn't hear. He was back down the other end. She watched him push off different walls, effortlessly, his body gliding. He zigzagged toward her. She watched his muscles flex and loosen. He came to the side and held his body parallel to the edge.

"I asked if you ate this morning," she said.

"Sardines," he said. Then: "Flipper allllwayyyys eattts sardiiiiineees." He splashed her again.

"How's your dad?

"Okay. Jenna is with him."

"Did you eat anything?"

"Not yet."

"Would you like me to cook you something? We should eat some of the eggs. We bought too many."

"No, thanks. I'll get something later." He looked around the pool and smiled. "Nothing floating this morning, huh?"

"I didn't really look."

He nodded. She finished the egg and ran her bread

around the plate. The design came clear: yellow birds flitting around two vases wrapped in vines. Noel pushed off the wall and treaded water. He said something, then spit water out of his mouth.

"What?" she asked.

"I said I'm sorry about last night. The drinking and everything."

"That's all right."

"No, I shouldn't do it. It's not you, you know."

"I know."

He grinned and said: "I always thought you had to be in World War Two to end up drinking beer in front of the television."

He laughed. She felt the tension cracking. There was always tension in the morning, always time to fill. But, she realized, the situation was harder on him. She could feel it fully only through him.

"Grant is coming over," he said, leaning on the wall, his chin on his hands. "He and Mary are bringing some steaks. He says there's a croquet set in the garage. He wants to play croquet."

"When did he call?"

"I called him. He says he has a surprise for us."

"Do you know what it is?"

"No idea."

"What should I fix?"

"Don't go to any trouble. I'll fix it if you want. Mary likes to do everything once she gets here. She's due to be canonized next week."

"They already have a Saint Mary."

"So they'll have another. The Virgin Mary, Mary Magdalene, and Mary Simpson, Saint Tupperware."

He sank and came up next to the ladder. He pulled him-

self out, the water streaming off him. Hopping on one foot
and shaking his head, he asked: "Did you ever play dibble?"

"Christ, you have more games."

"No, really. Did you?"

"No."

"Grant and I used to play it all the time. You get a golf
tee and take it down to the bottom. Then you climb out
and try to get it before the other guy."

"Is that it?"

He walked over and sat down. He leaned back and put
his face up to the sun. He put a finger in his belly button
and pushed it in and out. Over the liquid sound he said:
"I'm coming."

"Noel, stop it."

"I am." He turned to face her. "You should see Grant do
the woman hurdler with his belly button."

"I'd rather not."

"Anyway," he said, "dibble was the game. We used to
play it all day. We even thought we invented it. Then one
time we went to a friend's country club and every kid there
knew how to play. That ever happen to you?"

"My uncle thought he made up the violin thing." She
put the plate on the ground. "You know, when someone
starts telling you a sad story, you pretend to play the violin. I guess you're supposed to be a Gypsy. Anyway, he
thought he made that up."

"Was it sad when he found out?"

"It was for him. He was a strange man. He—"

She stopped. Noel was playing the violin. She laughed.
He lay back and asked: "You sure you don't want to see the
woman hurdler?"

"No, thanks. Listen, I'm going to start lunch before it
gets too hot. How about a salad?"

"Fine. I'll help if you want. It's really too hot already."
She picked up the plate. "Not like Africa. It's not that
hot, is it?"

"No."

"I'll see if Jenna wants anything. You relax."

"I'm getting good at that."

"Yes, well . . ." She did not go on. She walked back to the
house. She turned once and saw him sitting quietly, staring
straight ahead. She stepped into the kitchen and felt the
heat reduced, ran her plate under water, looked again to see
him. He hadn't moved. She wanted to call him, to say:
Come in, Noel; hold out the invitation for him to accept or
refuse. Yet she had a vague notion the distance was too
great. Her voice would have fallen between them, would
have been caught in the languid air, held, smothered. She
could not cross to him, imagined them now as a pair of
opened scissors, the knotting rivet Paris, the two ends
Africa and the present. She thought: The spread, felt,
momentarily, the press of the old man above, the sickness
somehow communicated to walls, floors, the air. In this she
felt herself a silent witness, powerless, a spectator of no importance to some debate between father and son, the flesh-
rich claims of responsibility. She could not understand it
completely, was surprised, even now, to find herself incon-
sequential beside a larger question, thought: It does not
change. Through the heat, the tree rustle surrounding him,
she watched Noel, his skin brown, his posture slumped.
She listened to the water lap, heard a bee pass close to the
window, its vibration pass to the window screen, go up in
light, and wondered about her own place, her own stance.
She saw herself moving closer to motherhood—not of children, but of her own husband, felt something long dormant
inside her tugged by demands to feed, clean, to observe
wordlessly. She did not want it, had never asked for it, but

she could feel it happening, saw the house being turned over to her, saw Noel's parents' bed slowly losing the weight of the dying man each day while she was granted parentage of a hundred memories. The house is ours, Noel had once told her. If you want it, the house is ours. She wondered now if she did want it. It would not be hard. It would be comfortable, perhaps too comfortable, and at this she rebelled, thinking briefly of Noel's father bating this snare with his own body. Come home, it said. Return, it said, echoing words spoken by the Africans a month ago.

Then she saw Noel stand, dive, heard the water slosh. He swam in an easy freestyle, palms cupped, fingers pointed. He swam five laps while she watched, his head turning only to take a breath twice every length. Each time he breathed she watched his lips pucker and his eyes close so that his expression was that of a man enduring great pain or the pinched features of a newborn child. She turned away and went to the sink. She heard him swimming over the jet of the faucet, heard him swimming still when she went upstairs to check on Jenna.

Frankenstein walked through the garden, careful not to step on the flowers. The dirt turned under his feet. A few clods of peat broke free and lifted with his step, fell, adding footfalls to his own. He bent over a small fountain and washed his face, drank. The water tasted of metal, cement, corrosion. He swished it in his mouth until it mingled with his own saliva, lost its taste, then swallowed. He drank three handfuls this way, then sat on the edge of the fountain, squinted, remembering now the ladies who had appeared in early spring to replant the garden. They had planted gardenias, marigolds, pansies, crawling around on their knees, wearing green gardening gloves, straw hats, their purses set in the middle of the plot like a leather campfire. He had watched this from the rhododendron patch, each day coming to see the soil new-turned and fresh. When the women were done, he had gone to Farley and bought his own flower seeds, had come at night to plant, throwing three seeds in each finger-poked hole. In moonlight he had planted; in moonlight he found the first green shoots and bent to lip one, tasting a vegetable flavor, sand, the iron of new earth.

Now, with memory fading, he stood and stepped carefully through the rows of pansies. His body was stiff. He felt a stone bruise his foot, stopped once to place his full weight on it, testing, then walked on. The slingshot tapped his chest, swung opposite the leg going forward. He saw the sun rising from the city buildings, the light divided by telephone wires, early smoke clouding it. He crossed Pleasant Street, feeling exposed, and hustled to regain the curb. He stopped then, raised one foot to a fire hydrant, and tied his boot. The leg he was standing on quivered. He let his foot swing down and moved closer to the buildings, felt himself grow smaller as he approached the city square.

He paused on the corner of Hope and Pleasant, listened to a telephone wire stretch and crackle, heard in his imagination the voice the line carried break free of the wired insulation, pour down like rain, garbled, pooled. He put a hand to his slingshot, took it away. A cat crossed the street running on bent legs, oblivious of him. He sucked his teeth, made a high shrill sound, and watched the cat suddenly gallop in a rabbit run, back legs tucking forward, front reaching. He sucked again, but the cat was gone.

He entered the town square from the north corner. The Protestant church took up one side, and he walked to it. He

*sat on the cold stone steps just as a street cleaner came up
Federal Street, circled, and left a wide arc of wet pavement.
He watched it move off, though its sound continued a block
away, the bristled churn of its underwheel grating gravel
and new tar. He reached into his pocket for bread crumbs,
then scattered them, flicking his hand in a seeding motion.
He was not quite finished with his first handful when he
saw a pigeon break free from a building and swoop down.
He let it come, let it attract others. He drew his slingshot
off his neck and arranged it, his movements causing small
surges in the pack of pigeons now circling him. He listened
to the birds, fed them more, checked the street, and saw
nothing. He loaded a rock in the leather pocket on the
elastic and settled it against his thigh. He raised his hands
twice, each time watching the reaction from the pigeons
grow weaker, less alarmed. The third time he raised, sighted,
fired.*

*The rock hit the bird on the shoulder. It fell back,
dragged a broken wing as he had seen pigeons do when
mating. It toppled to its side, rose, flew a foot off the
ground, then fell again. He loaded once more, standing in
his excitement, almost missing the approach of a woman
directly behind the pigeon. She was staring, a small dog in
front of her, her silence contained, then released in a wail.
The buildings echoed. She started walking toward him, her
heels clicking.*

*—Why did you do that? That was the cruelest thing I've
ever seen. Don't they call you Tommy? That's your name,
isn't it? Don't lie to me. I'm going to call the police. A man
your age shooting pigeons. Do you see how cruel it is?*

*And she walked across the street, sun flashing from the
shins of her stockings, her dog starting to yap. Frankenstein
raised his slingshot at her, saw her duck. The dog strained
at its leash, and he thought: Poodle dog. Q-tip dog.*

In midmorning heat Noel worked. He pulled weeds from the garden lining the front of the house, jerking the thin stalks free and shaking them to release the dirt from the roots. He smelled the soil, thicker here than it had been in Africa, and felt his hands covered by a resin of plant matter. The perimeter of the garden was overgrown, obscured by grass. He turned the soil to cover it, watching the roots appear in the churned clods, the dirt dissected by gray lines seeking moisture. Beetles scrambled for cover, slipping and falling in fresh pockmarks, shocked by the sudden exposure to light. He stopped once to watch two garden slugs dangling from their own mucus solution, saw them entwine, mating, their reproduction covered by a silver sheen. He saw one drop, sated, while the other climbed back up the strand of spittle, returned to the leafy branch, then proceeded in a hunched march down a slender limb. Farther on he came across a leaf blistered by a sawfly. He turned the leaf over, imagining as he did so the fly sawing between layers of leaf with its penis, depositing its eggs silently by night, ejaculating eggs into the epidermis of vegetation, hidden, secure, wrapped in a blanket of tissue. He thought: This knowledge handed down, and remembered his father, recalled his father leading him and Grant around the yard, an amateur naturalist restricted to his own backyard, giving lessons in birth and life, escape and predation. They had been stern lessons. Each portion of the yard had been subjected to intense scrutiny, so that even this play took on the aspect of work, preparation. Application, his father had said, as though knowledge should be used to garner power. In time, Noel remembered, the yard had lost its magic, had become something to be tested, examined. The stalkings and small wars that went on nightly in the garden, encircling the house, were held up as examples. Suffer, if need be. Defend. Noel thought this in connection with his father and wondered if the lessons did not have application now. He felt like a pupil drawn to his teacher in order to demonstrate the special knowledge gained by instruction.

He moved down the garden, his mind still working, the grass touching his bare legs. He felt the sun on him. His arms, when he touched them with his fingers, left white marks, which disappeared slowly into red. He was still at work when Jenna came onto the front porch and stretched. She didn't speak at first. She seemed shocked by the light, surprised it was still early morning. Finally, she came down the steps and sat on the bottom one and lit a cigarette. She said: "Hot. The heat's building upstairs."

"Do you feel all right?" Noel asked.

"Oh, I'm fine. I just came out to smoke. I don't like to smoke around him."

"How is he?"

She shrugged. "Who knows?" she said. "You never know, do you?"

"I guess not."

Noel pulled a weed free and put it on a pile of others. He got up and stretched himself, bending back from the waist and rolling his shoulders. A muscle caught, released. He walked to the steps and sat down beside her. He took a cigarette from his own pack and lit it. Jenna said again: "Hot."

"Could it affect him?"

"It might. Men like him—well, you know—they seem like flowers to me sometimes. The heat might be all right. You don't know. I think it's all right."

Noel watched a bird wing overhead. The bushes moved to a small breeze, then stopped, clinging and settling to the earth. Jenna shifted. Her sandal scraped the brick steps. She asked: "Was it always this hot in Africa?"

"Hotter. It was a dry heat."

"I can't imagine," she said, then paused. "You know," she began after a moment, "Willy wants to talk to you about Africa. He thinks his ancestors are from around where you were. In West Africa, right? He thinks they were captured by slavers. Was there much of that around there?"

"It was more to the south and west. I stayed in an old slave fort in Ghana once. They stuck the slaves in the basement, then turned the cannons inland. They were right on the coast, and they were less worried about attack from the sea than from the natives. The natives attacked anyway. They had some bloody battles."

Jenna shook her head and clicked her tongue. Noel glanced at her and saw her weighing the facts. With her, there was always this exchange of knowledge—Africa for the understanding of his father's condition. But he knew she was dissatisfied with his stories of Africa. It was not, she had told him, how she imagined it. Her image was closer to Willy's. Noel had the notion she was asking for Willy's benefit, that her questions were ones he had prompted her to ask.

She said: "You know, I tell Willy what's done is done. He always wants to root up the past. Sometimes, when I tell him things you say, he doesn't believe me. He had a brother who went back—he doesn't tell it the way you do."

"How's it different?"

"Oh, he just says he was accepted. He says the Africans still think of the black Americans as brothers."

"They might. Except that most of the people I worked with didn't even know where America was."

"Is that true?"

"Yes. In the bush it was true. The school kids knew."

She shook her head again and rubbed her cigarette out on the step. She said: "Willy," and smiled. He watched her accept this knowledge, wondering if she believed it. He wanted to go on. He wanted to explain the details of life there as if her seeing it would make it come back. He waited for her to ask another question, but she didn't.

"Where's Kathy?" he asked eventually. Jenna stood, stretched once more. He knew the conversation was over.

"She was cooking something a minute ago. I don't know. Around, I guess."

"I'd be glad to talk to Willy. Bring him over anytime."

"I don't know. I think his ideas might get a little busted up. Maybe it's better to leave it be."

"Whatever you think."

"I'll mention it to him, though," she said. "I'm going to go back up. You want me to tell Kathy you were looking for her?"

"No, that's all right."

Jenna left. Noel went to the pile of weeds and lifted them against his chest. He carried them behind the garage and threw them on the mound of clippings. A bur stuck to his shirt, and he picked it off. He touched the mound with his bare toes and felt the grass give, a scent stir. He held his foot parallel to the slope of the pile. He felt the heat of decomposition, the green warmth. He imagined the pile covered with snow, small rodents burrowing into it, the center a warm cave of field life. He let his weight move forward and sank his foot up to his ankle in the grass. A dragonfly, unseen before, broke and sped past him, wings blurring and fanning the smell. He removed his foot and wiped it clean.

When he got back to the front yard, Kathy was waiting. She said as soon as she saw him: "Shouldn't they be here by now?"

"They said they'd be over this afternoon."

"I just thought they'd be here by now," she said. He watched her turn, hesitate. She was dressed in shorts and a halter. He looked at her legs and felt desire come, go, saw her body retreat from this new presentation until it became something he knew and recognized without careful inspection.

"Will you be much longer?" she asked.

"I'm done. I always hated this kind of stuff."

"You're doing a lot of it."

"Duty. I think I'm still expecting an allowance."

She smiled and, reaching for the screen door at the same time, hit her elbow on the mailbox. "Damn," she said. She stepped inside. The screen door closed over her, turning her into a specter that disappeared slowly into the dimness of the house. He watched the door, half expecting her to reappear, thought briefly of their divided labor—his on the outside, hers within. He heard metal strike metal in the kitchen, heard, a few moments later, a vacuum start. He collected the gardening tools and carried them to the garage. He was conscious of his movements, aware of his own knowledge of the yard, the garage, the tools. It seemed to him a return to boyhood, and he recalled his ability to find things when his parents couldn't, remembering the use he made of his small body, the texture of corners, the floor underneath tables, the squash of his body behind a couch.

He opened the garage and put the tools away. He went around the house. He wanted a drink but was afraid of the petty accusations, the looks he knew he would receive. At the pool he sat and dangled his legs in the water. Grass from the bottom of his feet fell free and floated halfway down, hovering in refracted light.

"Do you remember? Jesus, we used to play this all the time, and now I don't even remember how to set the wickets up. Is it two here, or three?"

Grant was bent over the first post, hammering it with the end of his mallet. The post was banded in color: green, red, yellow, black. It looked to Noel like a coral snake stiffened and pounded upright into the ground.

"I think it's three," Noel told him.

Grant nodded. He had come ready to play. Noel had followed him to the garage and watched him dig through old tires and hoses, newspapers stacked for the Salvation Army. Grant had found the set wicket by wicket, trailing it through the debris until he uncovered the ball carrier and mallets.

"I'm going to need a swim after this," Grant said. "How about you?"

"I took one this morning. Kathy might be ready for one."

"Well, maybe Mary and I will."

"It's your house, too," Noel said.

Grant didn't look at him. He was too intent on lining everything up properly. Noel took a drink of beer, then rubbed the can over his forehead. He was hot. He had listened to the radio all morning, to the constant monologue about the heat. Warnings were out to old people, to anyone with a respiratory condition. Even Grant had mentioned the heat when he first arrived. His voice had been calm, but Noel had detected concern for their father, had felt the import of small events, the general made specific. He had seen Grant's anxiousness and sensed in himself some appreciation for the critical situation they found themselves in.

He discovered in Grant's actions his own attitude reflected, saw the comfort of illusion being stripped to reality. Noel realized survival was an issue, that survival brought with it sharper senses, that even the air had to be tested, remarked on, because it did have a bearing. It reminded him of minor catastrophes from childhood—when an electrical storm would knock out power, or rains would bring small floods— which they hated and enjoyed at once. His father's lingering near death brought a new level of awareness, and Noel understood they would be disappointed to see the problem resolved, that life, returned to the smooth flow of things, would lose certain meaning.

"That's right, huh?" Grant was asking. "Two, then one, then two again. Two on the post? Like an hourglass, right?"

"I think so. Maybe it's three on the post. I'm not sure."

"Do you want to play?"

"Sure, I want to play. I just don't remember whether you set it up right."

"You don't seem that interested."

"Come on, Grant. I'm interested," Noel said. Then, to change the subject, he asked: "What's the surprise, Grant?"

"Secret."

"What's it about?"

"Secret," Grant said again.

Noel didn't pursue it. He moved to a line of pine hedges and sat in the shade. He lit a cigarette. He didn't want to play croquet but knew there was no way out of it. He leaned back on one elbow and smelled the dead pine needles close to his head. It reminded him of Christmas, scented candles burning in gift shops. Grant was still moving in front of him, his white legs ridiculous in baggy shorts. Noel tried to remember a summer when his own legs hadn't been tan and couldn't.

"I think we're ready," Grant said. He walked to the edge of the shade and squinted.

"Do you remember the rules?" Noel asked.

"I'll make them up as I go. I always did, didn't I?"

Grant laughed. He walked off to get the women. Noel lay flat on his back. He could feel the beer turning in his stomach. He cupped a hand over his mouth and blew into it. Grass pressed against his back, making him feel buggy. He wanted to scratch, then felt the grass take the shape of his body. For a moment nothing moved. There were no clouds, no sound. Then the silence was broken by Kathy's yelling something. She was coming fast, screaming: Off with their heads! Off with their heads!

Noel sat up and saw Mary following Kathy.

"Grant, do you really remember how to play?" Kathy was asking. She ran forward and grabbed a mallet. It was red. Noel plucked a blade of grass and put it in his mouth. It tasted of lime, and he spit it out.

Grant said: "I think so. You start according to the colors on the post. Every time you go through a wicket you get another shot. If you go through the first three—we think there's supposed to be three anyway—you get three extra shots. See what I mean?"

Kathy nodded. Mary was standing with her arms across her chest. She said: "Why don't you all play without me? I can get dinner ready."

"Naaa, come on," Grant said, moving to her. "It's too early for dinner. It's easy, you'll see."

"I was never much good at games," Mary said.

"Tough," Noel said, and laughed.

"Noel!" Kathy pointed her mallet at him.

"I mean, what the hell? Let's all just play."

"Don't play just to make me happy," Grant said. He had

moved away from Mary and was now practicing hitting the ball at the post.

"I'll start," Kathy said. "Come on, Mary. Let's play; then we can take a swim."

Noel stood. He walked to the ball carrier and took the green mallet. He set his empty beer can down on the grass, end up. He stood on the balls of his feet, then swung the mallet like a worker, up and over his head. He hit the can on the edge but still managed to crush it.

"What are you doing?" Grant asked.

"John Henry."

"Come on," Grant said.

From a few feet away Kathy asked: "Straight through?"

"But easy," Grant told her. "You want to leave yourself in position for the next wicket."

Noel watched Kathy hit the ball too hard. It went through the three wickets and carried almost to the middle of the court. She giggled. Grant was trailing her, coaching her as she went.

"That's fine," he kept saying.

"I'm going to get another beer. Anybody else?" Noel asked. He saw Kathy glance at him. Grant shook his head. Mary unfolded her arm and wiped something from her skirt. "No, thanks," she said.

Noel walked across the lawn. The grass reached up over his tennis shoes and touched his ankles. He looked up at the window to his parents' bedroom and saw Jenna's profile. He wanted to call to her but could think of nothing to say. He climbed the back stoop two steps at a time, then pulled open the screen door. He felt the kitchen heat immediately. Something bubbled on the stove. He opened the refrigerator and stood in front of it, feeling the coolness on his legs. He reached in and took out a six-pack, twisted one out of the plastic, and put the other five back. He snapped the top and tossed the ring in the sink. He took a drink and stopped in the center of the kitchen. The bubbling on the stove sounded like an aquarium. It was better inside. He took another drink, feeling a limber drunkenness. The drunkenness was controllable. He could direct it. He let it climb him, then pushed it away, wondering at the same time at the feeling of relaxation the beer had produced, his own ability to gauge his intake.

He pushed out the door and saw Kathy coming toward him. Her shorts were rolled high on her thighs. Her breasts bobbed under the halter. He was surprised to see how well she fit here with the pool behind her, the croquet match sending up color. He thought: Tennis whites would suit her, though this caused a small measure of anger to appear on the edge of his mind, forced him to consider that he might fit as well. And it seemed to him then that the house was a reward to her and a penalty for him, that she had won finally, had managed to claim the house and lawn as her province. It was as if something were being re-created from his childhood, roles passed down, so that Kathy might be his mother and he his father. Then, behind him, a clock struck two, the chimes like Sanctus bells, and he imagined his father rising, being lifted by unseen hands, Kathy the first communicant to receive of the body, the blood.

"It's your turn," she said. "You'd better hurry. He's getting annoyed."

"Where are you going?"

"Did you check the potatoes? I called to you, but you were already inside."

"I didn't hear you."

"I know. That's why I'm going to do it. It's your turn," she said again.

She passed into the house. Noel let the screen door swing shut. He saw Mary standing next to her ball by the first wicket. Grant was taking golf swings at a few dandelions. He was already through the middle wicket. Kathy's ball was by the hedges, sent.

Noel asked: "Who sent Kathy?"

"I did," Grant said.

"Fine."

Noel hit his ball through the first three wickets. He didn't glance at the wicket to his right but lagged a shot close to Grant's, instead. Grant turned to look at him, saying: "Fuck it, Noel. If you're going to play that way."

"If I hit yours with my next shot, I can send you, right? That's right, isn't it?"

"Fuck it. I don't want to play if that's how you're going to play."

"That's the game."

"You're going to follow my ball around? Wonderful."

"That's the game. If I hit you, I can send you, right?"

Grant dropped his mallet and walked toward the pool. Noel nudged his ball forward, grazing Grant's. He set his ball against Grant's, putting his foot on his own.

"Grant," he called, starting to laugh.

But Grant drifted off, his white legs flexing. Noel hit the ball anyway and watched it roll across the lawn. It ran in a green line, a mole swimming through grass.

Frankenstein thought: Run. He backed off. The woman was standing near the sprawled bird. The dog was still pulling at its leash, undecided whether to go for the bird or him. He smelled her once—a perfume smell that drifted on the wind, coated it. She did not advance. The street cleaner changed gears somewhere in the distance. A store door opened and shut.

—You explain this to me. Why do you do it? Do you see that bird? Do you?

Her voice rose to a near scream. Her hand rested on her hip, her purse looped over her wrist. He felt himself locked in her gaze and did not turn as he retreated. She took a step with each of his, danced him backward, her high heels clicking. The dog sat on the cement, then rose, a worried whine breaking from its muzzle.

—I just can't believe this goes on. I can imagine how many times you've done this. Why would you kill a pigeon? What possible enjoyment could you get from it?

But he was too far away to be expected to answer. He turned his back and started to walk. He draped the slingshot over his neck and felt the old rhythm return: feathers, rocks, slingshot, knife. Each item marked one limb, patted him, called the march. He saw a light go on in a stationery store. He smelled eggs cooking in Teddy's Luncheonette, thinking: Feathers, rocks, slingshot, knife.

—you.

He heard only this last word. Half a block away he turned back and saw the woman in front of a phone. The dog was staring at him. Around the first corner he began to run. He felt his size, felt his legs jar on the hard concrete. His boots hit the walk. He thought: The police now. He ran harder, ducked a low-hanging branch, touched the bark of a tree. Across one street he saw a boy pass, a radio tucked to his ear. The radio let out a steady beat of music, and Frankenstein felt his body respond, felt panic come. He was conscious of a blurring, had felt it before. Things struggled in and out of his sight, slapped forward and back, up and down, by the motion of his body. A bush leaned at him, fell

back. He chanted: No, no, no, no, under his breath, exhal-
ing, leaning once on an iron fence and smelling the metal,
thinking of cages and the night wail of flannel-shirted men,
the nurses, the blue blink of a subdued television sucking
the room dry. Tommy, he thought. Tommy. He pressed his
cheek against the metal, then pushed violently away, ran on
in a stiff-legged gait, frightening birds by his approach, feel-
ing the old wildness in his soul loosed, crawling inside his
skin and seeking escape.

He slowed to a trot when he reached the park, though his
mind raced on, full of memories and fear of his own be-
havior. He fell to his knees, his lungs pumping, sweat drip-
ping, combing the grass silently, smoothing it. No, no, no,
no, he chanted again, still smoothing the grass, picking
from it twigs, impurities, his mind focused on the slipper
walk through long hallways, the quiet voices, the nurse
hands reaching, guiding him through doors, past other
men, whose eyes looked out in bathrobe emptiness. He lis-
tened for the sound of the siren. He heard it break, turned
to an electric hum that now covered the morning air, and
scrambled to his feet. He lunged forward, his hands out-
stretched, trying to determine his name somewhere in the
siren yowl. He touched the slingshot around his throat,
then ran as the siren picked up tempo, turned faster on the
car coming to collect him. He skirted the border of the park
until he came to the pine grove. He bent and duck-walked
in. It was dark under the boughs. The branches went
straight up above him, and he reached for them, planting
one boot on the side of the tree, hoisting his weight up.
After he had attained the first rung, the climbing went
easier. He smelled pinesap and licked it on his hands, tast-
ing the bitter sweetness, tonguing the web of his thumb.
The siren lifted with him, caught the branches, and rinsed

the tree. He climbed on, a worried gurgle in his throat, his voice sometimes breaking silence, saying: No, no, no, no. Thirty feet above the ground he found a resting place and sat. The needles turned to spider legs in the wind, running on invisible currents. He put one arm around the trunk, then curled his body around it, hugging it, pressing himself into the resin. The squad car passed in a shark swim.

Kathy's feet padded on the tile. She felt the kitchen around her, felt the organization behind it. The arrangement of furniture still held a woman's movement. Pans were in easy reach. A pegboard glistened with kitchen gadgets: eggbeaters, graters, spoons, measuring cups, a colander. The room was functional. Meals were put together here; the day was planned. The few boards that squeaked marked a daily passage: counter to refrigerator, refrigerator to stove. She knew if she walked to the dining room, the creaking would increase. Miles could be paced back and forth, carrying food, feeding a family.

She turned on the tap and filled the kettle for iced tea. An air bubble shook the pipes, and she was forced to increase the pressure. The pipes rattled even louder. The house was old. At night she could sometimes hear it groan. It would lean into the wind, a momentary break in the rush of air to the sea. The timber would creak as if something inside the beams had never been killed.

She set the pot on high, then checked the potatoes. She poked a fork into one and felt it was still hard. She ran through the menu in her mind: barbecued steak, potato salad, tossed salad. She could feel the focus of the day narrowing, the slow movement toward the inevitable meal. Noel would drink and lose his appetite. Grant would eat enough for two. Then Mary would clean the kitchen, a robot let loose in the house. She thought: Repetition, imagining a metronome for their own activity tied to the pulse of the dying man. She hated him for this, could not free him from her judgment. Leaning against the smooth metal of the stove, she tried to see Noel out in the yard, but succeeded only in producing thoughts of him, veiled images in which his face would sometimes displace his father's so that it was Noel in the bed, his death superimposed on his father's. It was not the first time she had thought this, not the first time she suspected Noel of being linked to the man upstairs in some indecipherable way. Noel's moods reflected his father's health, responded to a change in air, breath. She thought: In the end, Noel will kill him, because she could no longer believe the man would die. His hold had been too strong—Noel and Grant admitted that. He was not the sort of man to fade into oblivion, to give up his soul without a last vengeance. It was merely a matter of time. Noel was receiving the disease of his father in daily doses, succumbing. It was an anticipated transference, and she could not liberate him. She could not even think to liberate him.

Now, in the stillness, she heard something stir above her. There was a loud thump, then silence. She went up the stairs, feeling the heat climb with her. A clock ticked on the wall, the pendulum heavy and slow. She pushed open the bedroom door and saw Jenna setting her transistor back on the night table.

"You okay?" Kathy asked.

"It's too hot. I fell asleep. Just dozed off, you know? The radio slid off my lap."

Kathy avoided looking at the bed. "Can I get you anything? Something to drink?"

"I got some water earlier. It's too hot. It's not good for him." She nodded at Noel's father.

"They don't have an air conditioner. It's normally so cool. Do you think we should go out and get one?"

"It'd be good for him. How about a fan?"

"I'll talk to Noel."

"It's up to you all."

"I'll tell him." Kathy moved to the door. "Sure I can't get you anything? I just put some water on for iced tea."

"I'll take a glass, thank you."

Kathy nodded and went out. She heard the radio switch on behind her. Jenna was humming with it, her voice low. The clock seemed to pick up her rhythm. Time passing, Kathy thought. Noel had once forced her to hold a palmful of sand, saying: Time made visible. But now, in the steaming hallway, the clock made more sense. Time, she thought, passed in seconds. It was slower than anyone imagined, more methodical. The pendulum made an almost violent sound, a scythe cutting dead air. Her fingers tracing the wallpaper, she thought of Noel looking at the sand, his imagination running to the slow erosion of rock. He saw the sea coming closer, washing over the land, rubbing it to fine particles. She saw the urgency behind the hands of a clock. That was the difference between them.

Halfway down the stairs she smelled something burning. She ran into the kitchen. She saw she had turned on the wrong coil. An empty pot smoked heavily, staining the ceiling black. She cursed and took it off. The bottom of the pot was ruined, the white Teflon coating burned and cracked. She reached across the stove and turned on the exhaust fan. There was a coughing sound, followed by an electric hum. Finally, the fan kicked into motion.

Hay fell, then sticks and twigs. Blood splattered on the ceiling. She reached to turn off the switch but could already see the edge of the nest coming through the grating. The metal blades whirled faster. She heard birds cheeping, their cries gobbled by the fan.

She reached across and slammed the switch down. The fan quieted, giving way to the sound of one bird still calling. She heard it echoing in the vent. She backed away from the stove, wiping her hands on her bare legs. She felt blood and hay mixed between her fingers.

Noel came through the door, and it was only then she realized she had screamed. She heard Jenna coming down the stairs. Noel was close to her, saying: "Shit, shit." She leaned against him, afraid to move her hands, afraid to touch her hair.

"Are you okay?" Jenna asked from the door. "You didn't hurt yourself, did you?"

Kathy shook her head. Noel was dabbing her face and hands with a wet cloth. Mary was reaching under the sink. The bird was calling from the vent, louder than any of the words.

"They must have built it this spring," Grant said. "It's a natural place for them. Protected and all. I thought I heard something the other day."

"You're okay," Noel was saying in her ear.

"Take me upstairs," Kathy said.

"We'll have to get the bird out," Grant said. "I guess we can take down the vent."

"Not now, Grant," Noel said. Kathy looked and saw Jenna still standing in the doorway, shaking her head. Grant was looking at the ceiling. Mary was cleaning.

"I want to shower," Kathy said to Noel.

"All right, I'll walk you up."

They climbed the steps slowly. Kathy no longer felt anything. She closed her eyes. In the bathroom Noel made her sit on the toilet while he undressed her. He piled the clothes in a corner. Kathy sat quietly remembering the nest coming through the grate.

"I'll get the water right," Noel said.

"I'm okay."

"You sure? I'll tell you what. I'll get rid of these clothes and come back. Okay?"

"All right."

Noel carried the clothes out. She stood and turned on the water. She wanted to be clean. She kept her back to the mirror. When the water was right, she stepped into the spray. She rubbed herself with soap. She glanced down at the drain and saw a faint pink. She scrubbed harder, then poured three capfuls of shampoo on her hair. She reached behind her and inched the water hotter.

"You okay?" Noel asked, opening the door. She looked out and saw him sit on the toilet.

"I'm all right."

"I'm sorry."

"It's not your fault."

"I know. I'm just sorry it had to happen."

She heard him lighting a cigarette. She wanted to be alone but didn't know how to tell him. The smoke mixed with the steam, making it hard to breathe. She looked out again and saw him through a cloud, his bare legs crossed, his head turned to the window.

"This sucks," he said. Then: "Doesn't it?"

"It's not your fault."

"I mean the whole thing. We're just sitting around waiting for him to die. We shouldn't have come back. We should have stayed in Africa."

"Noel, I don't really want to go into that right now."

"You're right," he said, standing. "Maybe I'll go down and help Grant."

"Go ahead."

"Why don't you take a nap afterward? I'll go down and help Grant."

"Yes," she said, releasing him, hearing in his last statement a drunken repetitiveness. The door opened, shut. She turned the water hotter and let it run over her body.

Grant was up on the ladder. He had his arm deep in the vent. He smiled at Noel and shook his head.

"I think it's a boy," he said.

Noel watched him fishing with his hand, his head turned sideways against the wall. "Is it okay?" Noel asked. Grant didn't say anything. He was concentrating, his eyes nearly closed. The bird was calling loudly. Noel wondered if Kathy could hear it upstairs.

"I feel something," Grant said. "We might have to perform a Caesarean—no, no, wait a minute. I think I've got it."

He leaned away from the house, barely able to turn his arm. "It's pecking the hell out of my hand," he said. But he was still pulling. The aluminum ladder shimmied under his weight. Finally, he winked at Noel and pulled the bird free. The bird was bigger than Noel had expected. It was black and fully shaped. It pecked at Grant's hand and flapped its wings once.

"There you go," Grant said.

"It's big."

"Looks like it should have been out on its own long ago, don't you think?" He was holding the bird for Noel to take.

"It looks like it."

"This late in the season? I mean, it's still early summer, but you'd think it would be flying by now."

"Think we should call someone?"

"Like who?" Grant laughed. "Here, take the goddamned thing. Hold it around the legs so it doesn't jump off."

Noel took it. The bird began pecking his hands. It flapped its wings weakly. Noel cradled it to his chest, thinking the warmth from his body would soothe it, but the bird started pecking his shirt. He looked up at Grant. Grant was busy putting the cover back on the vent. He was grunting softly, pressing the screwdriver against the house. Noel wanted to let the bird down. It made him nervous to hold it.

"What should we do with it?" he asked.

Grant didn't bother to look. "I'd kill it if I were you."

"Why?"

"What else are you going to do with it? You can try feeding it," Grant said, putting the last screw in. "Still, it might not make it. You'll have to fix up a box or something and dig worms. Maybe it will eat hamburger, I don't know. I'd kill it."

"Go ahead." Noel held the bird out.

Grant started down the ladder. The bird settled on Noel's hand, but its eyes still watched sharply, its head darting back and forth. Grant pulled the ladder away from the house. Mary came onto the porch and said everything was clean inside. She came down the stairs and tried to pet the bird. It bent back and nipped at her fingers.

She said: "It must be hungry."

"You think so?" Noel asked.

"Sure. I'll see if there's anything inside. You think it would eat hamburger?"

"If it won't, I will," Grant said. He picked up the ladder and began walking to the garage.

"Kathy all right?" Mary asked.

"I think so."

"Terrible thing to happen. My mother did something like it once. She closed the lid on a garbage can and didn't see a little raccoon inside it. I guess they didn't open the can for a while. Those were the days when you separated the burning trash and the regular garbage. Anyway, the thing died in there. It was trapped. My mother still doesn't like to talk about it."

Noel nodded. Mary shuffled her feet, half smiling. The bird squirmed in his hand. They could hear Grant rattling the ladder into place. The croquet match was forgotten.

"You think we should kill the bird?" Noel asked.

"No, why?"

"Because it will die anyway."

"If it dies, it dies," she said, and reached out to touch it again. "I don't see why you have to kill it."

"Neither do I."

She sighed and said: "I'm going to get dinner ready." She walked back up the steps. Noel watched her for a moment before starting toward the pool. He walked slowly. The bird fluttered on his arm, then leaned awkwardly against his T-shirt. He stared down at the feathers, watching the colors held in the blackness. He saw red, purple, green. With each shift of the bird the color changed.

At the pine hedge bordering the pool he stopped. He held the bird up and tilted it onto a branch. The bird reached out its feet, and Noel steadied it while it gained its balance. He let it go when he was sure it was all right. The bird squatted on the branch, its head tucked into its body. The feathers were ruffled; the iridescence was gone. Noel saw it stiffen, slowly becoming part of the tree.

"You think it will be all right there?" Grant said behind him. He had taken off his shirt and changed into swimming trunks. Noel looked at the band of fat around his middle, the stretch marks at his hips.

"I don't know. It's old enough, isn't it?"

"Christ, who cares? You want to swim?"

"Not right now."

Grant threw his towel onto a chaise longue and walked around the pool to the shallow end. He climbed down the ladder, easing his body in. The water refracted and bent his limbs. He swam slowly, keeping his head above the water. Noel crossed to a lawn chair and sat down. He took a cigarette out of his pocket and lit it. He glanced back but couldn't see the bird.

"By the way," Grant said when he was close enough, "you were being a jackass."

"So were you."

Grant laughed, then shrugged. He pulled himself up onto the edge and left his feet dangling. Water dripped through his chest hair. His swimming trunks pulled at his waist to show the top of his rear end.

"The water feels great," Grant said.

"Yep."

Without looking, Grant asked: "How do you think Dad looks?"

"How do you think?"

"He can't hang on much longer." Grant ran his fingers through the water. "He looked worse to me today. He's awfully pale."

Noel leaned back in his chair. He took a deep drag on his cigarette. A piece of tobacco worked free and stuck to his top lip.

"You ever think about killing him?" Grant asked. The question was matter-of-fact. Noel's chest tightened.

"Sometimes," he answered.

"I was just wondering. I guess the bird made me think of it." Grant slipped back into the water. He hung on the edge, only his head visible. He smiled, then shook his head.

"You don't have to," he said. "Nobody has to. He's not suffering."

"How do you know?"

"I don't, I guess. Not really. But I do know you'd think of that. I think he sent for you because, well—almost as insurance."

"How do you mean?"

"I don't know exactly. It isn't easy, is it? It just seemed like he felt he could count on you to do the difficult thing. He couldn't count on me. Does that make sense?"

"Sort of. Did he ever say anything to you? Before, I mean."

Grant rested his chin on his hands. "He knew what it was going to be like. It worried him, I think. He didn't want to end up like this. Hell, you know how he was. I still can't even believe it's him up there. He's too weak to be our father."

"Did he ask you? Did he ask you to do anything?"

Grant waited for a moment, then pushed off the wall. He didn't speak. "Grant?" Noel asked again. He felt the conversation closing. "Did he?" he asked, but Grant only shook his head and ducked under the water. He swam underwater, moving quietly. When he surfaced, he rubbed his face and pushed back his hair.

"Dibble?" he asked.

"No, not right now."

Grant began swimming laps. Noel threw his cigarette away and turned to look for the bird. He couldn't see it.

Pine. Frankenstein thought: Needles of pine. He ran his hand over the earth. His shirt was part of his skin. It coated his body, moved when he did in moist rhythm. His feet were hot, sore. He looked up through the branches and saw only green. The air was filtered to coolness.

He reached to his pocket for his flask. He drained the last of it, holding it to his lips in hopes of a last drop. When he was sure it was finished, he set it beside him, propped against the tree trunk. He saw a few people now walking through the park grounds. A woman passed close by but did not see him. A child came forward, rocking on hesitant legs, then teetered away, running in choppy steps. Frankenstein saw all this, though his mind sometimes pictured the woman talking into the phone, her red lady lips explaining the incident. He thought when the heat moved off, it would be all right. He could not think farther than that.

He felt sleep coming as if from a distance. It moved to him slowly, a dream of itself before causing dreams. Gnats circled his head, were blown off, returned with new vigor. He felt them brush his forehead, his eyes. He took a handful of yellow tansy from his pocket and rubbed it over his face. He touched the tansy to his nose, sniffing its rank odor, then continued rubbing the plant over his neck and ears. A voice came to him. He heard it speaking through time and remembered Borg sitting on the flat bed, his flip-flops scuffing on the waxed floors, telling of a wild dog he had found once back in an old dried sump pit. He had said the dog was dead from biting itself continually, trying to escape the insect pressure of black flies and no-seeums. Borg's voice was called back to him now. Frankenstein could see the dog, curled head to tail, the silver slaver turned yellow in *its fur. He moved toward it, reaching forward, crawling into the black pit, and was only mildly surprised when the dog jumped at him.*

It jolted him awake. His muscles loosened only by an act of will. Finally, he lay quietly, looking up. He hooked one finger under a pencil-thin root, thinking of roots separating and dividing, a river of seeking carried on in a black world.

Kathy was half asleep. She curled her legs under the sheet, tucking them close to her body. She listened to the house, surprised at her ability to unravel the noises, to picture motion from sound: Mary cooking, three steps to the refrigerator and back; Noel lingering, talking with her, his steps somehow circular; Grant yelling in from the backyard, the steaks turning brown.

She opened her eyes and watched dust whirl in the eddies of light that filtered through the room. She tapped the bed once and watched it release more dust, saw the dust hang suspended in indecision, then slowly succumb to gravity. She listened for the sound of Jenna's radio but could not find it. Instead, she heard Noel laugh in a quick burst, the sound scaling the wall and entering by the window. Grant's voice came, too, and she felt a tear form in the corner of her eye, then slide silently to the sheet. She did not know why she cried, though various explanations came and passed, leaving only despair, the pain of something unfulfilled. She twisted one end of the pillowcase, tucking it tighter and tighter until she could no longer hold it. She let it go and watched it curl back, its motion almost cartoonlike, starting and stopping at unpredictable intervals. She thought of

Africa, thought of the nest coming through the grating, saw blood speckle the ceiling, and felt her despair increase. She had the notion nothing would work, that things would continue to falter, to start well but end flawed somehow, ruined by fate, by inattention. Noel, she knew, was the cause of her despair, though he lingered inside it as well, was both affected and the father of it. She had marked his relentless swims, the laps, uncounted, going on for what seemed like hours, his drinking, his preoccupation with all aspects of his father. All these things moved in her mind, pushing her to think: I must leave him. But she could not entertain the idea completely. It was too hard, too final. Besides, she realized she wanted him, though it was no longer the Noel of her imagination, but a person as real as herself, who was broken, flawed, imperfect. And she felt for this a wave of self-pity, grieved silently over the loss of a girl's illusion, which had been transformed into a woman's acceptance.

She rolled onto her side then and heard Noel coming down the hallway. She closed her eyes. He paused in the doorway, and she imagined him standing with his hand on the pull-up bar. She wondered what he saw, what he thought when he looked at her. A moment later she felt the bed sink as he sat on it. He patted her legs.

"Kathy, dinner's ready," he said.

She pushed around onto her back. She smelled beer and cigarettes. She felt lines on her face from the wrinkled pillowcase. It was an effort to move. The heat pushed at her, draining her energy. She had to blink twice before her eyes would open fully.

Noel's voice came from far away. "You awake?"

"I didn't mean to sleep so long."

"The steaks are ready."

"What time is it?"

"Around five-thirty."

She stretched. Noel ran a hand over her waist and stomach. She pushed back into the mattress, leaving his hand momentarily suspended. He stood and yawned.

"What did you do about the bird?" she asked.

"Grant got it out. I set it in the branches down by the pool."

"Did you feed it?"

"Mary tried to, but it wouldn't eat anything. It sits there looking kind of stupid actually."

"I still can't believe it happened."

"It was an accident."

"I know," she said, and put her legs over the side of the bed. "My mother always said a bird in the house was a sign of death."

"That's a pretty safe bet around here."

"I didn't mean it that way. I don't know what I meant. I was just thinking out loud."

The heat moved. Kathy stood and pulled back her hair. She saw his eyes in the mirror over the dresser. She thought when people's eyes met in a mirror, they were supposed to fall in love or turn into killers. But Noel's eyes were blank. She pinned her hair up and said: "Is Jenna gone?"

"She left a little while ago. Willy came to pick her up. They make a nice-looking couple."

"It's hot still, isn't it?"

"Yep, still hot. I'm going to go down," he said.

She followed him out of the bedroom and went into the bathroom. From the back window she heard Grant yelling to Mary. She bent to the sink and washed her face. She cupped her hands over her eyes, letting the water form pools in her palms. She counted to ten, then patted her face dry. She felt cooler.

She walked downstairs. In the kitchen Mary was bent over the stove, her hair dripping down her back. Her shoulders were hunched. She turned and smiled.

"How'd you sleep?" she asked.

"Fine, thanks. Can I help you with anything? I'm sorry you had to do everything."

"No, I think everything's ready. I had them set the picnic table. I thought it would be cooler under the trees."

"Can I take anything out?"

"You can take the potato salad. I'm just waiting on the corn."

Kathy lifted the silver bowl. It was cold in her hands. She walked down the porch steps, slightly surprised the day had passed.

"Kathy," Grant said, "how do you feel?"

"Fine. I'm okay."

"Your husband was just telling me about the tomato war they hold between Boston and New York."

"The thing in Vermont?" she asked, putting down the salad. Noel was folding napkins and sliding them under the forks.

"He says they play army with Volkswagens for jeeps or tanks. When you get hit by a tomato, you're out. Sounds like something he'd enjoy." Grant nodded his head toward Noel. Noel pulled a squirt gun from behind his back and spritzed Grant twice.

"That damn thing," Grant said.

"What are you doing with a squirt gun?" Kathy asked.

"I used it to keep down the flames from the steaks and grease. Damn it," Grant said again as Noel shot. He turned back to Kathy. "Did you?" he asked.

"Did I what?"

"Did you ever hear of it?"

"I've heard about it. You're getting senile, Grant."

"You know," he said, "I've heard of groups of people getting together and actually playing war. They shoot stuff, I guess some sort of dye pellet, and crawl around all night. They use flares, the whole bit. It's kind of scary."

Grant stood next to the grill. Mary came out of the house. A mosquito buzzed Kathy's ear, and she slapped at it. She wanted to ask where the bird was, but there wasn't time.

"Come, my beauties," Grant said, lifting the steaks.

"Does everyone have something to drink?" Mary asked. "There's a pitcher of iced tea."

Grant brought the steaks to the table on a meat platter. Red juice ran down the grooves and collected in small hollows near the handles. The corn steamed. Kathy saw a platter of tomatoes beside the steak.

"Would anyone mind if I said grace?" Mary asked.

"First holy water," Noel said. He squirted Grant. Grant held up his plate like a shield. They both were laughing.

"Come on," Mary said.

Noel put the squirt gun down. He made a quick move for it, and Grant grabbed his plate again. They were laughing louder. Mary crossed herself, shaking her head at the same time.

She said: "Bless us, O Lord, for these Thy gifts, which we are about to receive, from Thy bounty, through Christ, the Lord, Amen."

And then there was the quick cross again, the trinity of mystery. Mary sat next to Grant and smiled at them all.

"Muss mu me steakum," Noel said.

"What did you say?" Grant laughed.

"Steakum steadieus."

Kathy looked and shook her head. "He's speaking in tongues," she said. "After anyone prays, he speaks in tongues."

Noel took a swallow of beer. He started to laugh, and Grant joined him. They both looked guilty. Kathy noticed they avoided looking at Mary.

"I'm sorry," Noel said after a bit.

Mary nodded and finally smiled. The food was passed. Kathy took an ear of corn and buttered it. She wanted only vegetables, but Grant was handing out slices of steak, the meat too red. She held out her plate and took a piece, knowing she wouldn't eat it.

"Are you going to tell us your secret?" Noel asked.

Kathy watched Grant bend close to Mary and whisper something. Mary nodded. She rested a hand on Grant's shoulder and said aloud: "You tell them."

She patted her mouth with her napkin while Grant pushed back in his seat. Kathy poured herself a glass of iced tea and covered the glass with her napkin.

Finally, Grant said: "It's a long story."

"Do you want us to beg? Come on," Noel said.

"Well, I won't bore you with all the details." Grant shifted in his seat. Kathy noticed he wasn't eating.

"Tell them everything," Mary said.

"Okay, okay. You both know," he began again, "how we tried to adopt a child, right? Well, I know someone from the office who adopted a South American baby. The baby is Colombian, from Bogotá, I think. Anyway, there's a group of people that formed . . . a society I guess you'd call it, and they help American couples adopt children. So we got a call yesterday from this man, and he said there was a baby available right now. We're going to go down Monday morning."

Grant pushed back even farther in his chair, grinning and rocking. Mary kissed him on the cheek. She saw Noel jump up and kiss Mary. Kathy saw Noel look happy for the first time in weeks.

"That's terrific," Noel said.

Kathy ran around the table and kissed them both. Grant was saying: "I plan to turn him into a jockey. No Little League baseball for him. I'm going to buy him a pony for his fifth birthday."

"Will it be a boy then?" Noel asked.

"That's what they said." Mary laughed. "It's not certain. I mean, anything can still happen. We're trying not to get too excited."

"Any cigars?" Noel asked.

"Not yet. When we get the baby, I'll give you a big one. Like Mary said, things could go wrong. There was a couple that went down and came back empty-handed. There were problems about papers—something like that. But it's hard not to get excited."

Kathy moved back around the table and sat down. Grant was pulling closer to his plate, picking up his knife and fork.

Kathy asked: "Any names in mind?"

"Maybe Paul," Mary said. "We wanted to ask you, you know, what you thought about naming him after your father."

Kathy glanced at Noel. She saw him pause for a moment, his eyes flicking up to the bedroom window. "I think that's great," he said.

But Kathy saw him still glancing at the bedroom window. She wanted to say something to him. She felt him drifting off, his happiness fading. Come back, she started to say. Be here.

Noel watched Grant's car pull into the darkness. The engine stalled at the corner, then started again with a short burst and a rush of gas. Noel took a cigarette out of his pocket and lit it.

"We need milk," Kathy said.

Noel didn't turn to look at her. He sat across the picnic table, smoking. He felt the insects swarming, moving around him in tiny clusters. He wondered why the smoke didn't stop them. He thought of punks made of brown fur on black wires. He had bought them at a corner store until his father showed him how to dry out cattails and light them. The odor was like incense inside a church. Deep and heavy, it turned mosquitoes away.

"What did you think of their plan?" he asked.

"Whose? Grant and Mary's? I think it's fine. Why? Don't you?"

"I don't know. I was just thinking how the Africans would never think of giving a child up."

He watched Kathy wipe some crumbs off the table. She pulled her hair back over her ears and said: "We need milk."

"I won't drink coffee tomorrow."

"I will. Don't be so lazy. I'd like to take a ride anyway."

"Then you can get the milk, right?" he said.

"Fine."

"I'm only kidding. I'll go with you. I've got the keys right here."

"Do you want to check on your father?" she asked.

"No, let's just go. You want to come right back, don't you?"

"Maybe I'll drop you off. I'll see. I should see Joan one of these nights."

She stood, rubbing the backs of her thighs. Noel flicked his cigarette away and watched it glow in the grass. He could see the tree where the bird waited, hungry, alone for the first time. He had gone with Kathy and tried to feed it meat, lettuce, seeds. The bird had turned its head away. Kathy had tried to force-feed it, but the bird moved from branch to branch. It was that much alive, a good sign he thought. Kathy said it would be hanging upside down by the end of the night, a wild canary upturned in a cage of pine.

"A&P or Quick-Mart?" he asked.

"Quick-Mart."

He smiled, but she didn't see. She was busy climbing into her side of the car. Noel walked around to the driver's seat, checking the rust. The car was being eaten. New England salt, the inspection man had said as he poked a finger through the holes. Next time, Noel knew, it would cost a couple of hundred just to get it in shape.

Kathy rolled down her window and rubbed her forehead. She crumpled up two empty packs of cigarettes that were on the dashboard and set them in the corner. She folded her hands in her lap and said: "Are you okay to drive?"

"Sure," he said, though he felt drunk. He started the engine. It died before he could give it enough gas. He shifted it to neutral and let it coast down the hill. Near the street he turned the key again. The engine knocked but started. He pushed in the cigarette lighter, forgetting it didn't work. He patted his pockets as he turned onto the road leading to town.

He asked: "Are there matches over there?"

"I don't see any."

"Did you look?"

"Yes."

She was leaning close to the window, her hair blowing loose behind her. He found a match in his thigh pocket and had to lift himself to dig it out. His foot left the gas pedal for a moment, and the car lurched slightly, the momentum broken. Kathy reached out a hand to steady herself. Noel let the wheel go to light the cigarette.

"Are you all right?" she asked.

He ignored her and said: "Do you realize nobody I know has a nice car? My father let this thing run down."

"What brought that up?"

"I don't know. I was just thinking. But it's true, wouldn't you say?"

She shrugged. Noel flicked ashes out the window. Sprinklers threw fans of water onto summer lawns in the twilight. A group of boys were sitting on the front steps of one house, their faces sweaty, balls and bats scattered on the grass around them. Noel followed the road without thinking, allowing his senses to work. His headlights caught the eyes of a cat and held them for a count before the cat moved, or blinked, and disappeared.

He pulled the car into the Quick-Mart parking lot. Kathy pushed open her door as soon as the car had stopped. Noel watched her walk. Her wooden sandals were loud on the cement. He got out and leaned against the fender. Cars pulled in and out. A Chevy, jacked up in back, idled thickly at the rear of the lot. Two girls bent close to the window, talking to the driver. Their shorts showed two handfuls of flesh on their thighs, rounded, curving into cut-offs. One girl reached behind her and pulled a comb out of her back pocket. She leaned her head to one side and ran the comb through her hair quickly, shaking it back and to the side. Then she slid the comb back in her pocket and continued talking. The driver revved his engine.

"Noel?" Kathy stood on the step up to the door. "I need money."

"I don't have any. I thought you brought some."

"Oh, Christ," she said. She let the door swing shut and started across the parking lot. Noel dropped his cigarette and stepped on it.

"Wait a second," he said.

"Let's just go."

"I'll get the milk."

"You don't have any money."

"I'll pay him tomorrow. They'll let me take a quart on credit."

"Don't be ridiculous."

"Wait and see," he said, starting for the store. He heard her open the car door. There were moths around the store light. A woman came out, leaning on a cane. He let her pass, then stepped inside. A young girl was behind the counter reading a magazine. She didn't look up.

"Excuse me," he said. "My wife was just in here. We forgot our money at home. Could I just take a quart of milk and pay you tomorrow?"

"I'm sorry," the girl said, standing next to the cash register. "The manager doesn't let anyone have anything on credit."

"I'll pay tomorrow. It wouldn't be credit. Come on." He smiled, testing his charm. The girl smiled back but shook her head.

"I'll tell you what then," he said. "I'll steal it. You can pretend you didn't see me; then tomorrow I'll come in and make a confession. Okay?"

She laughed this time. She started to shake her head again, but he was already moving. He walked to the dairy section and took a quart of milk. It was cold, sweating.

"Sir . . ." the girl said.

Noel kept walking. He bent over the carton, pretending to hide it. "Sir?" she said again. He put his fingers to his lips and said: "Tomorrow, I promise."

He pushed through the door. He held the quart over his head. He checked behind him. The girl had come around the counter, but she wasn't moving to catch him. Noel waved and put a hand over his heart. The girl shook her head and smiled.

"See?" he said, climbing into the car. "That wasn't so bad."

"She let you have it?"

"I stole it."

"You did not."

"Yes, I did. Don't worry. I charmed her."

Noel started the car, feeling better, stronger. He had charmed her, and he felt an odd sense of accomplishment. It was as if an old part of himself had been brought forward, observed, and set back into the past. He revved the engine and backed up close to the Chevy. He shifted and the car turned a small patch. He glanced in the rear-view mirror and saw the two girls watching him pull into traffic.

"Do you want to take a quick ride?" he asked.

"I don't want to hurry. Would you mind if I took one alone? I'll probably go see Joan. I'll stop and get some money for the milk."

"No, I don't mind."

"You sure?"

"Positive."

It was still hot. Noel wanted another cigarette but decided to wait. He turned on the radio. The Red Sox were playing at Fenway. He listened to the crowd noises in the background. Faintly he heard the hawkers, one calling for beer, another for hot dogs. He didn't recognize the names of the players. It seemed strange not to know, and he listened attentively, trying to remember the names.

Then: "Noel?" Kathy said, pointing. The boys they had passed on the way to the store were fighting. Two of them had ganged up on a third. They had him on the ground, kicking him. There was a red smear on his cheek.

Kathy said: "Slow down. Make them stop."

Noel saw the kicks were fake. He wanted to say: Suburban boys don't kick. He saw them start to laugh as he slowed the car.

"They're just fooling around," Noel said.

"Are you sure?"

"We used to do that all the time. They're just bored."

"Stop and see a minute."

He pulled the car over. The boys ran. They were laughing so hard it was difficult for them to run. The boy who had been on the ground fell on the small incline to their house. They ran around the corner and disappeared. Someone in the house next door turned on a porch lamp, then turned it off.

"I've never seen that before," Kathy said. Her voice sounded hollow, as though the sight had drained her. Noel lit a cigarette. He drove without speaking back to the house.

In final heat Frankenstein sat up, feeling the long notches the needles had made in his back. He felt it approaching hunting time, his senses already opening to the night chill, the blank sun sinking to the west. It was the best time to hunt, and he listened to birds calling up in the tree, his motion detected and communicated in wary cheeps.

He stood. His limbs were shaky. He felt a liquid need, a desire for drink. His hands trembled slightly. He leaned against the pine tree and pressed his forehead against the bark. He pissed onto the roots, passing scat, marking the tree as his territory, throwing his scent to wind. He finished and pressed back through the long branches, gaining his height as he stood in the park clearing. There were lilac smells and pine smells and a sea smell. He patted his pockets to make sure of his equipment, widening his nostrils at the same time, taking deep breaths. He was hungry. He stood for a moment watching bats start, glutting on insects, as the night chill ran along the top of the grass, took his ankles above his boots, pressing and saying: Twilight.

He crossed the park and started back toward town. He did his best to skirt the busiest sections. He walked quickly, mistrusting the cement. The light diminished, sliding off buildings, drawn back to the sun. He bent to tie his boot when a car passed and managed to keep his head hidden while the slingshot bobbed out of his shirt. He thought: Feathers, rocks, slingshot, knife. He straightened and continued on, touching the sides of buildings, bushes, fences, his hand an extension of sight. He stopped in front of one building and watched a man cross a room, his hand holding a pipe, the smoke rich and blue in the first inside light. There were other people in the room, a woman perhaps, he couldn't tell, but they were out of sight, simply varied presences that played on the man. Frankenstein watched for two or three minutes before moving on. He turned back once to see a shade drop, dividing night from warmth.

He hurried on when the church bell sounded. He tried to count the tolls but lost it in the suck of his own breath, the rhythm of his walking. He caught his reflection in a few windows, his shape broken by diamond-shaped grilles pulled over for protection, yet did not stop to examine it.

By some trick of light his reflection was sometimes cast forward so he had the sense of meeting it, becoming it, while it leaped forward to another window. He paused beside a barber pole, his fingers tracing the red lines. He watched the stores turning out their lights. When he saw the light to the hardware store extinguished, he jogged across the street, feeling the thrill of complete exposure, the challenge of possible capture. He went around the side of the store, down an alley and past half-loaded garbage cans, finally coming out in a small brick courtyard. He saw Farley's truck still in its parking slot. Near it there was a small shed covered with mangled hides: squirrels, groundhogs, beaver, dog, cat—all pinned to dry on the wall, the skins splayed like four-legged swastikas. He moved beside the truck and waited. He was watching the back door to the shop when Farley came out, turning off lights and locking the windows. Farley shook his head when he saw him and said:

—I was wondering when you'd get here. Sergeant Peters was here already. You killed a fucking pigeon in front of a woman on the damn Historic Preservation Commission. He told me not to buy anything from you.

Then Farley smiled, his lips pulling back to show a missing tooth in front. He pushed back a red hunter's hat and scratched his chest. He dipped a finger into his lower gum and pulled out a wad of tobacco, then flicked it sideways. He rubbed his finger against the brick wall.

Said: —You're something, Tommy. Fucking crazy, ain't you?

He held out his hand. Frankenstein handed him the plastic bag. Farley frowned and made a sound somewhere in his throat. He ran his fingers over the white feathers, a few pieces of squirrel skin.

—You want fifty cents for this crap? Shit. I can't make no

flies out of this here. You got to do better than this, Tommy. Too much time hiding out, huh? You're a regular bandit in these parts.

But he held out a dollar. Frankenstein took it, retreated to the side of the truck. He didn't speak. Farley finished locking up. When he turned back, he smiled, the gap in his teeth appearing first between his lips.

—I know you must have hid out all day, so it's all right this time. I'll give you the extra fifty on credit. Ain't no cop going to tell me what to buy.

Then he lost his thought and headed for the truck. He climbed in, and Frankenstein stood aside.

—You bring things by this time of night, hear? I'll buy them, don't worry.

The engine kicked. Farley backed out, slamming the gears. Frankenstein looked over the skins, trying to remember which ones he had killed. The last rays of the sun were inching down the wall, setting the skins to bake. But then the skins in the shade seemed to be crawling up to the sun. Frankenstein pocketed the dollar and left.

Kathy stood in line, letting the air conditioner cool her. The girl at the counter looked up once but didn't seem to recognize her. Kathy concentrated on seeing the store, looking at the items surrounding the cash register. There were magazines, razor blades, packs of chewing gum, a special on cap pistols. She reached out and spun a display of Gothic novels, reading the covers on some, trying to imagine from the pictures what the stories would be about. Every book showed a woman in décolletage set against the background of a swarthy man. The woman was invariably on the edge of some emotion: joy, hate, love, orgasm. Valium volumes, Noel called them.

A boy wearing an open shirt lined up behind her, and she thought about pretending she had forgotten something. He was holding a case of beer under his arm. He smelled of sweat and suntan lotion.

She turned and said: "That looks heavy. You can go in front of me if you like."

"I'm okay." He smiled.

"Really, I don't mind."

"If you're sure," he said, and moved up. Kathy glanced down and saw his bare feet. His hair was long and dirty. She tried to recall what his face looked like but couldn't. He was humming something under his breath, shifting from one foot to the other. The beer had made a wet stain on the side of his shirt.

"Next," the girl at the counter said.

He slid the beer around to show her the price, then reached behind him for his wallet.

"Do you have any proof?" the girl asked.

He sighed. He flicked open his wallet and set it on the counter. The girl bent over it, squinting to see the writing. "That's a New Jersey license," he said. "The whole thing is coded."

"What do you mean?"

"The back, it's coded. See, someone with brown hair is a three. If you weigh between one hundred and fifty and one hundred and seventy-five, you're a six. Something like that."

"Where's the birth date?"

"Right here." He pointed. The girl nodded and rang up the price. She made change of a ten. He jammed the bills and coins into his pocket and turned to Kathy.

"Thanks," he said.

"No problem."

The girl said: "Next."

Kathy stepped up. She said: "My husband was in for a quart of milk a little while ago, and we didn't have our money with us."

"The guy who stole it?" The girl laughed. "I didn't think he'd be back."

"Why didn't you stop him then?"

"I don't care. It's not my store. Was it skim or regular?"

"Skim."

"Sixty-two cents."

Kathy handed her a dollar. The girl dug into the drawer, saying: "Actually we lose about a hundred dollars a week in shoplifting. The manager figures it into his budget. People come in all the time and open a box of cookies, eat a couple, then leave the package there. I guess they don't think that's stealing."

"I guess not."

"Well, I'm glad you came back anyway."

She handed Kathy the change, then sat back on her stool and opened another magazine. Kathy turned and left. After the air conditioning, the night felt even hotter. She walked to the car, lifting her hair off her neck. The boy with the beer was sitting on the trunk of his car, talking to a young girl. He waved, and Kathy waved back. Kathy saw the girl edge closer, staking out her turf.

"Want one?" the boy called, holding up a beer.

"No, thanks."

She climbed into her car. She turned on the radio and heard the D.J. break for news. The announcer came on and said the heat wave over the Southwest was still on. Cows and poultry were dropping. Water was short. The pools were open to midnight, and emergency centers were set up in high schools. Kathy wondered briefly who set up the centers, what kind of person would take it upon himself to stand waiting for catastrophe. She had a second image of old people lined up in an Olympic-sized pool, their arms crossed, their skin puckering with age and water, while doctors hovered close by with stethoscopes and blood pressure gauges.

She shook the image away and drove. The news fed back into a golden oldie. The Beatles were harmonizing, the song sounding hopelessly sentimental. She sang a little, then turned it off. She heard nothing but the chug of the engine and flicked the station back on. She sang again, forgetting some of the words and compensating by doubling her volume on the refrain, feeling her mind float free, backing toward years in high school and long nights in cars. Various remembrances came: prom night; a trip, as seniors, to toilet-paper the football players' homes; beer; a girl friend throwing up. The images came without reason, moving to the rhythm of the Beatles song. She felt nostalgic, felt mourning begin for her own youth, the potential that had been hers. She tried to remember what her dreams had been, but they were vaporous, too far removed. She thought: Husband. Thought: I am married, feeling vaguely that some dream had been betrayed, condensed, perhaps too heavy for her years.

At an intersection she pulled to the right to allow traffic to move past her. She adjusted the driver's shade to cut off the glare. When the light turned green, she drove off slowly, feeling lost momentarily, unsure of her surroundings. More cars passed her, cruising, searching for a place to stop. She felt out of place, felt old in an area designed for the young. Blinking neon formed a tunnel stretching into the sky, fading finally in lighted wisps. A large sign showing a lumberjack putting a golf ball with his ax marked a miniature golf course. She saw families walking along tiny

paths of green, mothers and fathers and children. She heard
a whistle go off, on top of it a machine-gun sound from an
arcade.

She saw a blinking sign ahead: HAMBURGER JUNCTION.
She recognized the name, remembering Noel had mentioned it. She turned off the road and parked near the entrance. The sign was buzzing. It was held up by thin wires
which ran back along the roof. She heard a low mechanical
moan and looked around. The parking lot was nearly
empty. A piece of tissue flapped from a bush near the back
of the building. A man in a white kitchen apron was smoking on the back step. He was waving his apron softly, leaning against the back wall.

Kathy climbed out. She was not sure what she was doing,
did not know exactly why she had stopped. She closed the
door and heard the buzz from the ignition. She opened the
door again and pulled out the keys. As she straightened, a
letter on the sign blinked once, hissed for a moment, then
snapped back on. She heard the moan again, a sound string
moving in a thin line. She walked to the door of the restaurant, conscious of her wooden clogs scraping on the pavement. Just before she entered, she saw the man leaning
against the wall throw his cigarette away and step back into
the kitchen.

The moaning was louder. It met her at the door, pushing
the night out behind her. She stood in the doorway for a
second, amazed at what she saw. A miniature world spread
over the counter top, perfect in detail, everything to scale.
Someone had created a tiny world across the entire dining
area, complete with mountains and waterfalls.

She moved to a stool in the center, letting her eyes run.
She saw a farm in the farthest corner. It was suspended in
time, a hay bale lifted halfway to an open loft window. A
woman in a white apron was hanging out wash. A boy sat

under an elm, holding a fishing pole over a blue pond. Lily pads grew across the water, a minuscule frog crouching on one. Looming over everything was a papier-mâché mountain. Its sides were covered with pine twigs, stopping only at an imaginary timber line. There was a mountain-climbing team a third of the way up, their size gauged for perspective.

To her right, a struggling city was being built. Six or seven stores faced each other across a dirt main street. In the middle of the town a large bank was being constructed. She saw the wooden frame springing up, men walking along the beams with hammers dangling from carpenter's aprons. A woman with a parasol sat in a horse-drawn carriage, her eyes lifted to watch the men. A dog barked at the horse; a cat lay on a porch railing. One detail blended into the next, guiding her eyes over the contours of an early American city.

The moan marked the approach of the train. Kathy looked up and saw it coming out of the kitchen, a thin wedge of smoke trailing over the flatbed cars. The Lionel engine pulled easily up the side of the mountain, then stopped in front of her. Someone in the kitchen tapped the whistle twice, and Kathy saw an order form tucked into the caboose. She pulled it out and read the menu: TRANS-SIBERIAN SHAKE, READING ROCKET ICE CREAM, B&O BURGERS. She circled a CHATTANOOGA COLA and put the order form back in the caboose.

The train pulled away, weaving slowly toward the kitchen. Kathy watched it go. Then, without stopping, it reappeared at the other side of the kitchen, a tall glass of soda balanced on one of the flat-bed cars. The whistle blew when it reached her. She took the soda off and put a straw in it.

The man she had seen behind the building stepped out

of the kitchen and sat on a stool close to the swinging doors.
He was smoking again. He smiled, and for the first time
Kathy noticed she was the only customer.

"It's wonderful," she said.

The man nodded. He had taken off his white paper hat,
and she could see his hair was combed straight back. He
took deep drags from the cigarette.

Kathy asked: "Is it your place?"

"My brother's and mine," he answered with a Greek accent.

"The kids must love it." She took a sip of Coke. The man
smiled, then shook his head.

"Some do, some don't, you know? Too many star movies.
Kids like to see rockets."

"Still, it's unique."

"I call it silly. My brother, he loves the train. He's always
changing the scenery. Sometimes it's a circus; sometimes it's
Russian. He did a Wild West scene once. He read somewhere that cowboys used to shoot buffaloes out of train windows. A woman got mad. Said all the fake blood made her
lose her appetite."

He laughed at this. He stubbed out his cigarette and lit
another. "At least we don't have to pay no waitress, huh?"
he said.

"I'm surprised the kids don't love it."

"Like I say, some do. They see everything on TV, and
they think it should be like that. The little ones still got
their imagination, they like it. It all depends."

The door opened behind her. Three boys came in. They
moved quickly to stools by the farm, pushing each other as
they sat. Kathy heard the train start, but she was no longer
paying attention. She let her mind move into the scenery.
With little effort, she became the woman in the carriage.
She could feel the jog of the horse, the sway of the carriage.

Above her, she heard the crack of hammers on wood, the beating that grew louder as the nail sank deeper. Gradually she added to the scene, imagining a pig snuffling in the gutter, a man standing on the raised wooden sidewalk sweeping out his store.

Then: "Cut it out," she heard one of the boys say.

She looked up, thinking for an instant they were talking to her. Instead, she saw one of the boys with a straw to his mouth, shooting wet balls of paper at the figures. He was aiming at the hay bale. She saw gray wads sticking to the side of the barn.

One of the older boys said: "Jesus, stop it, would you?"

The train was coming. Kathy watched it glide past the boys and come slowly toward her. It wheezed to a stop nearby, the smoke going straight up, the electrical runners smelling warm. There was a note tucked into the engineer's compartment. She took it out and uncurled it. It was written in block letters on an order form. It asked: "WILL YOU BE MY DATE?"

Kathy read it again. She kept her eyes lowered, afraid to glance at the kitchen. The words rearranged themselves: Date, will you be my? My date, will you be? She couldn't completely understand. She felt angry, confused.

She folded the note and put it in her pocket. She slipped a dollar under the place mat and stood. The train remained stationary, waiting for an answer.

Date, she thought, will you be my?

Frankenstein walked into his camp in near darkness. An owl passed overhead, tucked its wings, and left in the rise and fall of gravity. Something ran quickly into the sur-

rounding debris, its path marked by the clink of cans in the dump. In the distance he saw the cemetery, the hills covered by rounded headstones, thought: Arrows to heaven, though the stones were blunted. A mist covered the cemetery. He spoke to the nearest headstone, the name recalled from a summer of companionship, saying aloud: "Gregory." His voice surprised him. He did not expect an answer but continued speaking anyway, listening to the sound go off, recoil in silence. Said again: "Gregory," at the same time setting out his bags: two of white feathers taken from a gull lured by a ham sandwich. He had plucked it sharp, without water, leaving behind the pimpled corpse, the skin puckered and marred by blood.

When he was finished, he made a brief inspection of his camp. There was an old bench, a table, and a small sitting space beneath a sheet of tin stretched between two trees. In one corner of the clearing he examined a glass telephone booth, checking the blankets inside to make sure no one had tampered with them. Afterward he moved to the border of the clearing and inspected the tin cans he had set up. Each can was tied to the next by thread, forming a circle of defense. None had been tripped.

Satisfied no one had come, he walked back and sat on the bench. He put his feet up on the telephone booth and watched the insects sink. They came down like air, falling as the heat released them. Their buzz decreased, giving over to the rattle of rats scraping in the distance, the tentative search of a nightly raccoon.

In time he heard the squad car coming, heard it prowling in the near distance, stopping and going, the engine an animal sound. He felt the dump come alive around him, unseen animals waiting as their bodies translated the sounds, their instincts filtering the present moment through a thousand ancestors. He thought: No, no, no, no, said: "Gregory." Then there was a squawk from a patrol car, a red light flashing, its beam broken and diffused by shards of glass, can tops, waste. Frankenstein stood and moved off, crouching behind a tree while a flashlight played over the dump, fingering items in a slow sweep, catching insects whirling. He knew they would not come. They would not chance the dump, the cemetery, this close to night.

—Tommy?

The voice came. It was the old name, a child's name, before children gave him the name of Frankenstein. He bent back, avoiding the light once more.

—Tommy, come out.

He heard someone curse. The dump suddenly quieted. He could hear only the static of the microphone, a breath passing unaware into the darkness.

—Tommy, if you can hear me, come in tomorrow for a talk. Nobody's mad at you. Come in, that's all.

A door slammed. The car rumbled, the engine powerful, Frankenstein thinking: The grind of taxes. He stepped forward as the light disappeared, retracting in silent ripples over the dump. He stepped into the phone booth and slid down. He wrapped one blanket over him and stared up at the sky. Stars were coming out. His breath clouded the glass. He kept the glass shut anyway, not wanting the insects inside. He watched the night deepen and felt himself sinking and slowly spinning with the earth.

Noel pushed the pine needles apart, looking for the bird. It was gone. He stepped back to see if he had the right hedge, the right group of branches. He looked down near the roots and squatted, trying to see through shadows. He stood and rustled the branches, thinking a sudden motion might make it cry out. The odor of pine stirred up to him, but the bird was silent.

He turned away, glancing at the pool to make sure everything was secured for the night. He saw the pool alarm drifting near the metal ladder. The cushions were locked in the small cabana directly behind the shallow end. He felt the night closing in.

For a moment he debated whether to put the croquet set away. Grant would want to play again. Given the chance, Grant would think up fifteen variations on the game: croquet on bikes, boccie ball, horseshoes by throwing the wickets at the posts. Let Grant pick it up, he thought, even as he moved to do it. He took a mallet and pulled up each wicket, yanking it sharply and catching it in the air. He thought of Grant picking up clothes around his room with his toes. See, he would say, balancing on one foot and lifting a dirty sock to his drawer. He had moved like a stork or an arcade crane, wobbling until the sock was over the drawer, then dropping it.

Noel placed the wickets over his arm. At the first post he had to bend over and pull hard. He felt his testicles flatten, his back strain. The post came up, leaving a dark, narrow hole in the grass. He looked up and saw his father's window, believing for a second he could hear the lungs working. He heard the heart beating, echoing softly over the yard until it obscured everything else. Without thinking he plucked a blade of grass and held it between his thumbs. He blew against it, the grass acting as a reed, vibrating into a hollow sound which covered the beat of the heart. He blew again. The sound was picked up by the rustle of the pines.

He finished picking up the wickets, stopping near the last

post to watch a cricket rub its back legs. Its sound came: Is it? Is it? He pulled the last post and carried the set to the garage. He rolled open the door, listening to the springs shake. He had to turn sideways to edge past the debris. Along the wall, hanging on nails, were rakes, shovels, hoses, hedge clippers, a hoe. He leaned away from the tools until he could tuck the croquet set under a small workbench his father had built at the back of the garage. A ball rattled off and bounced on the floor, finally finding a path through the boxes to the other side.

He worked his way out, feeling sweat sticking his shirt to him. His blue jeans grabbed at his knees. Outside, he closed the door and lit a cigarette. The moon had come up. It was round, full, and he thought: The moon is a hole to heaven.

He took long drags, trying to taste this cigarette. He blew smoke out his nostrils, feeling the slight pain and enjoying it. He wanted a beer. He wanted the day to end so the next day would come more quickly and also end. The cricket said again: Is it? Is it? It was joined by others, the sound swelling and receding on the breeze. He took another drag and threw the cigarette away. A gust of wind took it and made it skid along the driveway. It glowed brighter, rolling toward the street. He watched until it finally veered to the side and stopped; then he started back toward the house. He caught different scents as he walked: roses, clover, grass. Insects moved around him, finding his skin. A firefly burned near the pine hedge, its light fading in a yellow arc. He stopped to watch it, remembering other summer nights, the insect chigger of early evening when he and Grant had moved through the darkest parts of the yard armed with baseball bats. Crouching, they had waited for a firefly to light, then swung, hitting the light up and sideways, the phosphorus flecking the ash of the bat. Between the stiff grass blades, they had bent to find the fly, its glow now permanent. And Grant, in acts of cruelty uncharacteristic of him, had taken the phosphorus and wiped it on his face—over his brows, under his mouth, along his cheeks. Noel remembered this, recalled Grant wandering in the darkness, an outline of his face glowing, the sweat and sheen catching the light of the house, whispering: Here's one. There, over there. Noel had bathed his own face in the phosphorus and followed Grant on these small pillages, the destruction in opposition to their father's lessons.

These thoughts held him. He did not move for what seemed a long time. He watched the moonlight spread across the lawn. A dog, deep in the yard, ran unseen with its collar jangling, called by scents left and recorded on grass and bark. Noel whistled softly and heard, almost in answer, a night bird echo.

He continued across the yard and went inside. He turned on the outside light and went to the refrigerator. He took out a beer. A pain was running along his hairline, gradually working into his skull. He opened the beer and took a long swallow, throwing the ring on the counter. He took another swallow, swishing the beer in his mouth. He sat at the kitchen table next to the open back door, watching moths land on the screen and spread their wings. He wanted to touch one, to feel it beat against his closed fist, frantic, trapped. He imagined the chalky smoothness of the wings, the powdered resin that would shake free onto his skin.

He took another drink. Above him he felt the pull of the sickroom, could smell, even here, the musk of medicine and illness. It reached from the stairs, like a tongue of ether, stretching, almost in invitation. He was afraid of it, had felt it before. His fear fed his imagination, allowed him to envision a dappled white cloud, low-hanging, forming a smothering carpet above the stairs. The image closed in on him, taking his breath away. He felt strangely drawn to some mystery of death, thinking: He is still powerful. Oddly he thought of prayer, mumbled words long forgotten, sensing in this awkward turn to piety an acknowledgment of evil. He wondered if death wasn't always evil because it was not the first time he had been aware of the weight of his father, the pull he exerted on them all. He knew, too, that Grant had felt it, had seen the chipped features, the teeth and jaws protruding, the bladelike cheekbones, and had been forced to a reckoning of his own. That was the reason for the conversation by the pool. Grant had seen the hyena laugh of his father, framed for eternity, perhaps spreading malevolently inside them all. Now he thought: It should be stopped, thinking: I was called, summoned for this.

He drew a steady breath, smelling the air as it was expelled to discover his own drunkenness. He stood and carried his beer to his father's study. The room was dark. He switched on the outside lights and sat in his father's chair. He swiveled so he could watch the pool, the blue water flat and cool. He saw the gun propped in the corner and picked it up. He checked the pellet compartment to make sure it was loaded. He dumped the pellets into his hand, then pulled the trigger. A small whooshing sound came out of the barrel, followed by the snap of the trigger back into position.

He stood and opened the French doors. He put the pellets back in the gun and aimed it at the pool. He squeezed a shot and saw the water skip white. The pellet barely made a splash, but he liked the gentle kick the gun gave off. He thought about floating a beer can in the water for target practice, then decided against it. He put the gun back, stood, and closed the doors.

A car passed, and Noel listened, wondering if it was Kathy. He heard it move on. Someone shouted from the car, and a beer can rattled on the pavement. The engine gunned, thick and metallic, then screeched to a stop farther off. Noel could just make out the heavy idle stringing through hot air. He rocked back in the swivel chair, feeling restless, drunk. In the upper right-hand corner of the window he could see a quarter of the moon perfectly cut off in a triangle. He bent forward. A thin cloud rowed smoothly across the orange surface. As he looked, the moon seemed to move forward and back, shrinking for a moment before growing larger. It was a harvest moon except for the heat surrounding it and the steady strum of insects.

He rocked out of his chair and crossed the study, closing the door carefully behind him. He climbed the stairs, a sensation of compliance climbing with him, the beer can at his side. He glanced at the family pictures running diagonally up the wall. The pictures were arranged chronologically, though they came to him in no particular order. He saw a picture of Grant's graduation from high school, only then remembering an earlier picture, already passed, of his parents' wedding. He saw himself peering out from under a Little League cap and for a moment stood transfixed, feeling, through the years, the woolen rub of the stockings, the spring smell of red lettering at the front of the shirt. He stared at his own face, unable to recognize it, found only vague hints of what he imagined his face to look like now. He leaned forward, almost touching the photograph with his forehead, and said: Noel. He saw his own reflection, dimmed by moonlight, superimposed on the body of the boy, and waited, trying to match his present smile with the boy's, feeling in the small muscles of his mouth years unknown to this smaller image, disappointment unfathomed.

He climbed again, stopping suddenly as a car pulled into the driveway. He crouched, not knowing why, while the lights moved through the house, picking out items, lamps, chairs, patterns, flecking them all with intrusion, interruption. But the car merely turned, its lights flowing up the wall just beneath the pictures, illuminating finally the door at the top, causing Noel to think: Yes, this photo. It did seem to him a photo, the doorframe wide and trimmed with white, the man inside it no less held by time. He walked to it as the car pulled away, the last trace of its coming a horn punched in the distance.

He pushed open the bedroom door and heard the hum of the fan Jenna had helped him dig out of the attic. He remembered her bending close to him, her smell rich in the languid air, pulling with him at the old fan. There, among crates, trunks, clothes bags, she had struggled beside him, short grunts working from her throat, her blouse knotted above her waist, a line of sweat running to the button of her khaki slacks. They had set it up close to the bed, aimed directly at Noel's father. "There we go. There we go," Jenna had said. And now Noel stood in the doorway watching the white sheets flap weakly, the curtains pressed back against the wall. He wondered if the fan could steal air from his father's lungs, push it past the open mouth too quickly for his father to draw it in. But he saw the chest rise, still panting, the flesh bellows working.

He stepped into the room and sat on the straight-backed chair. He listened to the liquid lungs, rasping, making a sound like the last suck of a drain. The odor he had smelled before was here. He recognized it, though his proximity canceled fear. He let it climb him, enfold him, bending closer to see the open mouth, the sealed eyes. As he listened, the breath clogged, halting for a moment and forcing him to bend closer. Then, steadily, it began again. He felt the rhythm, imagined his father's being carried back and forth between life and death, now here, now gone, his breath tidal. Closing his eyes completely, he reached out a hand and rested it on his father's forehead. He stroked the brittle hair once, twice. Then, feeling his own blood begin to race, he moved his hand down to his father's nose. He thought: Kill him. The thought came forward, released now, clear, precise, naked. It was a simple thing. He knew, his hand on his father's flesh, that it had been with him since receiving the letter in Africa, had lingered in unconsciousness alive, awaiting discovery. He thought: Father, son, seeing in it no escape, some inevitable question perpetually unresolved, but one touching his own death, life. He felt, then, the freedom of resolution, for his father had granted him power over his life by letter, by rearing; his days and experience had prepared him for this last action.

Telling himself he was only experimenting, he pinched the nostrils shut. He heard the breathing change, the mouth gag and hiss. Noel felt himself calm. He thought: it ends here. He reached out his other hand and held it suspended over the mouth. He could feel hot air on his palm, quicker now, the chest panting. He opened his eyes and saw only bones in front of him, a cadaverous man impatient for death. He covered the mouth with his hand.

And then the breath came. He saw the chest rise, sink halfway, and catch nothing. It began to push upward again, and Noel watched it, mesmerized. He saw a line of drool squeeze between his thumb and index finger. The nostrils flexed slightly. The color drained from the face, whiteness spreading.

Then, without warning, his father's eyelid flickered. A twitch, a nervous reaction, nothing more. Noel almost dropped his hands. The eye stared at him, quivering, half-shut. He pressed his hands tighter, closing the nostrils and mouth. He tried to say a prayer, but his mind stayed on the expanded chest, and he realized he was now holding the dead air in. He removed his hands and heard the final hiss, the air passing for the last time out of the body.

The sound pushed him back, crying, his chair skidding away. He stood, paralyzed, not knowing how to move. In his mind he could still feel the rush of air down the thin nostrils, the hot sucking of the mouth. He saw the flicker of the eyelid again. He hurried out of the room, hearing, over it all, the hum of the fan, the night stirring.

In the light of a telephone booth Kathy watched the moths cluster. They came out of the darkness, whirling in frenzy, their bodies striking the glass. She listened to them, thinking they sounded like rain, hearing the pelt and scratch of wings, the electric singe of the neon. The phone rang uselessly in her hand. She counted with it, imagining its ringing in Joan's apartment. Joan would not have needed more than three rings to answer. The apartment was too small, and though Kathy knew this, she let it ring anyway.

After a time she hung up. She pushed the door open and saw the light go out, the insects hang for a moment without purpose. She walked quickly to her car and started the engine. When she turned on the headlights, she saw the insects advance, pulled by the light. She worked her way into the traffic and followed it. The car, somehow, did not seem the same. It was no longer familiar. It blocked nothing out, as it once had, but fanned noise and heat inside, wrapped it around her. She had the sensation of moving in a river, the parking lots she passed pools and eddies of a larger source. She did not turn on the radio but drove in silence, letting her mind wander. Without order, images came. She recollected a pink dress she had worn at eight; a glass ball with a village scene inside it, which could be shaken to produce snow; a dance, held in a gymnasium, and a boy's damp hand on the small of her back. Through these memories came another image, this one of Noel standing in the snow, slowly rolling a ball larger and larger, building a snowman's stomach. She had helped him, both of them aware it was a courting gesture, that the snowman was not as important as the innocence it exhibited in each of them, the childlike grace that was a gift. And she had provided the carrot nose, the briquette eyes, going back time and again into her apartment and returning to Noel, who shaped and chiseled with his hands. The snowman was not original. It followed a pattern prescribed by cartoons, by primitive paintings: round head, round stomach, round base. She, for her part, had wanted it that way. The snowman was ritualized, childlike; it had stayed through an early thaw, dripping softly, shrunk by the weight of sun and moisture. It had remained, she remembered, some sort of gauge, always ensuring an introductory remark so that he might say: The snowman is melting, isn't it? Their love had grown in opposite proportion. The snowman took on a nostalgia it had never earned, becoming, in time, a signpost, something they could look back to in order to claim what they had since become.

She remembered this now while driving through the hot, quiet streets, and she expanded the image, thinking of it now as a small example of larger issues. It had been, she realized, through its conventionality, a way to mask reality. It had been romance handed down from movie screens, love generated from the want of love. She was ashamed at how easily she had been fooled—not by Noel, but by herself, by a societal image she had adopted. She thought: Build me a snowman, feeling the treachery of small favors.

She drove on, finally pulling into the driveway. Once the engine was off, she heard the breeze riffling through leaves. It was cooler. She got out and stood a moment beside the car. A bush near the front door bent suddenly under the wind, its branches painting the wall. She tried to smell rain, unconsciously going up on her toes, her hand still on the door handle of the car. A faint odor of moisture came, lingered, left. She turned her head, trying to follow it, but could not. Two wires flapped together near the road, their rubber coating making a threshing sound. She traced the wires with her eyes and saw them separate farther down the street, saw a single strand reach out and connect with the house. She assumed it was the telephone line and for a moment thought of the blackbird sitting propped on it, its feet choking voices, cutting off with its small talons the people trying to reach them.

Finally, she moved away from the car. The house was dark in front of her. The same bush shrugged once more, branches tapping a dark window. She reached a hand to touch it and felt it suddenly grow still, the branches pulling back. She fumbled with her keys and let herself in.

"Noel?" she called.

She heard a chair scrape. She reached for the light and turned it on, called again: "Noel?" She stepped forward and turned another light on, going from pool to pool, darkness at the perimeter.

"Noel?"

She called louder this time. His voice came from his father's study. She walked to it. A gear settled in the clock, preparing to chime. But the chime did not come, and she heard, instead, a draw cord on a curtain bounce against the window. Far away, a foghorn sounded, droning through miles of evening mist, the rivers now charted by sound, echo, pitched voices passing each to the other. She listened, almost unconsciously, for another, imagining green water churned by thrashing propellers, the rock-quiet glide of fresh water on barnacled posts. Then, breaking the silence, she asked: "Noel? Are you in there?"

She was reluctant to open the door. She stared at it, her eyes tracing the grain, the hinge, aware of his presence behind it. She was frightened, though she would not admit it to herself, and reshaped her fear to include him. It was him she was afraid for—his power, released on himself, which she would have to react to, understand, perhaps share. She did not feel up to it and waited at the door, wondering if he would let her pass.

"Kathy?" he asked.

She opened the door. She did not see him at first. The air in the room was stale. She smelled smoke, warmth, alcohol. His outline came clear then, illuminated by the pool lights outside. The French doors were open. He was there, in a chair by the doors, a ghost, a cigarette burning in one hand. Behind him on the patio deck were other cigarettes, white curls of time marked.

"Noel? What are you doing? What is it?"

He did not respond. She knew, then, what it was, saw his cheeks colored with tears. He seemed suddenly like an animal curled from light, suspended between attack and retreat. She tried to make herself cross to him and even took a step before stopping, her movement causing a reaction, a squeak from the swivel chair.

"When?" she asked.

"A little while ago. After you dropped me off."

"Have you called anyone? Grant?"

"Not yet. I haven't done anything."

"All right. I'll call, then come right back. You stay here," she added.

She was relieved to close the door. She could feel no

difference in the house. The atmosphere was no lighter, something she had always supposed would occur. There had been no change whatsoever. She wondered why she had always presumed death would rinse the house, cleanse it. It made no sense to her now. If anything, she felt a change occurring in herself, a new briskness, and was even thankful for a direction to take. This, she realized, was what she was good at—order, instructions, detail. She wanted people in the house. She did not like the silence and felt it seeping inside, closing, as though, if it settled, the house would never be rid of it.

She was brought up short at the top of the stairs when she saw Noel's father still there, his face uncovered, a glimmer from his left eye where it teared from the fan. She felt herself pulled into the room, drawn by decency to cover the face. She flicked off the fan and heard it drone quietly, eventually starting to squeak, then beat in descending slowness. She waited for it to stop while the heat seemed to take new license and close once more. She averted her eyes and felt for the sheet. She lifted it, flapping it first to work over the head. In the noise it made she almost missed the shallow intake of breath, the lungs of Noel's father still working.

She took a step backward, compelled by instinct to shrink away in an animal mistrust of sudden movement. She felt a scream rising which she caught in time, stifled, though it seemed to peal back down through her limbs. She stood perfectly still, watching the breath come once more, judging the intervals, counting, detecting now much longer pauses. She glanced at the clock on the night table and saw the sweep hand move, circle, while no breath came. She said once, twice: You're not dead, you're not dead, and found herself wanting the chest to rise no more, the lungs to cease. Thoughts moved through her mind, animated, wild. She realized she was still holding the sheet and let it drop, one of the old man's shoulders coming bare. She stared at the white skin, trying to shape her thoughts, collect them, but they moved too fast, came and went in confusion.

Finally, she turned. She started out the room, prepared to call Noel, when it suddenly struck her that the man was already dead in Noel's mind. He had died. She stopped in the doorway, feeling now the first impulses slow. Just beneath her she heard the swivel chair groan and wondered if Noel was listening, whether he expected a cry, a scream, some mark of emotion. Then, without knowing she had come to it, she thought: Noel has killed him. The idea would not stay with her, but she forced herself to concentrate. Again: Noel has killed him. She took a step back into the room. The old man hissed out his breath, a wet sound which did not seem to stop for minutes. A breeze sank in the room, falling from the wind outside.

"Noel," she said aloud.

She was alarmed at her next thought. She took a step toward the bed, thinking: I can end it. It is over to all minds but mine. It surprised her to think this, surprised her even to consider it. She wondered if it would be hard, wondered, too, how it had come down to her, how this choice had been left for her to make. She had never before been in such a position—completely free to act without the slightest chance of reprisal. It would be over in minutes, seconds. The mere freedom seemed almost impetus enough to do it; to retreat would be to deny an opportunity to bring peace, to survive, to pull out of circumstances that controlled them.

She put one hand on the bed and ran her fingers over the white coolness. Noel's father took another breath then, and she pushed back. She wondered, briefly, how many times he had been close to death, how many times Noel, or perhaps Grant, had been in her position. But she realized in the same instant it all could have been a mistake. Noel might have misread the signs; he might have grown nervous, convinced himself, panicked. Jenna had told them both that the man might not breathe for ten minutes or longer at a time. Perhaps Noel had seen that and forgotten.

She stood next to the bed, unable to move. She listened to a faucet drip in the bathroom down the hall. A few minutes later she turned and walked to the top of the stairs.

"Noel," she called. "Noel, come here."

Two

Frankenstein squatted in shadow, listening to the water. He could smell it, the chlorine reminding him of the YMCA. He saw the net leaning against the cabana. He rose and looked across the surface. There was nothing floating, but the animals could be down, dead things not yet buoyant. He had found them there before. A foot under they would be suspended, drifting, their bodies glowing green-blue.

He inched closer. He looked at the house and saw it was summer-lazy. There was a lamp on, nothing more. He had heard, earlier, voices calling. He had watched lights come on, climb the house. Now there was only one light remaining. He watched it, waiting for movement. The crickets called. A mosquito passed close to his ear, then wandered off.

He reached behind him for his flask. He took a short drink, stopping the flow of alcohol with his tongue. A bead of sweat slipped free of his sternum and rolled down to his navel. He pressed his shirt against it, rubbing in a circular motion across his stomach. He took another drink, short, bitten, this one finding a cavity in a back molar. He clenched his teeth and waited for the pain to pass. When it did he took a third drink, keeping the liquid in the sac of his cheek, warming it first before swallowing it.

In time he moved forward. He stood at the edge of the pool, no longer needing to hide. He checked the area once more, staring at the house first, then sweeping his eyes across the quiet lawn, the fanning hedges. He inspected the water last, walking slowly around the rectangle, trying, in darkness, to see what animals might be floating. He saw nothing except for three small frogs kicking at the sides. They rushed off at his approach, flicking the water with their hind legs and causing a small splash. It reminded him of walking beside a lake, the frogs releasing tender springs of leg and back muscles at the small quake of earth.

He did not take up the net. He passed it, ducking through the pine hedge. He crossed a small rock wall and entered an open meadow. He smelled rotted apples and saw the moon hanging like a scythe above the deep green of the trees. A cat crossed his path, its legs bent, its back level, a rodent dangling from its mouth. He sucked his teeth to chase it and watched it sprint off, sometimes turning back with white eyes, the rodent tail a gentle whip.

In the center of the field he urinated. Grass, knee-high, bent and nodded with the wind. Clouds passed over the moon, lending shadow to shadow, darkness passing. He hummed under his breath, the song unrecognizable, without name. He zipped up his fly and crossed the meadow. Sea *air came to him. He left it for the fragrant warmth of an old orchard near a second wall. He stripped his shirt and stood, shivering, in quiet moonlight. He pulled two apples, green and untended, off the trees. Twisting the apples in his hands, he broke them in half. He bathed in the moonlight, rubbing the apple cores over his body, under his arms. He did not take off his pants, but rubbed along his belt line. He took the scent for his own, still humming, the trees sometimes knocking with wood too damp to produce real sound.*

Noel pushed a wheelbarrow through the woods behind the pool. It rumbled softly, the metal bed empty except for a spade. He listed the trees as he passed them: oak, maple, birch, pine. The sun was cut off here, and he took quick breaths of the forest smell. The air was cooler. He glanced up and to his right and saw the tree fort he and Grant had built years ago. The plank steps were twisted, some of them forcing the bark to grow around them. In the first large fork of the tree the old boards were rotted. The wood was black, damp-looking even in the heat. Farther up along the trunk a squirrel had made a nest. It was the same color as the tree fort.

He walked on. The wheelbarrow bounced over roots and rocks. A swarm of gnats circled, black flecks rolling from the ground. They hung suspended over the dead leaves, roiling, and he stopped for a moment to watch them. A breeze pushed them toward a patch of staghorn sumac. He lifted the shovel out and swung it through the center of the swarm, watching the air current pull them apart. They re-

mained scattered for an instant before the circle was re-
joined. The wind lifted them into the darkness around the
sumac.

He threw the shovel back in the wheelbarrow and
pushed again. He stopped near a rock wall that ran for a
quarter mile in either direction. A small field spread out
beyond it, the brown grass mixed with meadow sweet and
rabbit-foot clover. He leaned the wheelbarrow against the
wall and began rolling the loose rocks. The insects beneath
them scattered at the touch of light, some digging into holes
in the soft earth. He brushed a slug onto the grass and
watched it curl, its saliva skin reacting to the dryness.
Crickets shot up out of the long grass near the base of the
wall, their quick wings sounding like sugar spilled on
linoleum.

When he had enough rocks, he threw the jagged ones
into the wheelbarrow. A few splintered, spraying chips
against the sides of the wheelbarrow. At ten, he stopped. He
lifted the handles of the wheelbarrow, testing the weight.
He set it down and added five more stones. He set the
shovel on top, then sat on the wall.

He lit a cigarette. The heat was fuller now. He smelled it
coming up from the earth, smelled lilac, bayberry, hawk-
weed. A chipmunk ran down the trunk of a maple and
made it to the stone wall. It sat for a moment on the edge,
then ducked into a hole. Noel smoked, waiting to see more
animals, but nothing came. He held his mind in check, not
letting it go completely. He began to think of his father,
but he forced the image to remain unfocused. He allowed
himself to remember the night in parts, never permitting
the whole to come together, deliberately separating each
section so it could be turned, controlled, forgotten. He
thought once: I killed him, though it was not true. He had
not killed him but only pushed him closer to the death that

eventually came, unbidden, to take him. Three days had
passed before real death came, yet he was sure he had
started it, had closed life in some way, though he could not
be held responsible. The real death, he remembered now,
had been far more formal, had been foreseen by Jenna in
staggered signs. The pulse had grown weaker; the breathing
had become labored, stopping and starting at indefinite intervals, life, hope, ushered back with the drawn intake of
breath; death a final prize. And they had circled him—
Grant, Mary, Kathy, and himself—while a priest prayed,
gave extreme unction to a soul killed once already, a dark
afternoon passing unnoticed outside the windows. Noel had
listened, had heard his father's sins forgiven, aware, at the
same time, that his own sin was not absolved. He felt no
forgiveness. The act remained the same regardless of its
outcome. The intention had been there. He had recalled,
while standing at the bed, the pinched nostrils, the air held
in the hollow chest, the scene frozen and stitched through
his thoughts. I have killed him, he thought. Only Kathy
knew of the mistake, and she had passed it off as his confusion, saying: Jenna told me they can sometimes go without
breathing for quite a while. But he was not sure he believed
her, was not sure she believed him. Twice, since then, he
had started to tell her, managed even to say: It started that
night, knowing she would need no reminder, hoping she
would understand. Yet she had not taken up the line of his
thoughts, and he had seen his guilt compounded and wondered: Who would it benefit to tell? He had avoided
Kathy's eyes instead, avoided her knowledge, handing to
her his tears and false grief while he watched his father die
naturally, cleansed by ancient rites. Forgive me, he had
wanted to whisper at the last, though his father was without
power to do so.

He ground out his cigarette on the wall and stood. He

lifted the handles of the wheelbarrow. The weight on his shoulders spread, pulling at the muscles along his neck. He took a step and felt the wheelbarrow start to twist. He managed to balance it, grunting softly, his legs trembling. It was overloaded, but he didn't care. He pushed at it, rocking it over roots and twigs. A drop of sweat stung his eye, and he blinked it back, hoping it would travel to his mouth, where he could taste the salt.

After twenty yards he set the load down. His muscles contracted, settling back into position. He was panting. He stuck his hands in his back pockets, touching the wetness that formed a wedge at his belt. He counted to ten, then lifted again. He grunted loudly, throwing his weight forward, the skin on his hands pinching. His foot slipped on a leaf, and he nearly lost his balance. The wheelbarrow lurched, but he caught it, something straining near his rib cage.

He stopped, holding his side, his breath hurting him. He took shallow breaths, sensing the air running over his ribs. He stretched backward, rolling his head on his shoulders. He saw the gnats again and watched them whirl in a ray of sun.

He lifted. The pain in his side caused him to cry out softly. He felt the muscles of his chest pulling at his sternum. He pushed forward, using his strength in short bursts. The pain grew, but he pushed until the wheelbarrow lowered on its own, sinking in his hands, dragging him toward the ground. He set it down finally and leaned forward, his hands on the rocks, his stomach suddenly churning. He knelt and put his head on top of his hands. He waited for the sickness to pass, but it grew, instead, expanding in his throat and stomach.

He retched to one side, short and violent, pulling his legs back to avoid the liquid. The pain in his ribs fluttered rapidly with his breath. He could see the yard in front of him, ten, maybe fifteen feet away. He forced himself to stand. In one motion he lifted and pushed. The wheelbarrow rattled forward, jarring his shoulders. It broke through the pine hedge, and then he was in full light, the house white in front of him. He leaned harder into the weight, his knees rocking, the cartilage knotting between bones. He started to put the wheelbarrow down but then pushed on, feeling a laugh, a dizziness begin in him. He pushed, no longer conscious of the pain, his eyes fixed on the spot he had chosen.

Nearly collapsing, he turned the wheelbarrow on one side and watched the rocks slide to the ground, their dull thuds shaking the soil. He threw the wheelbarrow ahead and watched it wobble, then fall, the metal now hollow-sounding. He stared down at the rocks, letting his body relax. He squatted and rubbed a blister which had formed below his index finger. He rubbed it harder, letting the small pain distract him from his exhaustion.

The sun moved behind a cloud, and the yard went dark for a moment. He could smell rain faintly, the air turning moist. He glanced at the sky and saw a dark bank of clouds settling above him. He wanted it to be gray. He hoped the rain would come early, covering the funeral, hiding the transfer of the coffin to earth.

He leaned forward and ran his hands over the surfaces of the rocks. He sized them up with his eyes, their shapes working into his mind. He picked up one rock, turned it, then set it down. He took another and placed it on the grass. Still squatting, he arranged the rocks end to end, fitting the angles together. He worked slowly. His ribs hurt, and he was conscious of each movement, aware of his skin gliding over bone. Sweat freed his skin of friction.

After fifteen minutes he stood. The base of the barbecue

pit was arranged. The rocks fitted together in a U shape, the front open so the ashes could be swept out. The nausea was gone. In its place there was only a weakness. His muscles seemed like cord, no longer elastic. His hands trembled, and he tucked them in his pockets, pushing them deeper into the lining until they were still.

He rolled his head on his shoulders again, thinking: Three sand, two gravel, one cement. He opened a bag of cement and poured it into a bucket. The cement was old, caked from years in the garage, but it still sifted into the wheelbarrow when he poured it from the bucket. He added sand and gravel, then walked to the house and turned on the hose. He let a little water trickle in and reached for the shovel. He stirred the cement, forming pools in the mixture and gradually wetting each small avalanche, spreading the grayness. He added a little more water, then squeezed a palmful of the cement in his hands. It stayed balled in his outspread fingers.

He pushed the wheelbarrow to the edge of the foundation and set it within reach. Moving quickly, he began troweling the cement into the crevices, walling up the rocks. He spread the cement in circular motions, his arm steadier now. He found himself watching his hands work, surprised at their ability. They smoothed the cement, filling in slots between the rocks with confidence, tapping each rock with the handle of the trowel to make sure it was in place.

"Isn't it hot enough for you?" Kathy called. Noel turned to see her, smiling, feeling somehow guilty. She was standing on the back steps, dressed in a new outfit.

"I like it," he answered.

He worked faster. The cement was drying. He sprinkled more water on it. He heard Kathy coming across the yard, the swish of her slip mixing with the sound of her shoes hitting the lawn. She stopped just short of him, her shadow taking the sun off his back.

She said: "Noel, you should get dressed."

"I will."

"Grant and Mary will be here in about fifteen minutes."

"Okay."

He stood and mixed the cement again. He added water, then turned to face her. Everything except the last rock was covered.

"How do you think it looks?" he asked.

"Pretty good. Is it crooked there?" She pointed.

"Where?"

"Right there."

He stepped back and looked. The left edge was slightly higher. He reached forward and dabbed a little cement on the right.

"How about now?"

"Okay."

She ran her hands down her dress, smoothing it. Noel bent to cover the last rock. He scooped the remaining cement out and smeared it across the top.

"Want to draw your initials in it?" he asked.

"Noel . . ." she started.

"I know, I'll get ready."

She nodded and walked back to the house. He picked up a twig and wrote his initials. He drew a line underneath, then added another. The letters held.

He threw the trowel and spade into the wheelbarrow and pushed it to the garage. The sky was darker. The wind cooled his back, pressing his damp shirt against him. He felt the pain along his ribs as he opened the garage door. He had to turn to raise it with his other arm. He wedged the wheelbarrow against the wall, then hung the tools back in place.

"Noel?" Kathy called again.

He shut the door and crossed the yard. He opened the screen door and grabbed a cleanser from under the sink.

"Is it going to rain?" Kathy asked from the kitchen table.

"I think so."

She shook her head and stared out the back door. Then she said: "You really should hurry."

"I will."

He carried the cleanser at his side. As he climbed the stairs, he felt a breeze working through the house. It came down the hallway and hit softly against the closed bedroom door. He stood for a moment beside the door, remembering the men carrying the stretcher down the staircase. It had been angled dangerously, his father strapped in by white bands around his chest and legs. But the head had been loose, lolling on a soft neck. Noel could not recall thinking anything but that he had acted too soon, that death would have come, had come, without him.

Kathy stood in the kitchen, looking out the window. She saw the foundation for the barbecue pit, the white lines of cement bright beside the dullness of the fieldstone. She wasn't sure what to make of it. Noel had spent the entire morning working, cleaning a patch of soil, digging up rocks, pushing the wheelbarrow. His movements had not been rushed. They had been slow and deliberate, so tightly controlled as to be almost frightening. She had watched him, his skin glistening, the heat hovering near ninety-five. He had worked without water, worked ceaselessly. She had wanted to say: Noel, we are burying your father today, but there had been something in the manner of his working which prevented it. He had worked with an animal patience, plodding, somehow deadly. It reminded her of his swimming, of the laps he swam in precise rhythm, turning from side to side, the gasping face coming free time and again from the water. His exercise had always had some measure of punishment contained in it, but this was something more, something almost brutal. She had seen him sweating twenty minutes afterward, his body finally releasing the moisture held by the blue water, a damp spot left on the cement deck to mark where he had been. Watching him these last few days, she had thought: He killed his father, and wondered at the face coming free of the water, the pinched pain it expressed, thinking: He cannot resolve it.

She turned on the tap and ran a glass of water. The house was quiet except for the sound of Noel's shower. She could feel the tension returning, the pressure from his father undiminished. It remained like a residue, no different in any way from the medicine bottles she still found in odd places, the receipts she located in drawers, all acting as reminders. She knew Noel felt this, too. For the three nights of the wake he had been restless. He had cleaned out his father's desk, had stripped the bed of its sheets and carried the mattress down to the basement. It had been useless to tell him there would be time for that. His own silence had demanded her silence. But she could not stop her alarm at seeing him in such constant motion, building, cleaning, moving in endless cycles which did not seem to tire him. He hardly slept. Instead, late at night she heard him prowling the house or yard, the sounds of his movement passing through the walls to find her in bed, awake, listening to him struggling with himself. His drinking, too, had increased. He drank to deaden, she knew that. But now he no longer seemed aware of his consumption—or perhaps he was too aware, relied on it, administered glasses like medicine.

Through it all she felt clinical, detached somehow. He seemed to her to be on the edge of something she could not touch. More than once she had thought: Now, now he will break down, not at first seeing the significance of the word. Because it was like a breakdown, the manic energy a last grasp at protection. She had watched the tension grow from the night he had mistakenly reported his father's death, loom stronger each day until it seemed he must snap. She waited, feeling pity, but knowing she must not voice it. This was something she could not claim to know.

Now she set her glass down and walked through the house. The dining room was ready. She reminded herself to leave the back door open for Mamie, the caterer. Grant had insisted on a catered reception. Together with Mary, she had arranged the menu, keeping it light because of the heat, making sure there would be enough to drink. Noel hadn't helped. Somehow his constant motion had absolved him from responsibility. He had remained unaffected, passive, letting Grant see to the details.

From the dining room she heard Grant's car pull into the driveway. She went to the front door and stood for a moment in the dimness, trying to compose herself. She glanced at her image in the wall mirror and straightened her dress. It was already clinging to her, the heat pushing it against her slip.

"Noel? They're here," she called up the stairs.

She heard the shower click off and water rush into the tub. From outside, two doors slammed. She pulled open the front door. It came away shaking, the doorjamb swelled. Mary was just ahead of Grant. She wore a lace veil over her head.

"Hello," Grant said.

Kathy held the door open for them. Grant bent and kissed her cheek. Mary said simply: "Hot."

"It is," Kathy said, leading them inside. Mary moved to the dining-room table and casually straightened the cloth.

"Mamie should be here any minute," she said.

"I thought we'd just leave the back door open for her," Kathy said.

"Oh?" Mary asked. "I don't know. Thieves sometimes read the obituaries to find out when a house will be empty."

"Funerals and weddings," Grant said.

"Mamie will be here, though," Kathy said. "As long as she's here, I don't think there's any problem."

"I don't know," Mary said.

Kathy suddenly felt tired. It was warm. Mary was edging around the table, checking the silverware. Grant dropped into a chair along the wall. Kathy moved for something to do. She stepped to the bottom of the stairs and called to Noel. He yelled back that he was almost ready.

"I got a card from Mr. Sheppard," Grant said when she stepped back in the room. "He won't be able to make it."

"We still have—what?" Mary asked, "about twenty, twenty-five?"

"I think so," Kathy said.

"It doesn't really matter," Grant said.

Kathy felt her stomach turn. She wondered if they were as close to losing control as she. She thought: They lost a baby to this, remembering the phone calls, the anxious questions to find out if another child would be available later. She stared down at her hands and watched them moving. She tried to think of an excuse to get out of the room, but everything was done. The house was clean; the kitchen was ready for the caterers.

"Hot," Mary said again.

Kathy moved to the picture window. She looked out at the brown lawn, now and then hearing a gentle click from the silverware. It wasn't their fault, she realized. The thought failed to comfort her. She wondered what it would be like to scream. She wondered if she screamed once whether she would be able to stop. She could imagine the sound building, rising through her body until it blocked out everything. She thought, just for an instant: In heat, people go mad.

"Is that Mamie?" Mary moved up behind her and leaned to look through the window. Kathy smelled perfume and baby powder.

"It's a van, I think. It must be Mamie," Mary said.

"Driving a van?" Grant asked.

"She's the boss. She has a couple of people working with her," Mary explained, going to the front door. She opened it and walked outside. Kathy heard her telling Mamie to pull the van closer.

"How's Noel?" Grant asked.

Kathy turned. Grant was sprawled out in his chair, the back of his head resting against the wall.

"I don't know. He started building a barbecue pit this morning."

"Why?"

"No idea. He's taking it hard."

Grant leaned forward. He put his arms on the table. When he spoke, his voice was low. He said: "Kathy, are you going back to Africa with him?"

She was not ready for the question. She touched her throat. "I don't know," she said. "I'm not sure. Is he going?"

"He talks about it. If he goes, would you?"

"I don't think I can go back."

"Because of him or because of Africa?"

"Mostly Africa."

Grant nodded. He pushed away from the table and sat back, wiping his brow with his hand. Kathy realized she hadn't seen before how tired he was.

"Is Noel good in Africa?" he asked. "Do you know what I mean?"

"He's very good."

"Better than you? Better adapted?"

Kathy had never heard Grant speak so frankly. She leaned against the windowsill, her elbows pressed on the glass behind her. She said: "In some ways he is. I think he probably is."

"Do you know, when Noel writes home, he never mentions his work? The first time I really knew what he was doing was when he came home the last time—when he met you. He never talks about it."

"Most people don't listen."

"I know. I know they don't." Grant sat forward again. He put his hands on his knees, then stood. He blew air straight up at his face, his hair moving slightly. He said: "He loved Dad an awful lot. Dad loved him, too. Whenever Noel traveled, Dad would pull out his maps and globe and figure out where he was. He'd follow him with his finger, reading up on the different countries, wondering whether Noel went overland or by air. A letter from Noel was an event around here. I don't think Noel ever knew Dad took such an interest."

"I don't think he did either. Were you jealous?"

Grant reached forward and fingered one of the napkins. He rubbed it for a second, then let it drop. "A little," he said. "Mostly at first. I wasn't really close enough to be jealous—do you know what I mean? I wasn't allowed in. Noel went away because he was so much like our father. I only realized that later on. I could stay because I wasn't."

Grant moved back and sat down. Kathy had the feeling he had delivered his speech especially for her benefit. It sounded, uncomfortably, like a warning, like advice. She also saw Grant in a new light—lonely, isolated, yet, oddly, the person keeping everything together. He seemed to her a bear, a huge creature who was capable of sustaining injury without others' being aware of it. She wanted to say something to him, perhaps that she felt much the same way, that, at least for a time, she had adopted his place between Noel and his father. She started to speak, had even said: "Grant—" when Noel came around the corner. He was dressed in a navy blue suit. His hair was still wet.

"Ready?" he asked.

Kathy spun and went into the kitchen. She heard Noel ask from the dining room: "Should we go?"

Outside the back door, Mary was leading Mamie up the walk. She was saying: "The stove has four burners. You can serve inside or outside. Will that be all right?"

"That's fine, that's fine," Mamie said.

Kathy ran a glass of water and stared at the half-formed barbecue pit.

Frankenstein returned to camp in first light. His plastic bag was weighted with skins, feathers, souls. They would bring, he knew, about five dollars from Farley. He threw the bag on the table. He was hungry. He opened a can of spaghetti and a loaf of white bread. He used his knife to open the can, used the fork to spear the noodles. He ate slowly, pushing the bread down in the can, forcing the tomato paste to climb. He rolled one piece of bread between his palms until it was hard, candy, a bread pill. He sucked it to clear his palate, then ate another forkful of noodles.

He watched the clouds building seaward. The sun was a dim glow, threatening to remain hidden. The wind faltered, the stillness a measure of the rain to come. The grass pulled back against its roots. A can jumped off a pile of rubbish, the insides caught by a rag of wind. He could feel the dump growing behind him. It rose quietly, yielding sections as the sun found them. He felt the moisture rotting the ground, seeping into paper bags to spin them brown. He took a long drink from his water canteen. He spared some to trickle over his forehead, tilting his head back so the water would be held in his hair. He felt some collect in the lines around his neck, more in the sockets of his collarbones.

He listened to the wind start. It came from the southeast, carrying fish smells. He leaned toward it, discovering it among the stronger odors of the dump. He remembered Borg's saying: You can't smell the sea new. Just before you think you smell it for the first time, you remember you already know it, that you smelled it before. This made sense to him now. He rocked on the bench, letting the scent go just to catch it again.

The rain started without his knowing it. The first drops were large. He carried the spaghetti to the telephone booth, opened the door, and climbed in. The door shut on easy hinges, folding off the day. Pools of water were already forming. The morning light was refracted, broken. He watched the wind pass through a tree. The metal coil from the old phone lay in the corner. Sleep came like the grayness while the rain did a water dance on the clean glass.

"In the name of the Father, and of the Son, and of the Holy Spirit, amen."

The priest's voice mixed with the rain. The priest had started with the rain, drops hitting on the green awning. Noel had listened, catching bits and pieces of the brief sermon, heard his father portrayed in a light neither true nor false. It felt strange to hear his father eulogized in this way, strange to have a man, even though a priest, speak from an assumed position of long acquaintanceship, while the guests shifted in their discomfort on the sodden ground.

In the new-won silence when the priest paused momentarily, Noel heard the nervous shifts and mutters of the people gathered. It was like a second voice running beneath everything, this one a practical voice which did not approve of being out in the rain. A woman coughed. Someone said in response: Are you all right? There were other sounds, some too muted for him to hear clearly, yet all, it seemed to him, with the purpose of distraction. It occurred to him the people were uncomfortable not only with the rain but with the solemnity as well. He felt a need to break the mood and cleared his throat, able for an instant to concentrate on the mundane, the mechanical. He cleared it a second time and waited for the sound to echo, repeated by those around him, matched finally by the drip of water from the canvas.

He stared at the piece of green artificial turf covering the hole. The center was bowed by gravity, the corners pinned by rocks. Maroon canvas straps peeked out beneath it, ready to lower, to drop at the touch of a button. A wreath blew off the coffin and rolled almost to the feet of the priest. Noel saw the black wood exposed. He thought of the coffin's being pulled from the hearse, the back doors open in a

cruel mocking of birth. He and Grant had carried it with
four others, men he barely knew, the weight distributed
among six hands. They had already started toward the plot
when Mr. Liott, the funeral director, had whispered:
You're at the wrong end. There had been an uncomfortable
moment while he and Grant switched with two older men,
Mr. Liott saying: Yes, yes.

Now the priest sprinkled holy water on the coffin, the
sacred mixing with the rain. The coffin gleamed, its sides
discreetly grained like a bullet. Noel saw in the watered
translucence of the wood his own image staring back at
him, his face bisected by lines of water. For a second he felt
the air coursing through his father's nostrils, pushing at his
fingers, the drool leaking between his hands. He hadn't
killed. He remembered this, thinking that, instead, his father had backed away, convulsing again and again, sinking
deeper and deeper until his soul was caught from some
other place. He imagined his father resting somewhere deep
in his own body, safe in the cartilage of his rib cage, watching.

He turned away, letting the image recede. He had learned
to control it and now waited for it to pass. He looked across
the acres of cemetery and saw the stones pegged into the
sides of gentle hills. He imagined that viewed from above,
they looked like white-toothed saw blades, slashes of jagged
white breaking the roll of smooth green across miles of
open woodland. Mist rose from the ground, carrying the
sound of another party, a second burial, its car doors snapping shut and engines starting, the combustions so many
small explosions. A buzzer sounded from an open door, and
he felt the people around him turning, straining, hoping to
have it shut. The commotion it had caused obscured the
ending of the rite. He had not heard it all. He cautioned
himself to listen, to pay attention, but he heard, instead, a

short cry near him. He turned to see Grant crying quietly, Mary beside him. He reached out a hand to Grant in reflex, but Grant was too far away, and he let his hand drop. Mary nodded at him. He whispered: Grant, feeling a warmth of affection for his brother, a final binding. But when Grant did not see him, he turned back, pretending to look at the priest. He watched for a minute or two, seeing the priest's lips move, though he had difficulty understanding. He thought: It will be over before you understand, but the thought did not help, did not break through his numbness, and he began watching the drivers of the limousines, Mr. Liott, another driver, all standing in the rain, smoking, sometimes looking up at them. He wanted to be with them but was aware he was expected to stand closest to the grave. He was expected to cry. He concentrated once more, searching for what his body would give him, but found nothing. He realized, then, that he had grieved before, that the death and burial now were formalities. He had thought this before, and he tried to remember when, where, feeling his memory more real than the actual event in front of him.

"Lamb of the world," the priest said.

He listened to the ritual, rubbed his fingers together, picking at the lines of dried cement running along his cuticles. From the corner of his eye he saw the priest make the sign of the cross. A drop of water found his neck somehow and ran down his spine. He shivered. In the road the drivers glanced up and threw their cigarettes away. He saw them step into their cars, ready to start their engines the moment the crowd broke.

Gently he felt his hand taken by Kathy. She was close. He smelled her perfume. A man passed near and said: "You don't know me, but your father and I shipped the monorails up to Montreal for the World's Fair. That was some time ago, of course."

Noel nodded, not understanding. He looked around him, surprised to see people milling. He nodded again when a woman said he was good to leave Africa to come home and take care of his father. He said: "Thank you," without seeing her completely, staring only at a wisp of hair, sprayed and tinted, that curled across her forehead. Kathy was still close to him, her breast against his elbow. He pressed his elbow back, sinking it in the warm flesh, oddly pleased by the firmness of her bra.

Mary was saying to another woman: "We hope you'll come back to the house."

"Certainly," the woman said.

The crowd began walking. Noel followed them with his eyes. The cars were too colorful. He saw a few people start to run, a man slipping to one knee. The man stood and stamped the dirt from his pants leg, brushing it and cursing softly.

"Thank you, Father," Grant said to the priest. "We hope you'll come back to the house."

"I'll stop by," the priest said.

Noel watched the movement around him, no longer a part of it. The motion was segmented—he saw arms moving, legs bending. He was aware of a numbness building inside him, spreading.

"We should go," Kathy said.

Noel felt his hand in hers. He hadn't cried. He remembered now that he had planned to, that he had prepared himself. He wondered if he could call them all back and begin again. He was sure he could cry if given another chance.

He felt the dirt under his feet turning to mud. The soles of his shoes were slick. The grass bent, matted, forming a slide. He put all his weight on each step, hearing the soil squish, watching the mud creep up and over his shoes.

Halfway down the hill he turned to look at the grave. A man in a green custodian's uniform had appeared from some place, and Noel wondered where he had been. The man was bent on some task, his hands sometimes appearing at the side of his body as if he were untying something. Noel realized he was not intended to see the mechanics of the actual burial. He turned away.

"Come on," Grant said.

Noel finally climbed into the car, and the driver shut the door. The heavy click sealed them inside. He watched out the side window, catching glimpses through the rain. He stared at the headstones mounting the sides of the hills. He thought of waves then. He thought of the dead climbing over each other, bony toes dug into the scaffolding of ribs and spines, moving, burrowing, to the top of the hill.

Noel stood with his back to the wall, aware he had deliberately positioned himself there, obliging people to come around, to face him. His taking this position was the last deliberate gesture he could remember. The rest—the greetings, the bleak conversations, the quick words given and received—was more closely aligned to dreams. Frequently he found himself reciting: Yes, well, you know how these things are, yes, of course, thank you, hearing in disbelief his own words, the phrases without substance. He was surprised, too, at his drunkenness. He had not detected its coming, had not noticed his drinks disappearing faster than usual. He was conscious only that he was constantly down to ice. Even now his top lip felt cold as he pushed it under a partially melted cube and tried to find liquor. It reminded him of the swollen lip of a cow or rhinoceros, nibbling at a thorny bush. The liquor taste came finally, but only as a weak shadow of what the drink had once tasted like. He wanted another but was reluctant to give up his spot. He watched Mamie pass through the crowd, her apron stiff white, her dress black, and he wanted to call her over and take a drink from the tray. He realized he no longer cared what he drank. His drunkenness was indestructible, could not be dulled by crackers and cheese.

He leaned forward to see the backyard through an open window. The lawn was wet. The pool was flecked by rain water. The smell of chlorine reached him, the chemical purity somehow reassuring in the swell of perfume, cologne, and food. He wondered if he could make it to the window without being stopped, spun, confronted with inane questions. It occurred to him he might make it if he looked busy. It was, he thought, the host's prerogative to adjust windows, pull drapes. It was possible. He looked around, gauging the line he would have to follow, looking for fissures among the dark-suited backs. Before he could move, he heard someone shout. A man stepped back, lifting his hands and looking down at the front of his pants. He had dropped something and looked around him now with a guilty expression that quickly changed to amusement. He lifted his hands higher, smiling still, the responsibility, in a way, no longer his.

"Oh, look what you've done," a woman near him said.

Noel took the moment of confusion to leave. He worked his way along the wall and made it to the kitchen. Two young girls were working at the counter, their hands covered with bread crumbs. They turned to look at him as he entered. He found himself raising his hands like the man in the other room, his wrists turning out to show he concealed nothing.

"I'm looking for the whiskey," he told them.

"There's a bar set up . . ." one began.

"Yes, I know. I live here."

The same girl said: "Well, I didn't—"

"That's all right. I'll just help myself."

He found the whiskey at the top of a broom closet. He noticed the girls glancing at him, their fingers still busy. He wanted to ask them something, to draw them into conversation. He searched for an opening but couldn't tell if they were in high school or college. He carried the bottle to the counter, then got ice out of the refrigerator. He filled his glass, adding, on second thought, a dash of water. They moved to make room for him, though he was not close. It was, he realized, an unconscious movement, the sideways step of a horse shying. The closer one smiled.

"Have a drink if you like," he said, regretting it as soon as he spoke the words. He saw them giggle, their secret communication inaccessible to him. "I mean," he said, stumbling, "if you like, help yourself."

They giggled again. He wondered what caused it. It occurred to him he might look old to them. It surprised him to think this. He wanted to say: Look, I know how this is. I know how it is to be working and see a drunken man come in, but I'm not like that. He realized, in time, that any excuse he might think of would only make the situation worse. He stood silently for a moment, swaying slightly, his drunkenness coming to him on sad waves. He looked at the closer girl's hair. It was soft, brown, curly, freshly combed. Staring at it, he suddenly felt nostalgic, wanted to reach and touch it if only for an instant, knowing he could make it seem a gesture of loneliness, convey that he intended nothing sexual by it. At the same time, however, he realized he had been standing too long gazing at them. A tightness had come into their bodies, their earlier giggling replaced by nervous awareness of a man's watching them.

"I'll just put this back," he said.

He walked back to the broom closet, hearing a short giggle erupt, released by his turned back. He replaced the bottle and walked out. People were now walking in a slow line around the dining-room table, bending with plates held like paupers' dishes, helping themselves to food. He said: "Dig in, dig in," feeling the inappropriateness of the words on the day of a funeral, changing them quickly to: "Eat up, eat up," finally falling to silence. He perceived the same hush he had experienced with the girls a moment before—the nervous concentration on the business at hand, the centered activity. Someone slapped him softly on the shoulder. He didn't see who it was. Grant stopped near him, appearing from out of the crowd. He said: "Dad never threw this good a party when he was alive." Grant laughed, trying to carry it off. Noel watched him, thinking he must join in. He laughed, feeling in the moment an effort on Grant's part toward union, an effort, already, to sort through the grief. Noel waited for another remark. He knew it would come, a probe by Grant to see how Noel had taken the death, underlying it the question How will we take this? It was also Catholic, Irish, a blood need to mingle death with laughter. Earlier, in a wave of sentimentality, Grant had shaken salt into both their pockets, holding out the flaps and goosing him with the shaker, saying: A little to keep the demons away. There had been a mixture of bluff and seriousness then, just as there was now.

"Who are these people?" Noel whispered.

"I have no idea."

Grant laughed once more, this time quietly, but it wasn't true. Noel had seen him speaking with different couples, stopping not merely from politeness or to talk about business, but because he was part of the community. Some of the guests were friends of his from the bank.

"Well, mingle," Noel said, moving off.

He went into the living room. He didn't see Kathy or Mary. The room was almost empty. He crossed it and took up a new spot by the open window. He put his hands on the window ledge. It was still raining. He raised the window a little higher, he heard voices from the back steps. A soft wind came through the window, carrying traces of mist. Behind him he heard the clatter of knives and forks and turned to see some of the people straggling in, taking up positions on the edges of couches and chairs to eat. He felt he should join them but couldn't. The drunkenness was moving through him, changing his mood. His stomach felt hollow. A woman taking a seat on the couch called: "You should try some, Noel," and held her fork up like a drumstick ready to tap on the china.

"I will, I will," he said. He took a drink and watched her bite off a small morsel of food. Too quickly he asked: "Is it good?"

"Delicious."

"Good, good."

There was a commotion near the front door. The priest walked in, rather dramatically, Noel thought, stripping his coat into Mary's hands. He stuck his head into the living room and waved. A man said through a cheekful of sandwich: "Too wet for golf, Father?"

Noel saw the priest cast a glance in his direction. The priest had left the man's dig hanging and said to cover it: "If you'll caddy, I'll play."

"Oh, no, too wet for me. Like carrying your own lightning rods, wouldn't you say?"

But the priest was gone, being, Noel supposed, ushered to the table. He tried to remember the priest's name. He thought it was something Italian, a name ending with an *O*. He concluded it didn't matter. He took a long drink from his glass and rattled the ice cubes. Thoughts of the priest pushed him to thoughts of his father. Guilt came, softly, almost pleasurably. He thought: I killed you. It no longer made any difference whether he had succeeded or not. He thought briefly, in connection with the priest: sins of volition, sins of omission, remembering the deadening questions of the catechism, the aged cardinal standing, asking: Who is God? He smiled remembering it, picturing himself going to the priest now and repeating it: Who is God, Father, he would ask. Who?

He let this thought pass, too. He turned back to the window. In the distance he heard a buoy bell ringing, the flapping sound rocking to the rhythm of his own drunkenness. A sad purring noise came from the people. He listened with fascination, only to realize a moment later that the priest had returned and was telling a dismally elegant story, archaic-sounding in its woe and righteousness, about an impoverished parishioner. Noel had to fight down the urge to interrupt. He did not like the shape of the man, did not like the black color censoring the movement of the people. Mary, beside the priest, was listening attentively. Noel knew she was being more than a kind hostess. She was encouraged by what the priest was saying, her ears picking up notes of salvation, duty. He wondered if there was some final rite they all would be subjected to now. It was possible something had been overlooked, though he knew Mary would see to it, would ask the father to bless the house, to set the tone of one last prayer reverberating in all of them.

He thought: Oh, Father.

Suddenly, beside him, a short man appeared. Noel saw a bald head near his chin. He had seen the man before, apparently without a wife or companion, moving from group to group. Now the man looked up and said: "I've wanted to talk to you."

"Really?"

"Yes, for quite some time. Your father was a friend of mine. I didn't know him long, but I felt I should come today. You understand?"

"Yes, of course."

"I was curious when I heard you were from Africa. That you had been working there, I mean."

The man was chewing something. His jaws worked athletically. A muscle rolled from the top of his jaw into his scalp. He seemed, somehow, to be a more efficient eater than most. Noel realized he had not bothered to introduce himself, but this, too, was in keeping with the man.

"We're having quite a time getting things through Lagos. Your father probably told you. Our ships have to lie off for four and five months at a time. There's all sorts of pirating going on. You probably know already about bribes, graft—the dockworkers are getting rich. It's crazy, of course. It's the oil over there. Everything's gone crazy."

"Yes, well—" Noel said. He glanced over the man's head. The room had quieted. People were eating. He saw Kathy finally, her face flushed, a sliver of her slip showing from beneath her skirt. He heard the man speaking but couldn't concentrate. The breeze caught him from behind and pushed its way under his suit jacket. His sweat turned cold, then warmed as the breeze failed.

The man was saying: "—I know you left something to come back, but we need a man over there to watch after our interests. The last one we sent—well, he hadn't any experience in Africa. It can be a shocking place if you're not prepared. He came home in a month. Would that interest you?"

"What's that?" Noel asked. He knew it was a proposition of some sort, though he did not understand it clearly. "I'm sorry," he said. "I wasn't listening closely."

"I know. I'm sorry. Perhaps I shouldn't have brought it up right now, but we do need a man over there. If you'd like, no, here, take my card and call me in a few days. We need a man who knows shipping and Africa."

The man produced a card. Noel wanted to be angry. It was in bad taste to be doing business now, yet there was something about the man that did not permit anger. It was a certain vitality—the teeth and skull of the man were strong, clean, defiant, causing Noel to think of a Prussian general. He took the card, saying: "Perhaps I'll call you then."

"I hope you will. Once again, my condolences."

Noel expected a short bow, a click of the heels. But the man turned and simply walked through the room. When he was gone from sight, Noel read the card. He recalled his father's mentioning the company name, though he could not place the man. He put the card away.

Ten minutes later Kathy came and got him. She took a breath of air before saying: "People are starting to leave. Maybe you should be near the door."

"I hardly know anyone."

"I know, but . . ."

He shrugged and followed her. The closet door near the stairs was open. Mary was pulling out jackets and hats. He saw the priest still near the table, still eating. A group of people were getting ready to leave. One, a tall man with long gray hair, pulled the front door open. Noel saw the rain falling, the sky still dark. The welcome mat was deep brown and covered with mud.

"Thank you all for coming," he said to no one in particular. The statement seemed to make people prepare more quickly. He watched a woman button up her raincoat. A man slipped his feet into rubbers.

"Thank you," he said again, thinking now he was too

drunk, that he should be quiet. Kathy's hand fluttered on his back. It was the consoling pat a mother might give a small child. He suddenly felt nervous. He reviewed the day in his mind, wondering where he had given offense, if any, what he had done that was not appropriate. There was nothing he could remember.

The people moved out into the rain. They stood on the steps a second before dashing toward their cars. Their leaving seemed a weight removed. Noel noticed the remaining voices, though they did not exactly echo, reverberated in the new emptiness as if they had required such space all along. Mamie passed by with a tray of empty glasses.

"I need another drink," he said.

"Noel . . ." Kathy began.

"Just one."

He grinned, wondering at the same time whether the grin would work, whether it meant anything between them any longer. He saw her soften, but again it seemed out of some sense of superiority—the mother again entering into conspiracy with the wayward child. Her hand reached once more to his back, dropped. She smiled back at him, her face weary, tired and tried, stretched somehow into acceptance. He wanted to say: Don't do this to me, feeling, too, that they had finally arrived at the point they were destined for, had worked to achieve unconsciously. With this thought came a degree of pleasure generated by final limits, dissolution. He thought: We begin to end here, immediately wondering if she felt it, too.

"Just one," he repeated and turned. He walked past the table and entered the kitchen. The girls were gone. He saw one carrying something out to the van. Mamie was washing dishes. He went to the broom closet and poured himself a drink. A laugh broke through from the dining room, and he recognized Grant's voice mixing with the priest's. He leaned his head against the open door, smelling floor wax, varnish, dust. He pushed away and went into the small bathroom just off the kitchen. He sat on the closed toilet and drank. He began to cry without being fully conscious of it. A sob started deep inside him, but he controlled it, smothered it until it came through his mouth with a liquid hiss. He smothered another, thinking that from beyond the door it might sound oddly like a laugh.

Kathy said: "Thank you, thank you for coming," and shut the door. She heard the woman's heels clicking down the front walk. She waited near the door, afraid to go past the picture window for fear one last gesture might be demanded of her. She would have to wave, to smile. She waited.

From the kitchen she could hear sounds of Mary cleaning. The faucet turned on and off; there were sponge sounds, jars and canisters being lifted and set back down.

When she heard the car start, she turned and went into the kitchen. Mary was wiping down the refrigerator. She asked: "They gone?"

"Yes," Kathy said. "They just left."

"Who were they anyway?" Grant asked from the table. He was eating a sandwich. "I've never seen them before in my life."

"They worked with your father," Mary said. "The Kings."

Kathy sat down. Noel was smoking next to Grant. He smiled at her, then turned to look out at the backyard.

"Did you see the—what the hell's their name?" Grant

asked. "You know, the fat woman in the kind of sailor suit."

"Mrs. Garret," Mary said. She put down her sponge and ran water in the sink.

"It was a sailor suit, wasn't it? Anyway, she didn't stop eating the whole time she was here. But her arms, you know? Like hams." Grant snorted. Mary shook her head and gave the sink one last cleaning. Kathy watched them, feeling giddy, relieved. Grant asked: "Wasn't it a sailor suit?"

"Just the trim," Noel said. "The dress had white trim."

"She looked like someone had colored her in," Grant said. "She looked like someone used a crayon on her and was afraid to go over the lines."

"But it was nice, wasn't it?" Mary asked. "I thought Mamie did a nice job."

Kathy watched Noel stand up and move to the center of the kitchen. He wobbled slightly, then curtsied and smiled. "Horse ovaries, mister?" he asked. "How about some horse ovaries?"

"Hors d'oeuvres," Mary said.

"That woman was saying 'horse ovaries.' Wasn't she, Grant?" Noel asked.

Grant was laughing. Kathy found herself smiling. She leaned back in her chair and watched Noel take a long drink from his glass.

"Her name isn't Mamie either," Grant said. "When I asked who she wanted the check made out to, she said Sally. Sally Peterson."

"Why does she call herself Mamie?" Kathy asked.

"It's French," Grant said. "She could speak French. Didn't you hear her calling bacon ba-coaun?"

"Or canapés canapsies?" Noel said.

"It was nice though, right?" Mary asked.

"Horse ovaries? How about some nice, warm horse ovaries?" Noel said.

Kathy said, realizing Mary was upset: "It was very nice, Mary. It was, really."

But Grant wasn't listening. He was laughing harder, no longer eating. He asked: "And who was the guy with the monorails? He kept telling me about monorails in Montreal. I honestly thought he was trying to sell me something."

"You guys, come on," Mary said. It was almost a whine. Then, to Grant: "We should get going."

"All right."

Grant stood and carried his plate to the sink. He rinsed it off and stuck it in the dishwasher. Noel rattled the ice in his drink and made slow rings on the table.

"I'm ready," Grant said. "Noel, how about fishing tomorrow?"

"Where?"

"Off the bridge. We can go for flounder."

"Sounds good."

"I'll call you."

Kathy stood. Mary already had her purse. Noel got up and leaned against the kitchen counter, smoking again. Kathy felt the atmosphere in the room suddenly constricting. Grant stood by the dishwasher, smiling, rocking slightly on his feet.

"You all don't have to go," Kathy said. She felt uncomfortable as soon as she said it. "There's food, I mean."

"No, everyone's tired."

"Fishing then?" Grant said, and began walking through the house. Kathy followed. Noel was behind her. She heard his steps as they walked single file through the house. Mary pulled open the front door. It was still raining.

"Good-bye," Mary said. Kathy wanted to say: This is not a party. Stay. But there was momentum now, a forward movement. She saw Grant step out onto the porch and stop. His foot was still on the doorjamb.

"It feels strange," Grant said. He paused, then jogged off, ducking into his collar. He took Mary's arm and pulled her close. Kathy watched them. She lingered in the open door, smelling the air and rain and grass.

"It's over," Noel said behind her. "Right?"

"Right."

"I'm going to take a nap."

"Okay."

"Want to come up?"

"No, not right now."

"Are you all right?" he asked.

"I'm fine."

He squeezed her arm once, then turned away and climbed the stairs. She listened to his feet strike the hall. She stayed in the doorway, breathing deeply. She was aware of the silence building behind her. She rocked the door on its hinges, needing the noise. It creaked softly, oilless, somehow nervous. She thought: This silence will not last. But it was large and thick. She didn't know whether to be afraid of its beginning or end.

She turned and walked back through the house. She heard each footstep, her own sometimes echoed by Noel's above her. She stopped to listen to his pulling out drawers, to hear the casters of the closet door shake. She was aware of something settling in the house. She touched the plaster on the walls, her ears still following the motion upstairs. "Noel?" she said aloud, thinking if he heard her, she would know what next to say. When there was no response, she walked into the kitchen.

She moved to the sink and looked out the window. The

umbrella near the pool was flapping. The white iron table which supported it was rocking on its legs. She watched it, occasionally glancing at the barbecue pit, debating whether to go out or not.

Finally, she walked out the door and ran down the steps. A leaf blew past her, stopping and starting like an animal. She slowed, feeling better. She thought: It is over. Thinking: Then what begins? She stood still for a moment, hearing the water run on the roof, the gutters flushing.

On the patio she reached for the umbrella. The steel supports felt cold. She pushed the button in to let it slide closed and scraped her knuckle. The umbrella closed viciously, a flytrap snapping. She stood for a moment sucking her knuckle, letting the wind cool her. From the corner of her eye she saw a rabbit staring at her, frozen, its brown body a stone. The wind moved its fur, brushing it to whiteness in places. She took a step toward it, but it didn't move. Rain fell, softer now, and she left it on her skin, made no move to wipe it off. The rabbit edged closer, inspecting her, before suddenly breaking. She watched it dodge into the pine hedge, its back legs kicking up to show long paws.

A sheet of rain scattered over the pool, rolling a chlorine smell into the air. A tin ashtray blew off the table and rattled to the hedge. It stopped just where the rabbit had disappeared. She felt the slightest bit of fear. She imagined the rabbit lurking, watching her, ready to leap at her if she made a move toward it. Rabbits are rodents, she thought, even as she forced herself to walk.

At the hedge her body became mechanical. She bent stiffly, noting the way her limbs worked, her joints flexed. The ashtray fit into her hand, and she had the impression it came to her. She couldn't recall grabbing it. With her head still bowed, she glanced at the pine hedge, expecting to see the rabbit crouching, the ancient eyes of the prey turned predatory. Instead, without completely understanding it, she saw the pimpled corpse of the blackbird. She gagged once as she saw the body had been plucked, the head twisted backward. It was flat on its stomach, its head pecking straight up at the sky. A mound of ants near its head sent a trail of black insects to the eyes.

She backed away. The rain broke harder. Her eyes remained fixed on the ants. They can carry ten times their weight, she thought, seeing the small feelers holding the flesh above their heads. She wanted to move forward and kick the bird free, bury it, but she kept moving backward. The wind behind her ran along the ground, gathering itself, crawling up the bark of trees.

She walked. Her limbs pushed at her to run, but she didn't listen. Somehow she knew to run would bring full panic. She made herself feel the soggy grass, the mud expanding. Her shoulders were wet and cold. She saw the screen door waiting, the bottom section bulging from the paws of the family dog, dead except in legend. Pulling it open, she paused in the doorway, not quite ready for the silence of the house.

Shivering, she finally stepped inside. She heard the refrigerator hum, the wooden click of the clock. She went into the bathroom and wrapped a towel around her hair. Her clothes were drenched, and she shucked them onto the floor. She looked at herself in the mirror, her skin raised, her nipples hard. She leaned her head over the sink and rubbed her hair until it was only moist, then stepped back into the kitchen.

The house was darker. An autumn coolness worked through the rooms. She crossed the kitchen, remotely aware of her breasts jogging. She folded her arms over her chest, hugging herself, her weight distributed on the balls of her feet. At the stairs she checked to make sure the front door was locked. She heard thunder.

She ran up the stairs. Warmer now, she moved down the hallway. She opened their door quickly and saw Noel asleep, his body turned to the far wall. She closed the door and crossed the room. She lifted the blanket, letting the rough wool scrape her. Then there was his skin, warm, muscles contracting from the sudden cold.

"Kathy?" he said, out of a dream.

She ran her hands over him, touching his thighs, his chest, his buttocks. She pushed her body into him, her breasts on either side of his backbone. She waited for him to turn, not sure what his reaction would be. When he did turn, his weight sank on her, digging lower and lower into her body. It was not sex, not intercourse, only the full pressure of his skin and smell.

He made a sound deep in his throat, and she bit him there. She guided him into her, wrapping herself around him, needing his weight as a shield against the storm, against, she knew, the loneliness. She felt like an animal, small and afraid, burrowing under him, prying him loose from the ground to escape in his shadow.

His muscles tightened. She held him close, knowing it was a way to hold herself. The rain drifted farther away, dried by the hot tent of the blankets.

The heat was already on the dump by the time Franken-
stein woke. He did not move at first. He remained still, his
eyes shaded by the red band around the telephone booth.
His sweat rolled freely, chiggering his skin. His eyes

opened, but his mind was stone. Memory pushed, faded. A nerve reacted to some unfelt pressure in his wrist, and he sensed his finger jumping, once, twice, the knuckle hitting glass. He pressed his finger against his side, running it smoothly up the seam of his pants leg.

He sat up after a while, his eyes already searching the dump. Tin glistened. Broken glass held light on razored edges. He climbed out slowly, stood, pushed the folding door shut over the blankets. He was hungry. He built a small fire at the edge of the clearing, feeding it sticks and paper until he had coals. He filled an old teakettle with water from his canteen, added coffee grounds, then set it on the fire. The smell started a few minutes later, and he bent over it, breathing slowly. He put more sticks around the base of the kettle and watched the flames leap up, a yellow dance in white sunlight. He went off to the left of the camp and urinated. When he came back, the coffee was boiling. He looped a coat hanger over the handle and swung the kettle in a large circle over his head. When he was sure the grounds had settled at the bottom, he put the kettle back on the fire. He poured himself a cup. He added whiskey, stirring it with his finger. He flicked the finger dry and took a sip, tasting the coffee, flat and dull, the whiskey playing. He cleared his throat, feeling his sinuses loosen. He spit to one side, then took another drink, hearing, almost before the sounds were perceptible, the squad car coming. It slowed to a crawl, and he wondered if they thought they could surprise him. Two doors slammed. He squatted closer to the fire, feeding it stray bits of sticks when his fingers found them.

—Tommy? someone called.

A second voice said:—I smell coffee.

Frankenstein rose to see the two patrolmen coming, picking their way through the debris. They both wore flat brimmed hats, reflector sunglasses. Cuffs jingled from their belts. Guns buggy-creaked in their holsters. Their uniforms were bluish green.

—Tommy? Sergeant Peters yelled.

Frankenstein stood. He hawked and spit toward the cemetery. Whiskey phlegm coated his throat. He watched the two patrolmen split apart, ready, he realized, for attack or defense.

—Tommy, Peters said. He stood in front of Frankenstein, lining his toes up. —I thought you were coming in today for a talk.

The other patrolman circled, looking over the camp. Frankenstein didn't recognize him.

—Tommy, you really stepped in it this time. That woman was on the Historic Preservation Committee. Her kind don't like to see pigeons killed, you understand me? She wants us to bring you in. Now Captain Walker talked her out of it, but if she sees you do anything like that again, we'll have to come get you. The captain wants you to stay out of town, hear? You can come in to sell to Farley in the evenings, but that's it, huh?

Frankenstein nodded. The second officer still circled behind him. Frankenstein turned and watched him nudge a bag of feathers with his boot toe. Two greenheads came off it, buzzing. The officer shook his head.

—Christ, he said.

—George, Peters said, then stopped.

Frankenstein spit again. It came too close to the new officer. He turned and squinted at Frankenstein.

—You dumb fucking animal, he said.

—George, Peters said.

—You hold your goddamn spit or I'll stick it right back down your throat.

Frankenstein felt his muscles tighten, his blood rise.

Then he calmed himself. But the officer was red-faced. He could not see the man's eyes.

—Come on, George, Peters said.

—Fucking animal, the officer said, this time slurring the words. He walked after Peters. He kicked the coffee off the small fire, said:—No fires here either, asshole.

Frankenstein patted his pockets. Feathers, rocks, slingshot, knife. He moved back into the shade. He watched the two cops talking, the new one gesturing. A garbled voice called over the radio. The doors slammed, and the giant antenna whipped back and forth with the chuck of the car.

The next day Noel stirred sugar into his coffee. He watched Kathy working near the sink. He listened to the water running, the stream broken now and then by the sound of washing. He heard a cake tin go under, then a glass. He lit a cigarette and watched her set dishes in the drainer.

"What time is Grant coming?" she asked.

"Pretty soon. Why?"

"I was hoping you'd take care of the bird first. Would you?"

"Sure."

"What do you think did it?" she asked.

"Did what?" he asked. "The bird?"

"Yes."

"I don't know."

She turned and glanced over her shoulder. She said: "It's not normal for the feathers to be gone, is it?"

"I don't think so. But you said there were ants, right?"

"What would they do with feathers? I've never seen a bird like that before."

He stood and carried his plate to the sink. He handed it to her, blowing the smoke from his cigarette away from her. He paused a moment, feeling the warmth rise from the sink. It steamed despite the heat.

"I don't think we should go fishing," he said.

"Why not? Grant wants to."

"Still . . ." he started, not quite clear.

"Go ahead. You should get away from the house."

He shifted his feet and asked: "What are you going to do?"

"I'm going to go downtown. I'll be home early."

"All right then, if you're sure."

He waited, thinking there was more to say. He couldn't convince himself things began again so easily. He had slept the night away, drunk, barely remembering Kathy's coming to bed, her warmth, the soft pull of her flesh. He hadn't dreamed. He had been afraid of dreaming.

"I wish you'd take care of that bird," she said.

He crossed the kitchen and stepped out onto the back porch. He could see silver lines thrown by inchworms, their strands catching the light whenever the wind stirred them. There were broken branches and twigs scattered all over the lawn. The heat was building. It came up from the earth, moist, humid, the grass matted as if to smother it.

He stepped down off the porch and walked to the pool, his ears tuned to the insect hum now muted by dampness. He saw the pink corpse waiting exactly where Kathy had said, the pale wings partially covered by pine needles. He stepped to the hedge and poked the bird with the toe of his shoe. The bird arched up. He moved back and stared at the body. He saw the thin line of ants moving to a brown mound a few feet away.

He stood on one leg and kicked the ground with his heel.

He kicked again, the dirt giving way. When the impression was deep enough, he nudged the bird into it. The ants scattered. With the side of his shoe, he scraped dirt onto the bird, covering it. He tamped the mound with his sole, feeling the body give and splinter. He thought he heard a squeak come from the bird's mouth, the hollow cavity of the body giving up air, but he couldn't be sure. He bent close to the soil and took up two handfuls of needles. He sprinkled them over the mound, careful to make it look natural. When he was finished, he stood away and appraised the job. The bird was gone.

He backed out of the pines. He saw the stack of rocks near the barbecue pit and walked to it. The rain had turned the cement gray. He stopped breathing and listened to the cement absorbing water. He checked his pockets for cigarettes. A breeze blew behind him, and he heard the drops going from leaf to leaf.

"Did you find it?" Kathy asked. She was standing on the back steps, her arms crossed.

"It's gone."

"It was strange, wasn't it? I mean, the feathers plucked like that?"

"Probably the ants."

"Do you really think so?"

"I don't know."

Kathy started to go back into the house, then stopped. She said: "I can make you all some sandwiches. What kind would you like?"

"Don't bother."

"It's no bother."

"What kind do you have?"

"Almost anything. There are a lot of cold cuts left."

"Roast beef?" he asked.

"Mayonnaise?"

"Please," he said.

She went into the house. He walked back to the pool, sat on the edge of a lawn chair, and lit a cigarette. He thought of the bird again, its neck twisted. The ants, he knew, hadn't taken the feathers. He tried to think of an animal that would take the feathers and leave the flesh, but there wasn't one.

He stood. He walked back to the pine hedge and squatted, reaching out a hand to support himself. He bent lower, checking under the branches. To his left he saw two footprints in the mud, one coming, one going. The prints were made by large boots. He pushed into the pine branches, seeing more prints the farther he penetrated. Some were blurred, smeared by rain or an indecisive step. Others were clearer, freshly made, the ridges of the boot sole still visible.

The branches slapped him as he crawled back out. He felt his mind clearing, touched alternately by fear and anger. Slowly he worked around the pool, noting the footprints, trying to see the man's motion. It was like following a dance pattern on a cement floor, the feet going in odd directions. They circled the cabana, then came back to the dark side of the pool. For a moment Noel imagined the man still lurking in shadows, watching the house, waiting.

"Noel?" Kathy called.

He looked up and saw her calling from the kitchen window, her head turned to shout through the screen. She said: "Grant's out front. Should I tell him to come around?"

"No, I'll be right there. Are the sandwiches ready?"

"Just about."

Noel watched Kathy pull away from the window. He thought suddenly: He watches her.

Kathy watched the pigeons ducking around her bench, their necks shiny with light. She threw a crumb from the cookie she had been eating and saw the birds scatter for a moment before falling on it. They reminded her of water, a ripple. When the traffic let up, she could hear their beaks pecking on the cement.

She glanced at the church steeple and read the time. It was almost noon. The traffic was increasing. She watched a woman dressed in a flowered skirt cross the street. The woman was carrying shopping bags, and Kathy tried to guess what she had bought. She thought of the groceries she had purchased earlier baking in the trunk of the car. The bread would be warm. She had deliberately avoided the dairy case so she wouldn't have to worry about perishables. Nothing would spoil.

Two men moved to a bench near her. The closer one began talking about the baby boom and the fall in real estate. He said: "Remember when they were short of teachers? Now teachers can't find a job. Two schools closed in this county alone last year. If there are fewer people, it only stands to reason we'll need less housing, right? That has to be right, doesn't it?"

Kathy tuned them out, concentrating, instead, on their colognes. She smelled Old Spice and something equally familiar, but the name wouldn't come to her. She tried to watch them from the corner of her eye, saw only muted colors, ties, pin stripes. The man farther from her was staring straight ahead, his legs stretched out in front of him. She heard business words: *deal, open house, party, loan, options.*

She threw the last crumbs to the pigeons and stood. She

began walking away from the car. She didn't want to go back to the house. She passed two storefronts and continued walking, conscious of the heat. She came to three circular racks set out on the sidewalk and stopped to browse. She flicked through the summer skirts, occasionally rubbing the material through her fingers. A woman on the other side said: "Purple is the color this year. It's in all the magazines."

"I know," a customer said, "but I hate it. It makes me look like an Easter egg."

"No, it won't. Look at this."

Kathy waited to hear more, but she could no longer make out the words. A bus passed. She saw the two businessmen who had been seated near her walk by, still talking, the taller one gesturing.

She let a skirt fall back into place and started to the car. She passed the hardware store and watched a man carrying a bag of grass seed out to a station wagon. An old woman opened the tailgate for him, saying: "The grass in back is all burned out, you know, Mr. Farley?" The man smiled, nodding his head. Kathy stared for a moment at the flies hooked into his hat—reds and greens, black ants, flying bugs. She saw the sun play on each insect, stirring it alive, making his head seem to crawl.

"Hi," the man said, and wiped his hands on his jeans. Kathy nodded. The old woman slammed the tailgate shut and reached into her purse.

Kathy hurried to the car, checking the clock as she walked. Inside the car she could smell faintly the bread from the back, a bakery smell. The vegetables were going over. She knew they would be softened, sweating. She leaned across the seat and rolled down the window. As she straightened, she picked up a manila folder she had placed neatly on the passenger seat. She flipped it open and read the résumé, surprised, as always, to see her experiences written down, contained on one sheet of paper. She pulled the car into traffic after carefully replacing the folder. She tried to remember a shortcut Noel had shown her but couldn't. She followed a slow line of traffic, her thighs taking the heat of the upholstery. Each time she was forced to stop, the air stilled. She fiddled with the radio, trying to find music, but all she could get was news. She turned it off and dangled her free hand out the window. She pressed her palm flat against the side of the door, traced the chrome strip with her fingers, finding it hotter than the paneling. The ball of her thumb touched a rust spot, and she chipped at it, her mind thankful for the diversion.

She turned at the first corner and pressed the accelerator quickly, trying to make a second light. She had to go through the orange. A car coming from the other direction honked, though it was in no danger, had not started across the intersection. The horn startled her, and she drove more carefully. She felt thirsty. She glanced at herself in the mirror and saw a white film coating her lips. She licked them and watched, between quick looks to the road, the whiteness returning, her lips cracked by fissures of dryness.

She drove a mile before seeing the junior high school. There were only five or six cars in the parking lot, and she pulled in beside a green Buick. As soon as she turned off the engine, she felt the heat coming off the pavement, saw the glare sent up by white lines painted for foursquare, bike tests, stickball. She picked up the manila folder and climbed out, smoothing her skirt, feeling suddenly apprehensive, secretive. She had not told Noel of the appointment—had not known herself, when she made the call that morning, exactly what she was doing—and now felt guilty because of it. It seemed an act of small treason, and she wondered what she would say if they offered her a job. It didn't seem likely. People did not get jobs so easily, yet it

was possible, and she tried to organize her mind, to prepare.
As she crossed the parking lot, she reviewed her job experi-
ence and found the answers came simply. She was qualified.
She decided not to worry.

She paused at the door, leaning against the pressure bar
for a moment, seeing beyond it the long, dark hallways
identical to hundreds around the state, the country. Scraps
of paper blew along the base of the building, rolling with
leaf sounds, finally pressing themselves against a window
grate. In the same instant a feeling of defeat enveloped her,
loss, and she thought: I have not escaped this. As she
pushed open the door and entered, the feeling was compounded, and she stood blinking in the dimness, suddenly
dizzy. She leaned forward against the tile wall and let the
coolness work into her temples. Thoughts continued to
come in confusing waves. She remembered, suddenly, her
own school days, a December, the halls long-shadowed, the
smell of steam heat and paper, while she cleaned out her
locker for the holidays. Bending over the pile of accumula-
tion, she had heard the clocks ticking, minutes passing from
wall to wall, checked off with electrical accuracy which was
not at all dehumanizing, but comfortable, warm. She had
closed the locker door and walked out, down through long
hallways emptying in shouts and screams of release, wrapping herself in winter clothes as she approached the doors.
Finally, she had pushed out into the evening only to find
the flagpole bare, the rope hitting it repeatedly, the metal
sound passing into the sky, the paved driveway. She recalled
standing beside it, taking off her glove to try to still it,
while teachers shouted to one another, their cars starting
like barking dogs, and she had felt, perhaps for the first
time, utter loneliness.

Now here it was again. Even as she pushed back from
the wall, she felt it. She tried to calm herself, but it was no

use. She looked up to see the hallways stretching out in gray stone, the lockers standing like sentinels along the wall. She knew what it would be. She did not have to enter. She could picture, without moving, the mute classrooms, their incompleteness when empty, the boards cleaned and black. She knew the shades would be drawn almost to the sill. Passing from room to room, the sun would be banded, interrupted only by the dividing walls, stretched until it appeared as light seen from a train window. There would be a wax smell, a janitor somewhere mopping in endless routine, the cement floors actually smoothed by his mop in combination with hundreds, thousands of feet sneakered and pumped.

She could not enter, though: This is defeat. She backed out, clutching the folder to her chest. She ran down the front steps, feeling a sense of panic, knowing again the schoolgirl thrill of dismissal. She laughed aloud, suddenly on the edge of hysteria, defeat and joy mingled. She threw the folder onto the seat and climbed in after it. She started the engine and slipped it in gear. She pressed too hard on the gas and felt the tires spin for a second on gravel. Then they caught, and she jumped off, a shock in the front of the car rocking without oil. She drove without thinking. The front yards passed, each blinking by in a quick vision of porches and houseplants. She saw an ice-cream truck pulled to the side of the road, a line of kids waiting. On impulse she stopped. She searched her purse for a dollar, laughing again, feeling crazy, yet enjoying it. She climbed out. A small girl was yelling at her brother to choose. Another boy was passing out gum.

"What can I get you?" the driver asked. He was about nineteen, dressed in a T-shirt and cutoffs. The T-shirt had a picture of a donkey and just above it a line of print which said: KISS MY.

"I want a Good Humor," she said.

"You mean a chocolate cover?"

"Just chocolate on the outside and vanilla inside. Don't tell me they don't make them anymore."

"They do, they do. They're called chocolate covers now," the driver said and spun away. Kathy watched his legs as he bent into the freezer and pulled out the ice cream.

"Thirty-five," he said.

Kathy handed him a dollar. He threw it into a shoe box and made change from a silver holder looped on his belt. He put the money in her palm, smiling as their skin touched.

"Anything else?" he asked.

"No, thanks."

She unwrapped the ice cream and threw the paper in the mouth of a clown painted on the door of the truck. Below it was written: WRAPPER SNAPPER. The driver began talking to some kids, telling them about a contest he was running. She took a bite of the ice cream, letting the cold sink into her before she tasted it.

She walked back to her car, feeling steadier. The ice cream dripped down the sides. A piece of chocolate broke free and fell on the ground. She pulled open her door, careful to keep the ice cream straight up. She saw two bikes skid in front of her, the boys laughing. She tried to remember if she had been as reckless on her bike when she was their age. She didn't think so. She watched them ride off, making motorcycle sounds, shifting imaginary gears as they pedaled.

She started the car and pulled out. She steered with one hand and ate with the other. When she was finished, she threw the stick out the window. She watched it in the rear-view mirror bounce once and then stop.

Three blocks farther along she braked to take the turn

into the driveway. As she stopped near the garage, she watched the house. It was empty. She got out of the car and opened the trunk. The groceries felt warm in her arms. She put her nose against the brown paper and smelled it. It reminded her of childhood, of carrying packages in to her mother.

She set the bags down on the back steps and dug in her purse for her keys. She pulled open the screen door. As she reached to insert the key, her foot hit something soft. She glanced down, expecting to see the paper. Instead, it was the body of a small rodent, skinned, the head crushed.

She backed away, knocking the bag on her left off the steps. She heard cans fall, paper rattle. A tomato rolled onto the brown lawn. For a second it looked like a croquet ball rolling smoothly.

Noel stood close to the counter, watching the bait man ladle sea worms from a cardboard box. The worms came up black, stretching their pinchers. The bait man handled them delicately.

He said: "Don't hurt you, but I don't like the feel of them. Never got used to it."

"I know what you mean," Noel said.

The bait man wiped his nose and put his handkerchief aside. His nose continued to run. He sniffed, then reached for the handkerchief again.

"Fish them off the bottom?" Noel asked.

"Just about. You might want to tease them. You'll catch a lot of crap fish anyways. Tommycod and clowns. Bridge fishing's for niggers."

"Can you do anything with the fish?"

The man was putting the top back on the box. Noel set two dollars on the counter.

"Tommycod makes a nice chowder," the man said. "Too much flesh for anything else. They're all flesh and grease. The clowns are just a nuisance."

The man sprinkled water on the box and stuck it back in the refrigerator. He turned back and took the two dollars. He rang it up on an old cash register. A picture of a woman in a red bikini was glued to the side. Her legs were torn off.

"That it?" the man asked.

Noel looked around the room, thinking there might be something they needed. It was part family room, part office. There were hooks on the center beam in the ceiling. The counter was part glass. More hooks were arranged on spotted green felt at the bottom.

"I think so," Noel said. "I don't think we need anything."

"There you go then." The man pushed a small container at Noel. It was a box for Chinese food. A stamp on the side read: POLYNESIAN GARDENS.

Noel took the package and stepped outside. An old Irish setter stood, its legs and hips arthritic. It sniffed the sea worms, then lay back down. It snorted once and crawled on its belly to a patch of sunlight.

"You get them?" Grant asked inside the car.

"Sure."

Grant opened the box. Noel started the car and pulled out the driveway. He saw the bait man come out of his office and look after them. The dog rolled onto its side.

"I've never understood why these things have pinchers," Grant said. "You?"

"I don't know. Maybe to hold onto the kelp on the bottom."

Grant pushed back in his seat. He had asked Noel to

drive. His eyes looked red and puffy, and Noel wondered if
Grant's grief was deeper than his own. He couldn't concentrate on the question. He lit a cigarette and tried to
figure out why he had come. He didn't want to fish. He
started to say so, then rolled the window lower. Grant
pushed a box of doughnuts across the seat between them.

"Aren't you going to eat any?" Grant asked.

"Not right now."

"Christ, I love those big things. The bullfrogs. I like the
cinnamon."

Noel nodded. The car was suddenly on the bridge grating. The tires made a low hum. Water looped out on both
sides of the bridge. Noel leaned closer to the window. Grant
pushed a button on the radio, then turned it off.

"Right here," Grant said.

Noel eased the car off the road. He parked it in a picnic
area. Near a patch of sumac there was a sign saying: NO
PARKING AFTER SUNSET. He got out of the car and held the
door open while he lifted the poles from the back seat. A
hook swung free and caught the foam of the dashboard.

"Grant, come here for a second, will you?"

"What?"

"Here, take these."

He handed the poles out, still working to free the hook.
Grant's shadow made it difficult to see. Noel knelt on the
seat and leaned closer. His cigarette dropped and rolled
under the seat. He cursed and finally retrieved it. He
yanked the hook out as he straightened. A small piece of
foam splintered from the dashboard.

"Shit," he said.

"What's wrong? Do you have the worms?"

"I've got everything."

Grant moved off to the sumac and pissed. Noel put the
worms on the roof and closed the door. The poles were

leaning against the trunk. He took a last drag from the cigarette and threw it away. Grant came back, zipping up his fly.

"You all set?" he asked.

"Yep."

"Won't be able to piss off the bridge. Too many cars."

"I don't have to piss," Noel said.

"It's a long walk back here."

"For God's sake, Grant."

"All right. I'm just telling you. You start pissing off the bridge and the salmon try to swim right up it."

Noel laughed and started walking close to the railing. A truck passed and almost blew the worms from his hand. He smelled oil, exhaust. Over it all was the rank odor of wild daisies mixing with kelp. Yellow tansy covered the hills below the bridge.

The tide was coming in. Through the grating Noel could see the current ripping at the bridge pilings. The water looked green under the bridge, blue beyond. A thin film of foam covered the rocks along the shore. There was a separate line for each segment of the tide, each marking where the water had reached. Noel thought it looked somehow like the rings of trees.

"Here?" Grant asked.

"Okay."

Noel squatted and helped Grant arrange the tackle. He opened the sea-worms and put one on the cement walkway. He severed the head with a rusty jackknife. The pinchers continued to open and close.

"It's not too cold," Grant said. "I was afraid it might be too cold over the water."

"It's nice."

"I just wanted to fish."

Grant smiled. Noel realized it was his way of explaining.

He felt a moment of tenderness for Grant. Thought: My brother, as if no other phrase could signify as much. He rocked back on his heels and watched Grant bait his hook. Grant skewered the worm, feeding the metal up through the body. The worm tried to back off it, each section of its body undulating.

Grant stood and put the pole over the rail. The reel made a whining noise as the sinkers carried the line to water. When the line stopped, Grant switched the drag. He stood staring out, his eyes not even watching his line.

Noel baited his own hook and let his line drop. He switched the drag when it reached bottom. He leaned the pole against the railing and took out a cigarette. He turned his back to the water, protecting the match from the breeze. His hands were cold. He had to strike three matches before he could coordinate his mouth and hands.

"At least it's cool here," Grant said.

"You just said it was warm a minute ago."

"You know what I mean."

"It's been hot," Noel said, turning back to the water. Grant was slowly reeling in his line. Noel propped his elbows on the railing and watched. He heard someone shouting farther along the bridge and turned to see a group of boys fishing. They had something landed and were kicking it, silver flashing in sunlight.

Noel said: "What's the word from Bogotá? Anything?"

"I almost forgot to tell you. We're going down in a couple of days—around the first of July. It didn't look good, having to put off the trip that way. A couple my friend knows got a little girl."

"So you would have had a girl? I thought it was supposed to be a boy?"

"I don't know. I guess it would have been a girl."

"I'm sorry it didn't work out."

"Well, we'll get one. We've been waiting a long time. Mary was upset. She was sure they wouldn't give us another chance. It makes you wonder, doesn't it? Talk about fate."

"How?"

"Just that the little girl would have had a different life with us than she will with the other couple. Not better or worse, just different. Now we might get another baby, and that's a whole other thing. You never know—wait a second," Grant said. He stopped reeling. Then: "A bite."

"Are you kidding?"

"No, look."

Grant's line was jerking. Grant lowered the tip of his rod and waited. The line was still. Grant cursed but then yanked the rod straight up.

"Got it," he said.

The line was cutting the water now, snapping back and forth. Noel saw the silver of the fish coming up through the water. Grant was reeling faster. The tail thrashed as it came free, dangling in their shadows as they bent over the railing.

"Shit," Grant said. It was a clown fish.

"They hang around the pilings," Noel said.

"I hate the cocksuckers. Do we have a cloth? I hate to touch them."

"Nope, no cloth."

"They are fucking scaly. Look at that mouth."

Grant held the fish over the bridge and tried to work the hook free. The fish squeaked. Grant seemed afraid to touch it. He tried to hold its tail between two fingers, but the fish kept getting loose.

"What did we call these things?" he asked Noel.

"Clowns?"

"No, after we unhooked them. You know. When the insides came out. It was something like gunner, brunner."

"Gummers," Noel said, remembering the word.

"No teeth, right? Gummers, that's it."

Grant set the fish on the cement and put his boot over it. He tugged gently. The hook came free with the fish jaws still intact. "A gummer," Grant said. "I knew it."

Noel started laughing, watching Grant kick the fish back in the water. There was a three-second count before it finally splashed. Grant said again: "I hate those things."

Noel turned back to his own line. He thought about reeling it in to check the bait but decided not to. He was enjoying the warmth, the sun coming off the water. He unzipped his jacket. The smell of water was not as strong now. The tide was climbing the shore, covering each ring of foam a little at a time. Beside him, Grant baited his hook again, saying from a squat position: "Noel, what are you going to do now? Any ideas?"

"I don't know."

"Think you'll go back to Africa?"

"I'm not sure. There was a guy at the funeral, maybe you know him, Carl Soltis?"

"I've heard of him."

"He more or less offered me a job in Lagos, Nigeria. It would be a lot of money."

"Are you going to take him up on it?"

"I'm going to talk to him. Africa's the frontier now. There's a lot of money to be made."

"I didn't know you were so interested in money."

"I'm not. I just thought it would be an angle you'd approve of."

Grant laughed. He stood up and dropped his line over the railing. "What about Kathy?" he asked. "What does she want?"

"She wasn't happy there."

"And so?"

Noel tried to think. He wondered, briefly, if Kathy had put Grant up to questioning him. But it would have been unlike her. He thought it was more probable Grant had seen it on his own, had seen Kathy's discomfort, the weariness that had slowly shredded through the time at home.

"I think," Noel said, "she might leave me if I want to go back. She might just stay here."

"Would you want that? Maybe want is the wrong word. Would you, what—settle for it?"

"Do I have a choice?"

"You always do, don't you?"

"I don't know if you always do. I've been thinking some sort of compromise might be possible. If I took a job in Lagos, at least it would be a city. She won't go back to the bush, I know that. Maybe she'd live in a city."

"Have you asked her?"

"Not yet."

"Why wouldn't you stay here?"

Noel ignored the question a moment, trying to think. He wanted to say: I am empty here, yet he could not explain it, could not bring it past words that sounded too simple. He said: "It's not for me. It never has been."

"Isn't that a little strong?"

"Maybe, I don't know."

Silence came. Noel listened to the tide lapping. In the distance he saw a motorboat jumping across the water, the engine, throttled by waves, giving off the sound of a power saw finding the grain of some wood tightly woven. He felt incomplete, felt the conversation should have gone on, though he could not continue it. He thought: Hearing my own words, I would know, believing suddenly that insight which could not be gained in thought would be provided in words said aloud. To distract himself, he reeled slowly, feeling the tug of the hook as it worked along the sandy bottom, imagining as he reeled the floor of the bay—kelp-sweet, the worm rolling in the current, touching old metal, beer cans, while the flounder swam in flat strokes, its body pressed by the pressure of water and adaptation. He remembered once standing in the same spot years ago, Grant and another boy beside him, when the water suddenly came alive. A school of flounder covered the entire area, rolling to the surface, catching the sun, the natural size of the school doubled, trebled, all of them following the tide and the ride of incoming fish, debris, their flat heads mowing the bottom, threshing it while animal eyes searched in dimness. It had been amazing, a dance of sun and light, perhaps, he had thought then, even a trick of eyesight. But the fish had continued to roll, the green water lathered, trampled beneath the throbbing fins of a sea herd set to graze on new pasture. Together they had set hooks frantically, trying to capture something that could not be captured.

It occurred to him now to remind Grant of the day, thinking it was an answer to Grant's question, because his sense of wonder then was what he now sought and could not find in the States. He almost said: It is too complicated here, unsure whether Grant would understand, whether he himself understood. He was on the verge of speaking when Grant interrupted, saying: "Christ, look at that."

Noel turned just as the boys along the bridge began to yell. One of them had thrown up a fish, or dangled it, Noel couldn't tell which. A sea gull had taken it, not seeing the line, and was now flying with the filament stringing behind it. The boy jerked the rod, and the sea gull dipped. The boy let the line out again, and the sea gull climbed, squawking, black wedges on its wings. Noel saw another boy reach out and tug the line. The sea gull spun and fell. It was a perverse form of kite flying.

"Hey," Noel yelled, but the boys ignored him.

Noel began walking. He watched them jerking the gull across the water. It was being towed, its neck stretched out, its feet paddling madly against the waves. The boys were yelling louder.

Noel shouted again. This time one of the boys turned to face him. Noel saw a hurried conference, heard one of the boys say: Here he comes.

And then the gull was in the air again. The boys were standing with open faces, innocent, two of them backing away. Noel walked faster. He was conscious of Grant behind him. The gull was squawking louder, circling, its flight unsteady.

"It just took it," one of the boys said when Noel was close enough. Another boy laughed. Noel reached out and put his hand on the closest boy's shoulder. He squeezed, letting his fingers dig under the muscles.

The boy squirmed, and Noel felt himself squeezing harder, enjoying the pain, the punishment.

"Hey," the boy said. "Hey, mister, you're hurting me."

"Cut the line," Noel said.

"Noel, okay. Noel," Grant said behind him.

"Cut the line."

"Who do you think you are?" the boy who had laughed said. But he was stepping forward with a knife.

"Cut it."

The boy cut the line. Noel saw the gull dip. It glided to the water, tucked, and sat on a wave. It sat in the water, its head low from the weight of the sinker. It rode the crests of the small chop, whiteness surrounded by blue.

Frankenstein stood at the back of the store, looking in. He saw polished wood floors, rubbed white by boot soles. There were rakes, shovels, and clippers hanging from the wall. He walked carefully between the aisles, arms in, elbows against his sides. He could see Farley counting money out of the register, dropping pennies onto a green nippled mat.

—I'll be with you, Farley said, looking up for just a second. Frankenstein patted his pockets, checking the feathers again.

He stepped to the glass counter of flies. The hooks were embedded in black felt. They stared up at him, wet flies, dry flies. He could name only a few, though his eyes took in color, thinking of animals to match.

—Shit, all right. What do you got?

Frankenstein held out the bags of feathers: white, black, the skin of a squirrel, red from a cardinal, brown from the back of a hedgehog.

—You owed me fifty, right? I'll give you five bucks for the whole mess, okay?

Frankenstein nodded. He set the skins on the counter, the feathers on top. —Here, Farley said, passing the bill. Frankenstein took it and rolled it into a tube. He backed out, passing the wheelbarrows of nails and screws. Farley mumbled something, but Frankenstein didn't hear.

He pushed out the door, returning to night, a gray sky. There was an early-evening feed of people shopping. He passed through them, keeping his eyes straight ahead, thinking that if eyes met, eyes locked. He walked, brick underneath and curling up the walls. There was no wind, and he felt the town pulled to stillness. The burnt odor of

popcorn came to him. It was a carnival smell, rich, somehow suggesting movement. He followed it, crossing the
street, picking up his stride again. He spotted the liquor
store and tapped the money tube in his pocket. He slowed
then, pretending interest in a window display while a
woman passed, a second, their paper bags snapping with
efficiency. He heard a sound above him and looked up to
see a fat man leaning out his window, smoking a cigar.

He moved on, finally coming to rest outside the liquor
store. He stood in darkness, watching the tambourine lady.
He could hear her shaking it as a man passed through the
doors, her voice saying:—God bless, God bless. He listened
to the tambourine shake, the money shake, the woman in
dark blue.

Breathing deeply, he walked in. He blinked at the harsh
electric light, the rows and rows of bottles. He turned his
head away so he wouldn't have to look at her. But he could
still feel her, shaking, tapping, clucking. He searched for
whiskey. He watched the woman in the shoplifting mirrors,
seeing her round, hawk-faced, different in each glance. She
was humming. She was religious, shaking her tambourine,
Salvation Army written on her hat.

He carried the whiskey to the cash register. He handed
the salesman the bill, listened as he said:—Two thirty-eight.
His mind was on the Salvation Army lady, clinking, holy.

He took the bottle and closed his eyes. He squinted
against the electric light, the money warm in his hand. He
heard the tambourine shake and in one motion dropped a
quarter into the woman's lap. —God bless, he heard. —God
bless.

Kathy felt the sun on her back. She had been standing on the porch, not moving, her eyes on the skinned body. It was a squirrel. She was certain it was a squirrel. She saw the muscles in the thighs, the rounded ears, the short front paws.

The squirrel was between her and the back door. She was afraid to come closer to it. It lay on its stomach. She believed for a second it was still alive. She could see the muscles too cleanly, the compact body coiling. She was frightened not of its attacking, but of its trying to move at all. She was not sure what she would do if one paw stirred forward, one muscle twitched.

But it is dead, she told herself.

Slowly she backed down the steps. Groceries were scattered across the walk. She picked them up, stuffing each item back into the brown bag, then lifted the bag away from the porch. She stood and saw a branch that had been knocked down in the storm. She picked it up and stood on the bottom step.

She thought of flies. She was worried about flies coming, settling on the naked body. She remembered greenheads she had seen once covering a dead animal in the road. The memory was unclear, and she forced herself to forget it, at the same time reaching forward with the branch.

She touched the squirrel in the midsection and saw it bend. The body was slack. She wedged the branch under it and tried to flick it off the porch. The squirrel did an uneven somersault and ended up on its back. She closed her eyes and scraped the branch along the cement. She felt it hit something, then heard the squirrel fall into the bushes.

She opened her eyes and waited, almost prepared to have the squirrel come to life, almost expecting it.

She stood still a moment, then grabbed the groceries. The vegetables were soft. She held the bag to one side and climbed the steps. She opened the door quickly, grabbed the second bag of groceries, and stepped inside. She locked the door and put the groceries on the kitchen table.

She went to the sink and washed her hands, letting the water run over her wrists, rubbing them softly together. A headache was beginning in her right temple. She could feel it expanding, filling her skull. She bent close to the sink and splashed water on her face. She patted her forehead. When she stood, the water dripped down her shirt.

Still wet, she put away the groceries. She listened to the house, listened to her own sounds. She heard her breath wheeze slightly, caught and strained by some congestion in her lungs. Bottles rattled in the refrigerator when she closed the door. Paper crinkled; the floor creaked. She was aware of creating noise for her own benefit. She felt her nerves close to her skin. Her mind suddenly centered on the fact she was alone. She slowed at this, standing silently in the middle of the kitchen. The house settled around her, producing old sounds, noises that went on unperceived every day. She thought it possible houses had their own lives, separate and apart from those who lived in them. She cleared her throat and heard the sound echo, pool in the corners of the kitchen.

The phone rang in the same instant, making her breathe quickly. She exhaled as it rang again, timing her breathing to the sound of the ring. She crossed the kitchen and picked up the receiver.

"Kathy?" Mary asked.

"Hi, Mary."

"I was just calling to see if they were over at your place."

"No, they're not back yet."

"Okay. Do you know when they'll be back?"

"No idea, really," Kathy said. "Not late."

"All right. I just wanted to check."

"Good-bye."

Kathy hung up reluctantly. She thought to call Mary back but decided against it. She walked out of the kitchen and climbed the stairs. The banister was warm under her hand. The clock ticked on the wall. She kept her eyes forward, not wanting to see the closed bedroom door.

She stopped in the bathroom and took off her shirt. It was wet from the kitchen sink. She draped it on the doorknob and turned on the water. She put a washcloth on the drain and let the water run over it. When she was sure it was drenched, she bathed herself. She unhooked her bra and put it over the shirt. She wiped her skin, squeezing some of the excess water from the washcloth between her breasts. Her headache retreated.

She put the washcloth back in the sink and turned to the tub. She wanted to powder herself, then nap. Already she could feel the coolness of white sheets, the heat pushed back.

She was near the back of the shower when she saw the man. She stepped behind the curtain, feeling her body tense. The man was stooped under the branches of the pine hedge. He was on one knee. She noticed his eyes were not on the house. He seemed to be staring at the pool.

Then he was moving. He was making his way back through the small copse. Kathy watched him go, ducking under branches, finally jumping the low rock wall. She stood quietly, still pressed behind the curtain.

Three

Frankenstein walked in the calm. He saw the sky turn white far away. He thought: Firecrackers, gun sounds. He put his hand to the bottle in his pocket and unscrewed the cap. He held his thumb over the hole: wetness, the whiskey sloshing. He ducked into the arms of a pine tree and took a quick drink. The whiskey went down, and the first numbness began. Tickling, deadening, it worked deeper.

He screwed the top back on. He watched two squirrels run along a telephone wire, tails outstretched for balance. One squirrel paused to watch him and sent up a chatter when he moved. It did not flee but stood on its back legs, paws curled in prayer, its left eye cocked in his direction. Frankenstein touched the slingshot around his neck, considered. But the squirrel ran off, finding the telephone pole and beginning a spider crawl downward, twisting around in blood knowledge of hunters.

He watched it out of sight, then stepped out of the branches and checked the sidewalk. No one was coming. He moved to the gutter and walked beside it, watching for animals. He kicked the gravel with his boot toes. He felt the insects find him and settle in whirls around his head. Fifty yards up he found a squirrel paper-thin on the road. The pelt was old. He kicked it and watched it skid. He kicked it again, aiming it at an open sewer. The carcass tipped and fell. He stepped closer and saw the squirrel floating on the sludge. Moisture seeped around the edges, turning it black.

He tapped the bottle in his pocket. Thought: Feathers, rocks, slingshot, knife. He walked, letting the numbness take him. He watched the tree branches handing out darkness.

Kathy sliced a tomato, the seeds spilling onto the cutting board. She spread mayonnaise on a piece of rye and arranged the slices neatly. She glanced up and saw darkness beginning in the yard. A firecracker sounded somewhere nearby. It was followed by a string of explosions, the last one delayed by a few seconds. She heard the snap of the diving board and then Noel's splash.

Another firecracker went off. She set the sandwich on a plate and carried it to the kitchen table. She bit into the tomato and felt suddenly nauseated by the mayonnaise. It lined her gums and covered her tongue. She set the sandwich back on the plate and stood to get some iced tea. Noel came in as she was putting it back in the refrigerator.

"Want some?" she asked.

"No, thanks," he said. He rubbed a white towel over his head and sat across the table from her.

"You should take a swim," he said. "The water's perfect right now."

"Maybe later," she said and sat down. Then she asked: "No more dead animals?"

"Nothing. I checked, but there was nothing."

"Did you check for footprints?"

He nodded. "It was just one of those things. Just a strange thing."

"I don't know. I think it was aimed at me."

"Who would do it? Kathy, we've been all through that, haven't we? Who even knows you around here?"

"You don't have to know a person . . ." she said, then stopped. It was useless to go on. They both had been over it time and again. Still, she could not dismiss it. She wondered if he would tell her if there had been footprints. He did not share her fear.

He said: "Do you want to go to the fireworks? Grant asked us to stop by afterward."

"Sure. You?"

"I guess so."

He reached across the table for his cigarettes. Kathy tilted her glass and took an ice cube in her mouth. She let it sting her palate, the sugar dissolving on her tongue.

"Do you want my sandwich?" she asked.

"Don't you?"

"I'm not hungry. It's too hot."

"Let's go to the fireworks then," he said, reaching for the plate. He put an unlit cigarette behind his ear and ate. She held her glass against her stomach, occasionally rubbing the bottom on her thighs.

"Remind me to take the camera to Grant's," she said. "I want to take some pictures of the baby."

"I still can't believe Grant's a father."

"He's been a father for only three days."

She reached and touched his arm. She felt the hair on his forearm, saw it turning lighter. She thought: He is making himself ready for Africa again. He is changing color.

"That's nice," he said.

"Touching you?"

"Yes."

She laughed. She got up from the table and circled it. She stood beside Noel's chair and put her arms around him. She kissed the side of his neck. He took a bite of the sandwich and smiled at her. He held a piece of tomato between his lips.

"You are gross," she said. "Do you know that?"

"Thank you."

He swallowed and kissed her. Two firecrackers went off almost simultaneously. He winked and finished his sandwich. He said: "You know what Grant and I used to do on the Fourth?"

"What?"

"Well." He took her hand and led her back to her seat. He lit a cigarette and said: "We used to spend all year making model airplanes. Then, on the Fourth, we'd string up a clothesline from a tree somewhere and rig it so the planes could slide down. Then we'd put firecrackers in the cockpits and light them. We got a big kick out of seeing them explode."

"Didn't your parents get mad?"

"No, I doubt they even knew about it. Grant knew a kid who went to South Carolina every summer. He'd get us firecrackers. He was one of those fat kids nobody liked but who always had little gimmicks the other guys wanted. I heard later that he'd become a millionaire."

"How?"

"I don't know for sure. He patented some sort of door lock or hinge. One of those things you never hear about but everyone uses. Something like that."

"Is that the story? There's no punch line?"

"That's it. He was a clever little bastard, though."

Noel put out his cigarette and stood. "I'm going to get dressed. Will you be ready?" he asked.

"Sure."

He left the room, his bare feet padding. Kathy went to the sink and washed the few dishes they had dirtied during the day. Outside the window night was closing. More fire-crackers went off at staggered distances from the house, the sound and light peeling the evening back momentarily. As soon as one stopped resonating, another would take its place. She turned the water off and listened more closely. The sounds came at her, mapping out a jagged grid.

She reached behind her and pulled the string for the overhead light. She turned the water back on and began humming tunelessly, letting the hum cover the popping firecrackers. She felt a tension growing in her, and it was futile to try and push her mind from it. The heat swelled around her, and she stood transfixed, her mind covered by half dreams of childish games played through green bushes, the tangled panic of lurches through branches, lawns, while some unseen playmate stalked, attempting to transfer the subtle ostracism of the hunter, of "it." She could recall the feeling, the absolute fear of running with the pack while looking for hiding places, settling into a leafy window well, clutching cover around her, burying herself into the earth, aware even then she was succumbing to atavistic pleasures of flight and pursuit. She recalled a fall moon, smelling the mosquito repellent on her skin, sweat, the grass taint of dirty jeans. She remembered, too, the disappointment when the hunter's feet had gone on, passed her, and she had been left to silence, her energy already gathered for the wild run. She thought it was like that now, for the same sense of the impending hunt was with her, and she could not believe it was really over. The present silence did not comfort her. She felt it cracking, felt the hunt resumed already, thought: Begin, begin, begin.

She was shaken from her thoughts by the stairs creaking behind her. She turned the water off again, suddenly afraid. Noel came in, rolling up the sleeves of his shirt.

"Ready?" he asked. Then: "What's wrong?"

"The fireworks are making me a little nervous. I was thinking of the dead animals."

"Shhh, it's nothing."

"I know it shouldn't be."

He crossed the kitchen and kissed her, then took his cigarettes off the table. He paused by the back door.

"Listen," he said, "they'll start at sundown."

"Okay. I'll be ready in a second."

He went out the back door. She hung the dish towel on the handle of the refrigerator, brushed her hair back from her forehead, then crossed to the sink. She watched Noel light a cigarette and walk to the half-built barbecue pit. She saw him crouch, bend his knees, then bring his hand up quickly. It was an odd gesture, and she watched more closely, trying to see. He swung again, pawing the air. This time she saw a firefly blink a moment before his hand closed on it. She saw the light blink on and off between his fingers, watched him bend to see it. When he opened his hand, the fly remained on his palm. He clutched it again and threw it. The yellow flicker was stretched into a long arc which disappeared finally in the summer lawn.

Noel leaned against a backstop, feeling the wire mesh dig into his back. He watched people moving in streams toward the baseball field. He squinted, blurring the people, mixing them together. He smelled hot dogs, peanuts, cotton candy, pretzels. A urine smell came from the portable toilets set up on the infield. He found himself wanting to smell gunpowder.

He smoked, watched women pushing strollers, men carrying blankets and lawn chairs. Two children walked past, wearing sneakers over footed pajamas. Noel smiled at one and saw it turn and grab its mother's hand. A third child passed, trailing a balloon. The balloon was tied to the child's wrist, jiggling whenever the child looked to see something new.

An ambulance nudged its way through the crowd slowly, its tires crushing paper cups. Noel heard its radio blare once, then stop. A man with a jacket of shiny black material rode on the hood, asking people to move. The jacket read: RESCUE SQUAD.

Noel bounced on the backstop, taking the spring from the metal on his shoulder blades. He felt uncomfortable surrounded by so many people. He stared at the ground and saw legs moving, feet hitting heel first, then heel again. He looked at his arms and saw the silt from the baseball field already finding his pores.

"Noel?" Kathy called. She walked up to him, holding a hot dog in her hand. "Want a bite?"

"No, thanks."

"Are you okay? You're sweating. Are you?"

"I'm fine," he said, bouncing again off the backstop. He

let the spring push him straight up, then said: "We should find a spot."

"We could sit up on the hill, over there."

Noel took the blanket from Kathy's shoulder and cut through the flow of people. Kathy walked slowly, stopping occasionally to bite her hot dog. Noel walked between the blankets of other people until he found an empty place.

He asked: "Here?"

"Sure."

He flapped the blanket out on the grass and watched it settle. The corners curled under, and he worked his way around it, straightening them. He slipped out of his sandals and stepped to the center. He felt the grass pushing up at the blanket, holding it an inch from the ground. He touched it in different places with his bare feet, finding the feeling old and somehow safe.

"Big crowd," Kathy said, sitting. "Sure you don't want a bite?"

"Positive."

Noel sat next to her. He could see where the small rockets were lined up—poles with Roman candles pinned to them. A fire truck was postitioned in the middle of the field. The ambulance had made it to the other side and was roped off beneath a Red Cross sign. The crowd was still coming in, gradually circling a small pond beyond the outfield.

"When does it start?" Kathy asked.

"Soon, I think. As soon as it's completely dark."

"It's getting misty. Look at it rolling in."

Noel glanced at the horizon and saw fog forming. It dipped with the hill, seemed bound by thermal pockets.

"It's going to be thick," he said.

"Look," she said suddenly.

In the distance the sky turned white. A second flash appeared, green, then blue. A few people near them began to clap. Someone said: Must be up in Maine.

Noel leaned back on his elbows. The sky seemed to be lowering on them. He saw lights from the baseball field taking form. The light worked into the darkness, met it a hundred yards above them, then gave way, finally defined. A sea smell came, pushed forward by the tide run of the pond.

"How do you feel?" Kathy asked. "All right?"

"Yep."

"It feels good to be out, doesn't it? I've always liked these kinds of things."

"How come?"

"They feel like a carnival. Just that."

A siren went off, and Noel sat up. He saw a man with a burning taper go to the first rocket. The bottom of the rocket turned white, hissing. It was in the air quicker than Noel had expected. A baby cried. Someone nearby drew in his breath.

The rocket burst in one stage. It was only white. The sparks fell, reflected in the pond, doubling as they approached the ground. Before they hit, another rocket went off. It screamed as it went, part of its sound obscured by a dog barking. It exploded twice, then three more times. The crowd clapped.

"They're loud," Kathy shouted as another one took off.

Noel heard the dog bark again and turned. The dog was a white malamute. It was tethered by a leather strap to a sapling. The dog looked in Noel's direction, and he saw its eyes were blue-white. It barked again.

Two rockets took off. Noel turned back to look at the field and saw the man touch flame to a third. Staggered, the rockets exploded in red, white, and blue. The crowd clapped louder, some people whistling.

Over the noise Noel heard the dog growling. He turned and saw a child tottering toward it. The dog stiffened; then its mouth opened. A white rocket went off, and Noel saw the red mouth, the tongue out. The dog strained at its leash, seeming to laugh, its white eyes taking in light. The child came closer, reaching out, trying to pet it.

Noel rolled into a crouch, then started to run. The dog looked back and forth, gauging the two distances, concentrating on the child. It's fur was whiter in the darkness, but the rockets exploding caught its eyes, revealed the smile. Noel was aware of the dog's intelligence. It was not at all frenzied. It was waiting, silently, backing on its leash, prepared to take the child.

Noel started to shout. He yelled just as the dog lunged. The white lips curled back, and it nipped, its claws digging at the grass. The leash pulled it up just short, and it snapped back toward the tree, still laughing. Only now the child cried. It turned back to the blankets, still walking slowly, a single finger held up. Noel stood frozen, the lights exploding around him.

"Noel?" Kathy said beside him.

"The dog. The kid was headed for it."

"Where?"

"Right there." Noel pointed, but the child was no longer visible.

"Hey, mister," a man in a red hat said to Noel. "Mister?" Noel said: "What?"

"That's the kid's dog. He was just going to pet it."

A few people who had seen what happened began to laugh. The man in the red hat was turning on his blanket, saying: That dog wouldn't hurt that kid. No way. It just loves to play with kids.

"Do you want to go to Grant's now?" Kathy asked. "Why don't we just go to Grant's?"

"I'm fine. Let's just sit down."

Noel followed her back to the blanket. A Roman candle went off, sizzling in bright circles on a brown pole. The crowd inhaled, exhaled. The candle threw sparks, and Noel noticed a fireman spraying the ground beneath it, his hat on the back of his head.

Noel felt Kathy take his hand. His head ached. He rubbed his eyes, then closed them. He let the rockets go off in his own darkness, the light sometimes appearing dimly through his eyelids. He listened to the sounds, the crack of fireworks, the response from the crowd. He thought: I must control this, this will consume me, felt his nerves close, frayed. He thought of his father briefly, saw, once again, the bloodless figure. He was touched by guilt, pain, and he kept his eyes shut, not daring to look in the direction of the dog, the child, the man in the red hat. He knew what he would see if he did. The dog laughing, its cruel mouth open, its eyes locked on his own.

Kathy thought: Venus. She stared at the planet hanging over the trees, watching it fade back in the light of a rocket. She held her breath. She saw the man with the burning taper scurrying from one rocket to another. There was a confusion of sound, hissings, cracks, and then five rockets took off all at once. Then there was only light, a fuse sound in the dead silence while the crowd looked up, waiting, drawing in breath, needing to be released by sound and more light. In the instant before the final explosion a man yelled: Here it comes. Then the sky blinked white, flashed, the five rockets going off on top of one another. The pond glistened and seemed to spin upward. A tree across the field was suddenly illuminated, sketched in charcoal against the still, dark sky. The upturned faces glowed. Kathy heard a long wheeze and saw a black canister spinning to the ground, smoke trailing it, and then a concentration of air as it sucked the night into its density. It exploded in sound. It choked on the sound, then exploded again, louder, echoing, sucking and releasing like a plunger.

As soon as it was gone, a tinny sound system began playing the national anthem. People started to their feet. Blankets fell from laps. Kathy smelled beer, cigarettes, popcorn. A child asked somewhere: Is that all? Is it? The sound system crackled. Kathy listened closely and heard the crickets returning, a frog calling from the pond.

"Let's go," Noel said.

"All right."

Noel folded the blanket and draped it over his shoulder. Kathy slipped on her sandals, her hand touching his arm for balance. The lights from the baseball field were blinking on. The national anthem fell into the shuffling feet, the whines of cranky children.

"I'm going to go home," Noel said close to her.

"What about Grant's?"

"You can take the car over there. I'll walk."

"I don't want to go without you."

Noel shrugged. He said: "Really, I'd just like to walk. Do you mind?"

"No," she said, trying to think, picturing him lifting off the blanket and running toward the dog. "No, of course not."

Kathy walked beside him until they reached the street. A traffic cop waved them across. Noel stopped and stepped to one side, up onto a lawn, to let people pass. He took the blanket off his shoulder and refolded it.

"Here you go," he said, handing it to her.

She took it and held it against her chest. It smelled of grass and sand. It reminded her of autumn, of carrying leaves to a large pile, the wool warm and scratchy on her skin. Noel leaned down and kissed her. The wool pressed between them. "See you later," he said. "Do you have a key?"

"For the back."

"Okay," he said and began walking.

Kathy watched him go. His back moved into the crowd. She saw him cut diagonally across the road. He moved more quickly than the other people, slicing through them, dodging, alert. She felt a mixture of abandonment and concern for Noel, thought: He is quivering, anyone can see that. But she was not sure what she meant.

She turned and started in the other direction. She held her purse clamped to her side, the blanket against her breasts. She found herself wanting to move quickly, to match Noel's pace, angry when an older person would slow the march of people. She stepped into the road and walked there, touching fenders, using the hoods to guide her. Moving cars inched past her. She looked in the car windows and saw families, a girl on a boy's lap.

As she walked, she debated whether to go to Grant's. She pictured the baby in her mind. She could see the black hair, the thin mustache already sprouting from the upper lip, the bony harp strings of its ribs. The boy's stomach was distended, filled with air and old hunger; the eyes were innocent, shocked, somehow, to be pulled back to life. Twice, on the first afternoon Kathy had seen him, Mary had lifted the tiny T-shirt to check the umbilical cord, rewrapping it with precision and care, saying: Sometimes the women cut the cord with the top of a can or an old razor blade. Kathy had nodded, knowing it, pushed to remembrance of Africa, seeing the baby flawed, deprived. The muscles from the abdomen had not closed around the umbilical cord, and now there was a small knot protruding from the mound of brown stomach. The navel was herniated.

"Get killed that way, lady," someone yelled at her from a passing car.

She stopped and pushed back against the cars lining the curb. She had wandered out a few feet into the road. She held the blanket tighter. She looked around her, feeling lost, confused. Another car pulled to a stop beside her. A teen-age boy poked his head out the window and said: "Lady, do you know where Ash Street is?"

Kathy shook her head, looking into the back seat, seeing the car jammed with kids. She said: "No, I don't live here."

"It's right over there." The boy pointed and laughed. The kids in the back seat erupted, slapping the boy on the back as he stepped on the gas.

Kathy moved up to the sidewalk and began walking faster. She turned her head when cars passed. She stayed on the farthest side, away from the street, avoiding lights, hurrying. She saw her car a block away. She began running, not quite sure why, but caught in the motion. Her sandals flapped. Her purse swung on her shoulder. She thought: Slow, slow, but kept running, her muscles stretching, her toes sometimes slipping far enough forward in her sandals to touch the rough cement.

As suddenly as she had begun, she stopped. She walked the sidewalk alone. She saw hedges pressed up against the walls of a white house, scaling them, a moat of greenery, the first wave of erosion. The heat moved with her. She had the sensation of dancing with the air, walking with it. It followed her legs, resting on her thighs until she broke its touch only to be met by another. At the car finally, she stood watching the stars, saw their distant light through windless night, heard the last firecrackers going off in heated explosions and imagined the boyish thrill at destruction, the quick run for cover gauged against a shimmering fuse.

She climbed into the car and started it. She threw the blanket onto the passenger seat and set her purse on top of it. She pulled the car out on the road, seeing her lights hit fog. It moved through the beams of her lights, pocketed, rolling, smoky. She drove automatically toward the house, realizing Noel would be home, that his way was more direct. She stopped at one light, then another. She opened her window to let the air in. It was moist, humid. Firecrackers were still going off. She waited at the light, tapping the steering wheel. She drove off, following the road, turning, braking, high beams, low beams. The fog was shoveled by the car hood and thrown at the windshield. It curled, seeping, only meeting the road again in her rear-view mirror.

A block from the house she slowed. She let the engine idle and coasted. She looked in the side mirror and saw the street was empty. She looked in front and behind and saw only the house coming up. She turned into the driveway and turned off the engine. She slammed the car door and ran to the house. She felt grass on her ankles, then cement beneath her. She ran up the front steps and pulled at the door. It was locked. It creaked against its frame, then stilled.

She backed away from the house. The fog rolled at her shins. She brought her legs forward, making holes, which were covered immediately in gray. Her feet were gone, and she had the impression of walking on her knees. She leaned close to the ground and trailed her fingers through the fog, straining it, testing its thickness. She thought: The ghost of snow. She circled the house, reaching out to touch the bushes as she walked. The trees bent under the heat. The pool light sent up a green light. The fog crept along the surface of the water, a chemistry experiment, dry ice frothing.

Then she saw the man. Her body stiffened. He was moving beside the pool, bent, slouched, his body enormous. She squatted, hiding in the shadow of the bushes, the fog covering her in silver. She could just make out his form against the green background. He stepped forward, rowing the blue water with the net. Once, for an instant, he looked up at the house. She felt his gaze run over her and pass, pushing to see inside.

She crawled, keeping her body low, beneath the sill of light that came out of the downstairs windows. The churn of water came to her ears. Her mind rolled, and she wondered if Noel was home. Her fingers dug in the soft soil, steadying each limb. Ahead, she saw the slant of light coming from the study. She moved closer to the garden, smelling the soil. The man continued to move, oblivious of her, his body hanging over the water.

Carefully she pushed herself up to a crouching position. The muscles in her thighs were binding. She rubbed her hands on her shirt, drying them. Then, wobbling, she ran into the light and ducked through the doors. She pressed her body against the wall and listened to the water sounds stirring, whirlpools. She heard the steady hum of crickets.

She reached for the pellet gun. In one motion she threw it to her shoulder, not aiming really, but pointing, and stepped into the open doorway. The man still hadn't seen her. She moved her finger to the trigger and was surprised at the calmness of her hands, their ability to function. She held the gun steady, narrowed her eyes, and fired. The kick of the gun was smooth. She heard a splash, a muffled curse, and then the water dripping and spilling over the cement edges of the pool. She saw the man in the shallow end, wading, his head jerking to look at the house.

She let the gun drop and slammed the French doors shut. It hit him, she thought. Until that moment, she realized, she had not expected to shoot near him. She leaned against the wall and ran the curtain closed, pulling hard on the cord, nearly yanking it from the wall. She heard the splashing stop. The curtain muffled everything. She reached across the desk and grabbed the phone. Dirt came free from her hands and scattered over the blotter. She dialed the operator. She waited, expecting at any moment the man would come through the door, bloody, his hair streaming fog.

"Can I help you?" a female voice asked. Kathy was taken aback by the calmness of the voice and tried to compose herself.

She said: "Please, call the police and tell them there's a man outside my house. Tell them I live at two-fourteen Middle Street."

"The address again?"

"Two-fourteen Middle Street."

Kathy hung up. Above her, she heard something stir. A sound drifted down the staircase. She reached behind her and propped the gun next to the desk. She heard more sounds from upstairs—a step, a door opened. Vaguely she realized she was holding the gun trained on the door. She could not remember picking it up, even though she had only just done so. She yelled for Noel and was shocked to hear her voice turn into a scream. Behind her, the French doors shattered, glass trinkling to the floor.

Frankenstein felt the fog around him. He stayed locked in the bushes, trying to see where the lawn gave way to water. He could see the green light rolling, mixing with the haze. He thought: House of the blackbird, and glanced up to her window. There was nothing there, no light. He inched forward. A light pushed from a room facing the pool, but it stopped short, fell to the grass. He walked to the cabana and found the net. It shook in his hands, the aluminum as gray as the fog. The white mesh quivered. He stood for a moment at the end of the pool and saw the house sink back.

He lowered the net and began sifting the water, the shaft bent by refraction. Two animals hovered five feet down. He ran the net toward them, careful to row softly. The pool alarm was out. He saw it sitting near the ladder, hatlike, safe in the dryness.

He circled the pool. A chipmunk was suspended, a black stripe running to its tail. He ladled the net beneath it and came up. The chipmunk weighted the center and rolled once, its body fat and bloated. He shook the net and watched the chipmunk come dry, rolling on the cement and landing face up. He stared at the tiny face and was tempted to crush the head, stop the eyes. But he moved on, instead, his mind on the pool.

He heard something move in the distance. A sound like an explosion popped. He thought it was a firecracker, but then he felt a hand tapping the back of his head, burning, searing. He fell forward, the water coming up at him. The burning went deeper, bone-hungry, causing his head to explode again and again with sound and pain.

He was not surprised to be in the water. He curled his feet under him and stood. He touched the back of his head and came away with blood. The water was brown around him. He looked at the house and saw the curtains drawing closed, the light disappearing. He splashed to the side, his hands pulling the water behind him. He hoisted himself up onto the edge and stayed close to the ground. He squirmed to the bushes, thinking he could hide in the green. He felt his chest dragging, his head clearing. He thought: Feathers, rocks, slingshot, knife. He felt them all pressed against his stomach, felt them all ready.

He stood, slowly, shadow-still. He took out his slingshot and loaded it. When it was set, he moved, creeping under the branches, taking aim. He sighted on the large doors, the hidden light, and fired. He heard the window crack and, before it finished, was patting his pocket, reloading, warring. He straightened only to shoot, then fell back into the bushes, green, cool now. He heard someone scream, but he shot again, then moved, swiftly, silently, taking up a new spot and firing again. He shot for glass, shot for the screen twang and then glass.

He circled, shooting, smiling. He patted his pockets, then shuffled, rocks, slingshot. He let the branches hit him, taking their pine whispers on his back, his cheek, his hair.

Noel stopped halfway down the stairs and listened to the window shatter. The sound rushed at him, moving through the house and funneling up the stairs. He crouched behind the banister and waited. He couldn't think clearly. He had a vague notion he should find a weapon, but he realized that with a weapon he would be forced to attack or defend.

He moved closer to the wall. He held his breath for a moment and listened as the next window went. He could hear each glass shard hit the floor, then gradually swell into a complete noise. He tried to figure out the direction of the attack.

Leaning against the wall, he continued down the steps. In the living room he saw the carpet covered with bits of glass. A breeze seeped through the broken window and brought the night closer. He paused as the house seemed to tighten, preparing itself for the next attack. He imagined a man outside using a muzzleloader, ramming powder and lead down the barrel of a gun, allowing the rhythm of his movements to time him.

When the next window broke, he ran down the remaining steps. He squatted near the wall, rubbing his hands on his jeans. He thought: Sniper. The word did not seem real to him. In the same instant he thought it, the picture window in the dining room splintered. The glass hung for a moment like a wave. Then it curled slightly and sloped forward, each piece collecting light and taking it to the floor.

He heard Kathy scream again from the study. He yelled to her. He stayed near the wall and watched the door open. "Get down," he shouted when he saw her. But she stood in the doorway, the pellet gun in her hands.

"Kathy, get down."

"Noel?"

"Get down."

"Who is it. Who's outside?"

He waited for the next window to go, feeling the rhythm himself. In the silence afterward he crouched and ran to her. She waited, tensed, coiling, the gun raising.

"Come here," he said. "It's all right. Come here."

She came into his arms. Her body was rigid. He held her, waiting for her to break.

"I'm going to go out," he said.

"No, I called the police."

"They'll break every window in the place. There's no gun sound. They're throwing things. It must be kids."

That's right, he thought. It must be kids. But he felt Kathy shaking, turning her head back and forth, saying: "No, Noel. It's not."

"Kathy, go upstairs and wait. Stay away from the windows. They're just kids."

She pushed away from him and said: "No, I shot him."

"Who?"

"A man down by the pool. I shot him with this."

She nodded at the gun still in her hands. He took it and held it across his chest.

"Did you hit him?"

"I think so, yes," she said.

"All right. Go up. Go ahead."

He didn't wait for her to answer. He ran into the kitchen and knelt near the back door. He heard crickets. He rocked to his heels. In one motion he jumped forward and opened the door. He scrambled off the porch, dropping into the garden. A branch wiped his cheek. He smelled fresh leaves, green sap. Another window went, the screen twanging first and then the glass cracking. He ducked closer to the bushes, his senses feeling the darkness around him.

He began moving cautiously, each step planned. He listened to his own sounds, hearing each mistake amplified across the yard. At the corner of the house he paused, checking the pool area, his eyes finally accustomed to darkness. The fog rolled along the grass, milky, chilled. A small cracking sound led his eyes to the pine hedge. He saw a man step forward, his body straight, and shoot something at the house. An instant later a window shattered, the sound dripping down the sides of the house.

The man sank back. Noel saw the hedge shake softly. His

mind was already working the details of the stalk. He knew the yard, knew the pool area. He started to rise but then saw the man circle the hedge, coming out into the open. The man moved slowly. He seemed to be keeping the hedge between himself and a darker form. He backed away, his shoulders catching the green light from the pool. Something stirred deeper in the bushes. The man panicked and began to run. Noel could see him clearly now. He heard deep breathing, saw the quick turn of the man's head to check behind him. He was pursued, afraid. The sound of his limbs and clothing joined. He was motion, fright. Noel took a step forward, rising, saw a light flash from the pine hedge, then heard a loud snap.

The man fell forward. Noel saw the last false step before he tumbled. Then there was the deadening squash of flesh on soil, the moist, humid smack of his body jolting in on itself. The man grunted. His boots hit a second later, landing on the toes, the momentum lifting them a half foot off the ground. Noel heard a second crack from the bushes, and this time the body only humped to one side, smothering the movement and sound and pressing it into the lawn.

"Fucker," Noel heard from the pine hedge.

Noel stood slowly and walked to the body. He bent over it, hearing a gurgle from the lungs. He felt sick. From behind him he heard someone say: "You, stay."

Noel turned. When his body was halfway around, he remembered the pellet gun. But he kept turning, too numb to act quickly. From what seemed like miles away, he heard the same crack he had heard before. He saw white light, felt pain in his thigh. He tried to throw the gun, but it twisted in his hands and fell. Only then did he realize he was falling backward. He put his hands up to surrender, then pulled them back to break his fall. The ground came up too quickly. His thoughts were disjointed. He smelled the grass, the soil smell, which was never quite new. He looked down and saw blood seeping through his pants, heard a policeman say: "Oh, shit, shit, shit."

He dug his fingers in the grass, tearing out handfuls. He thought: I accept this. There was pain, intense pain, working through him, running in shivers. He saw the finger falling into the well, and he was beneath it, looking up, the sun orange. He rolled his head, trying to shake the vision, seeing each time he turned the other man lying near him, his cheek against the grass, blood at his lips.

"Do you live here?" the cop asked. "Do you live here? Can you hear me? Do you live here?"

Noel tried to answer, thought he might have said yes, but he couldn't be sure. Sound stopped. He lay back, flat on his back, his shoulder blades melting, the sky stretching black.

He killed the pigeon, Frankenstein thought. He felt the pain spreading from his back, slowly climbing him. He fought to keep it from his head. Lady lips red, he thought, but a moment later he had forgotten it.

He tried to turn. A blade of grass crept up his nostril. His eyes were wet. His right hand was pressed against the knife on his thigh. He wondered if he could fish it out and still stab. And then his mind closed and the pain came, but it was warmer than he expected. He arched into it, lifting his body from the ground, pushing up against his spine. A voice said something nearby, and the words dropped onto the man's shoes and were licked clean by the grass.

The blood pumped closer. He wondered if it wasn't salt. He imagined Farley bending over him, working quickly to preserve the flesh. Your hair will be a wing. Your skin will be a nymph, water dancing across cold ponds. Again he tried to roll. His organs rocked inside him. He saw a blue cuff and another cuff, darker than the first. Then the feet moved away. He wanted to rise, to stand, but his legs were gone. He pictured the insect he would become and held the image in his mind. He drifted along the snow stream, feeling the first tremble of the feeding fish. The water built upward, ripples marking their approach. Beneath him he saw the silver glint of the trout, mouth wide, eyes like plates. The first tug freed him from the line, and he was carried down, the hook gone, his hair brushing the sweet mud. The wind disappeared. The churn of white water spread around him, and he waited with the fish, feeling the spring snow feed through his gills.

Joseph Monninger grew up in Westfield, New Jersey, and was educated at Temple University. After graduation, he served as a Peace Corps volunteer in Upper Volta, West Africa, before returning to graduate studies at the University of New Hampshire. His articles and short stories have appeared in *Glamour*, *Redbook* and *McCall's* magazines. Married to Amy Short, also a writer, Monninger now lives in Providence, Rhode Island. *The Summer Hunt* is his second novel.